Where the Stork Flies

By Linda C. Wisniewski

Where the Stork Flies

By Linda C. Wisniewski

Published by Sand Hill Review Press, LLC
www.sandhillreviewpress.com,
1 Baldwin Ave, #304, San Mateo, CA 94401

ISBN: 978-1-949534-16-0 paperback
ISBN: 978-1-949534-17-7 ebook

Library of Congress Control Number: 2020910071

© 2021 by Linda C. Wisniewski

CIP Data:
Names: Wisniewski, Linda C., author.
Title: Where the stork flies / by Linda C. Wisniewski.
Description: San Mateo, CA: Sand Hill Review Press, 2021.
Identifiers: LCCN: 2020910071 | ISBN: 978-1-949534-16-0
(print) | 978-1-949534-17-1 (ebook)
Subjects: LCSH Time-travel fiction. | Self-realization--Fiction.
| Jadwiga, Queen of Poland, approximately 1374-1399--Fiction.
| Queens--Poland--Fiction. | Our Lady of Częstochowa (Icon)-
-Fiction. | Poland--History--19th century--Fiction. | Post-
traumatic stress disorder--Fiction. | Middle-aged women-
-Fiction. | Friendship--Fiction. | Family--Fiction. | Science
fiction. | BISAC FICTION / General | FICTION / Science
Fiction / Time Travel
Classification: LCC PS3623.I86 W44 2021 | DDC 813.6--dc23

Where the Stork Flies is a work of fiction. Its characters,
scenes, and locales are the product of the author's imagination
or are used fictitiously. Any similarity of fictional characters to
people living or dead is purely coincidental.

SHRP
Sand Hill Review Press
1 BALDWIN AVE, #304, SAN MATEO, CA 94401

. Sainted ancestors, we beg you
Come, fly to us.

Polish prayer on the eve of All Souls' Day, November 2nd

For Lucille, Marianna, Angelika, and Regina

I stand on their shoulders.

Acknowledgments

Heartfelt thanks to the International Women's Writing Guild, Story Circle Network and Lauren B. Davis's Sharpening the Quill Writers Workshops for years of encouragement and helpful feedback. To Tory Hartmann of Sand Hill Review Press for taking on Kat's story. To Katarzyna Jakubiak, Ph.D., for her kind assistance with Polish words and phrases: *Dziękuję bardzo!* Any remaining errors are mine alone. To the librarians in Poland who responded to my emails in perfect English. To the wonderful writers Janet Benton, Lauren B. Davis and Caroline Leavitt for editorial advice and cheerleading. To the Plumstead Township officer who told me about the Language Line. To my cat, Denyse, for keeping me company at my desk and inspiring the character of Selene. And always, always, to my husband Steve and our sons, Aaron and Matt. Love goes both ways.

PART I

Chapter One

THE WINTER REGINA ARRIVED, I had a lot on my mind. My part-time job at the public library was going nowhere. My husband had left me over a crazy misunderstanding, and our 19-year-old daughter, who had always favored him, blamed me and followed him out the door. Lonely and confused by the turn my life had taken, I stumbled into the kitchen that morning and found the back door standing open, letting in a few flakes of snow.

Get a grip. I slammed the door closed. A whimper came from behind me. I whirled around to see an old woman in a long brown skirt, loose white blouse, and a muslin headscarf. She stood beside my kitchen table, shivering. A scream escaped my throat and then hers, both of us yelling like a crazy banshee duet.

"Who the hell are *you*?"

She jumped back, knocking over a chair. Selene, my old gray kitty, meowed loudly and ran from the room.

"What do you want?" I shouted as she scuttled over to a corner, clutching a piece of cheese. Her wide eyes looked so terrified I felt for a second as if I were the intruder, not she. Her face was wrinkled parchment and her hair around the edges of her headscarf was gray, but her round cheeks, those small brown eyes above a long straight nose: I had seen them before. On my grandmother's face. A woman who raised me from the age of ten. A woman who had died over thirty years before. It was her. And not her. A queasy little wave traveled through my stomach.

"Who *are* you?" I said again, my voice shaking. I wondered if she was some sort of hallucination brought on by lack of sleep. My hands groped for the back of a chair.

She licked dry lips and held out both trembling hands, still clutching the cheese.

"*Przepraszam,* she pleaded. "*Niech mi pani wybaczy!*"

A wash of pity flooded my heart. Her voice was soft and hoarse, and though I didn't understand her words, I knew their rhythm, the pattern of her sentence, the rise and fall and cadence. She spoke Polish like my Babcia, and my mind responded with words from my childhood to ask what she was doing.

"*Co pani robi?*"

The old woman's lips trembled. "*Niech mi pani wybaczy,*" she whispered and waved the cheese in her hands, still begging forgiveness as her gaze darted around the room as if she was expecting punishment to come from some corner.

I didn't know how to say, Relax, it's okay, so I grabbed another phrase from my childhood, the one that meant Hello. "*Dzień dobry.* My name is Kat. Katherine." I pointed at my chest, where my heart thumped a jagged rhythm. "*Katarzyna.*"

She nodded and positioned her feet on the floor as if ready to run. Her iron grip on the big hunk of Jarlsberg told me she wouldn't give it up without a fight. I had to let her know I would never take it from her.

"I'm sorry," I said, softening my tone. "I don't speak Polish very well. Do you speak English?"

Her only response was a shaky smile that made me want to put my arms around her. All the while I had been thinking of calling the cops, but my gut instinct told me she meant no harm. I looked from her to the door and back again, searching for a clue to my next move. We couldn't stay there forever, staring at each other. I had to step up and take charge. *Deep breath, Kat.* I picked up the overturned chair and gestured an invitation to sit. Then exhaling, I sank into a chair myself.

Her gaze went to my shelf of sacred objects in the corner near the sink. She frowned at the candles, acorns and feathers, then slowly moved her head to look at me, her frown still in place. I squirmed and gathered my bathrobe around me.

She took a nibble of the cheese and went back to sit on the chair I had righted for her. I smiled and nodded at the food in her hand and she set about eating the rest, her eyes never leaving my face. Her jaws moved quickly, both hands close to her mouth like an image of a cartoon mouse. I had never seen a person so ravenous. And for some unknown reason, she was in my kitchen. I could relieve her hunger and maybe even save her life.

I went to the fridge, pulled out the milk carton, and crossed to the cupboard for cereal, a bowl and a spoon. The inner voice that questioned everything I did woke up. *What are you doing? Have you finally lost your mind, making breakfast for a break-in?* Surely not. Maybe it was still last night, and this was an extremely realistic dream. I touched my hand to the counter. The cool, solid stone felt real beneath my fingers. I put the milk down and pinched myself. Ouch! There was a red mark on my arm. So, not a dream. Okay, I could do this.

With more hand gestures and a nervous smile, I set the bowl of cereal on the table and invited the old woman to eat. She peered at the little O's floating in the milk and lowered her face until it almost touched the bowl. Then she lifted the spoon and ate without stopping. *With her left hand, like I did. Like my Babcia.* I stared and held my breath, waiting for the Universe to give me an explanation for what I saw: something strangely as familiar as my own hands clenched on the table before me. When the bowl was empty, the woman picked up the big yellow box, shook it, and looked inside the waxed paper bag.

3

Watching her, I realized she wore no coat on in the dead of winter, and wondered if she was homeless. Or perhaps she was mentally ill and might turn on me at any moment. With a shudder, I reached behind me for my grandmother's shawl and pulled it around my shoulders. Its bright flowers on a black background had never faded and still gave me comfort long after she passed away. My visitor touched her headscarf and stared at my shawl, as if recognizing something there. Perhaps she had wandered away from an Alzheimer's unit. But I knew the nearest one was miles away, too far to walk without notice. I took the shawl from around me and held it out to her. She took it from my hands with a nod and a whisper, then wrapped it around her shoulders.

From the first moment I saw this lady, I was drawn to her, if for no other reason than she reminded me of my beloved *Babcia*, I had to get her some help. But the way my life was going, I was not who she needed. No, that would be someone who knew what to do.

Taking a deep, centering breath, I stood and walked to the wall phone. She watched me, openmouthed, as I pressed in the numbers: 911.

"I'd like to report a ...a person in my house," I told the dispatcher. "No, no, not a break-in. I, uh, think she may be... lost." I gave my name and address, feeling better already. The police would know how to handle this.

The woman's eyes narrowed as I hung up the phone. With careful steps, never taking her eyes off me, she moved to the wall, touched the other side where the phone would be if it went clear through to the dining room then peered back at me. I could see it in her eyes: she thought I was crazy, talking to a wall. She backed away until she tripped over a footstool and nearly lost her balance.

"It's okay, don't be afraid," I said, my throat tightening. "Someone is coming to help us."

From outside the drone of a siren came closer and louder, then cut off with a blip. The slam of a car door made us both jump. A few seconds later, my doorbell rang. The woman flinched and retreated, her back pressed against the granite

4

countertop, eyes wide and mumbling something I could not hear and probably wouldn't understand.

"It's okay." I made my voice soft and held up a hand for her to wait and she trembled but stayed where she was. *Think, Kat. You can do this.* My mind ran back to Babcia's house and found the Polish words. *"Tutaj."* I pointed to a chair. *"Usiądź tutaj."*

She stood frozen in place as sharp raps hit the front door, and I froze, too, unsure if I should answer it or get her to calm down first. A loud voice broke through.

"Police! Open up!" In a reflex, I obeyed, hurrying to unlock the deadbolt.

"Hold on!" I shouted through the door, my fingers fumbling with the lock. At last, I swung the door open. And looked straight into the face of Officer Braun, the cop who had pulled me over for speeding the previous weekend. *Shit.* My face grew hot. Not good. Not good at all.

He squinted down at me as if he could not believe I was on his radar again. Before he could say a word, I turned away to hide my embarrassment and walked back to the kitchen.

"This your intruder?" His deep baritone vibrated close behind me as the old woman cowered, glued to her spot against the counter.

In his black leather jacket, Braun was the biggest thing in the kitchen except for the fridge and for a second, I regretted letting him in. What if he recognized me? Would it affect how he treated this call? Hot waves of shame coursed through me. Would he help this poor woman or haul her off to jail? I scrambled for words.

"You won't believe it. *I* don't believe it." I motioned at her with one hand. "This lady, she was just...here when I got up this morning...and...and...she doesn't speak English. I don't know how she got into the house without a key but the back door was open. She doesn't have a coat or anything." My voice was high and tense and I struggled to bring it under control. "I didn't know who to call."

As soon as I said that, I imagined him wondering why I didn't call a neighbor. But the nearest house was a quarter mile down the road and I didn't know the people who lived there. They were probably peering out their windows right now, wondering what had brought a black and white to our stretch of the Pike. Had I done the right thing, calling 911? *Shit, shit, shit.* I had no friends to turn to anymore. No way to know what I should have done.

To my great relief, Officer Braun ignored me, nodded at the woman and took a step toward her but stopped when she let out a high-pitched squeak. He held up both his big stubby hands, exposing the handcuffs attached to his belt. I hoped he wouldn't try to use them. Putting this helpless old lady in cuffs would be the worst indignity. I wouldn't let him do it.

"Good morning, Ma'am. Mind telling me why you're in this lady's house here?" Silence followed by a whimper. He modulated his baritone. "I'm not going to hurt you, but you can't stay here." The woman's face flushed pink as she turned to me. I cleared my throat, conscious of my state of undress. At least I had put on my robe.

"She doesn't understand you. I think she speaks Polish, but my skills are rusty." I pointed to the empty cereal bowl on the table. "She was starving, so I gave her something to eat."

Braun's full lips curved in a smirk. Frantic to explain myself, my voice came out louder than I meant.

"She was eating a piece of cheese and I thought..." I sounded ridiculous. "I mean...she didn't look threatening. But she can't stay here with me, she needs help." *And so, too, do I, but you don't know the half of it, nor would you care.*

Braun's face was blank, his voice steady.

"Okay, I'll take her in."

The old woman flinched as he took her arm and pulled her away from the counter. Her look was stoic, as if she had expected exactly this, and my heart ached, feeling her resignation as if it were my own, as if it was me so helpless in the policeman's grip.

I waved my arms in the air. "I don't want her arrested. I just want her to get some help: a place to stay, if she's homeless. I don't know..."

As usual—as in all my life—I wanted to direct the outcome of the situation but I had no idea what that should be, and it frightened me beyond words. When I bit at my thumbnail Braun looked away.

"Okay. I'll take her in to the station and call the language line." He took the woman's arm above the elbow and guided her to my front door.

"Language line?" This was news to me.

"Yeah, they have interpreters twenty-four seven. They can ask her who she is, what she was doing here, et cetera, et cetera." His voice was deep, strong and all business.

They were at the door now, his hand on the knob. She looked over her shoulder at me, her large brown eyes unblinking as Braun ushered her outside. At the patrol car, she hesitated a moment, but he put his big hand firmly on top of her kerchiefed head and guided her into the back seat. Then he stepped around front, got in and started the engine.

Her round face stared at me through the rear window as the car moved past the bare trees bordering my driveway. I opened the glass storm door and stepped out into the crisp winter air. *Wait.* The car turned left onto the Pike, the words Plumstead Township in sharp black letters on its spotless white side. I thought of running after it, a thread of longing pulling me forward, the same longing I had felt when I was only ten.

Chapter Two

OUR LITTLE WHITE HOUSE was empty when I returned from school that afternoon. I walked into the kitchen and called for my mother but a strange silence echoed my footsteps. A white envelope lay in the center of the Formica table with my name on it. I recognized her handwriting. Beside it lay another, addressed to "Sam," my father. I tore open the one addressed to me.

"Dear Kathy," I read. "I am going away. Please try to understand. Daddy and I have been having problems for a long time. You are better off with him. I am with someone who makes me happy. This is something I have to do. Be a good girl. Love, Mommy."

Shards of the past few months cut through me. Angry words from another room as I lay awake in bed. Cold glances when they thought I wasn't looking. My eyes stung with tears. *Mommy*. Who let me eat cake for breakfast. Who let me stay up late reading in bed. Who wore bright red lipstick to her part-time job as a beautician. The room went pale around me. I couldn't breathe.

My legs refused to hold me up and I crumpled onto the kitchen floor. My head began to hurt but I couldn't stop my tears. My home was an echoing shell. My mother was gone. The kitchen swirled around me and I fought and fought for breath until a scream ripped through my throat, hoarse and filled with pain. The sound, like an animal, frightened me. I laid my head against a chair leg and whimpered. My school uniform twisted around me like a blue plaid rag. I touched my face. Snot and tears mingled in a crusted mess over my upper lip. I stayed there, on the floor, for a long time, but nothing changed. My house was empty. I was alone.

After a while, I struggled to my feet and went to the bathroom down the hall to wash my face. I felt a little better so I went back to the kitchen and made myself a snack. Graham crackers and cold milk, what my mother gave me every day, but I stared at the plate, unable to take a bite.

Being home by myself was not so new. Sometimes I got there before my mother, and let myself in with my own key. Then I'd start my homework and wait for her. But now, she wouldn't come. Her letter said she had gone away. Left me. What did that mean? Would she never come back? I needed someone to sort this out, to help me find my mother. My Babcia would help me. She was the only woman besides Mom I could always depend on. She would know what to do.

I went to the phone and dialed her number, which I knew by heart, but all I got was a busy signal. With a big sigh that nobody heard but me, I hung up the phone and tried to start my homework but ended up turning on the TV instead. Every few minutes, I tried Babcia's number again, but it was always busy. The Brady Bunch kept me company until my father came home right at five as he always did. That much was still as it had always been.

"Mommy's gone!" I cried as soon as the back door opened. "She left you a letter, and one for me, too! We have to go after her!"

He strode to the table, pulled out a chair, and sank into it, reaching for the envelope that bore his name. His big hands shook as he read the note inside then pulled out a big white hanky and passed it over his wide forehead. He put it back in his pocket and raked a hand through his dusty blond hair which stood up in peaks atop his head. He didn't seem to notice or care. He sniffed and moved his chair back from the table.

"We'll be okay, Kathy," he said, not looking at me, his voice soft and low. "What do you want for dinner?"

9

I couldn't believe what I was hearing. How could he even think about eating? Tears of frustration flooded my eyes and ran down my face.

"Aren't you going to find her?" I screamed, my hands in fists at my sides. "You can't just let her go and leave us!"

My nose dripped but I didn't care. He stood and I rushed at him, pushing at his chest as hard as I could.

"Kathy," he said, easily gripping both my hands in one of his, "things have not been right between your mom and me for a long time. She might come back on her own. She might not. We have to go on with our lives. We'll be all right, you'll see."

Even though his shoulders slumped, he still towered over me. He released my hands, patted me on the head and went to the bedroom he shared with Mom. The torn white envelopes and the open letters lay on the table like leftovers. I gathered them up in my hands and sank to the floor, crawled under the table, and sobbing, tore the letters into soggy little tear-stained bits.

Dad stayed in his room until dark. I watched more TV, because no one stopped me like before. When he came out, his face was drawn but he smiled at me and heated a can of alphabet soup, my favorite. We ate toasted cheese sandwiches, not talking. My head ached and I waited to hear the slightest word from him, but there were none.

"I want to call Babcia," I said. "Can I?"

He shrugged and went back to his room. Babcia came over right away, and her face looked worried. Her smile was sad as she took off her long gray coat and scarf. Her fluffy gray hair was all mussed up, and her glasses were smudged. I grabbed at her arm, pleading with her to find my mother.

"*Uspokój się Kasiu.* You will make yourself sick. Why don't we get you ready for bed," she said. "Things will look better in the morning."

She got out my pajamas while I took a Nancy Drew book from the little white shelf next to my bed. Nancy's mother was gone, just like mine, I told her, but she had died when Nancy was a baby. She didn't just decide to leave. And Nancy's dad was warm and kind and full of life, not sad like mine. He even encouraged her to solve mysteries all by herself.

"Nancy is good company for a girl like you," Babcia said, tucking me my yellow and white coverlet around me. It felt good, her hands pressing against my sides through the quilt.

During the night, I woke to hear Dad's footsteps on the stairs, in the kitchen, in the living room then back to his bedroom but I left him alone. I got out of bed to find Babcia but she was gone too. All right, if that was the way it was, I would become like Nancy: strong and on my own. And I would not have a little girl's name. I would call myself Kat.

After the Plumstead Township police car had left my driveway, my world was as quiet and still as the night forty years before when my mother had gone away. I fed Selene, then showered, dressed and went grocery shopping. After a quick stop at Starbucks for a latte, I went home and checked my email. No news from Alan, nothing from my daughter Jessica.

I went to the gym and clocked two miles on the treadmill, did my strength training workout, and tried to keep busy all day, just as I had for the past two weeks, trying and failing to keep my loneliness at bay.

That night, I tried to lose myself in a book. I hadn't slept well since Alan left, and *Wherever You Go There You Are* beckoned from my nightstand. Its due date was near, and the library where I worked had a long list of patrons on the waiting list. *Come on, Kat, focus.* Selene settled beside me on top of my quilt, and I began to read, but the words blurred as the old woman's face hovered before me until finally, I drifted off to sleep.

Hours later, I woke to the clangor of dump trucks on the highway outside. In the bathroom as I brushed my dark brown hair from my eyes, the faces of my mother and grandmother appeared in the mirror like a triple exposure photograph. I blinked and they were gone. I reached for my moisturizer and smoothed it over my face, but the wrinkles remained. The dark circles under my eyes were not from lack of sleep. It was time to face the truth: At fifty, I was getting older.

People said I looked like Mom– her hair, the brown eyes and the round face–and they were right. She never came back, but I still remembered her. Dad never remarried. My mother's mother took care of me at her house after school and when Dad worked on weekends. Once I asked her if it was my fault Mom left.

"Not at all, Kathy," she said. She always forgot to use my new name. "Some people, like your mom, are never really happy with what they have. They keep looking around the next corner for something better." She smiled at me and gave me a little hug. "She's my daughter, and I love her, but she was wrong to leave you. There's no better little girl in the world."

The memory of that hug made me smile now, as I got ready for the day. I wondered if in some way, I really was like my mom. I was often preoccupied. A multitude of choices cluttered my mind every day. I found it hard to keep my commitments when so many new and more exciting things beckoned. Sometimes, after I was grown, I tried to find her, but there was no one to ask about her after Dad and *Babcia* died. After all these years, she might be dead as well. A little wisp of sadness touched my shoulder.

I reached for my toothbrush, and looked in the mirror to see another face: the face of the Polish-speaking woman in the old-fashioned clothes, the one I had turned in to the police. I blinked and shut my eyes tight. Opened them again. Just me in the mirror, no one else. *Deep breath, Kat. Relax.*

The bathroom was chilly and I shivered as I turned on the shower. Soothing warm water poured over my head and back as I talked myself out of anxiety. *Lots of Polish American women have round faces and brown eyes. That doesn't mean you have to take responsibility for whatever mess she's got herself into. It's not like you don't have enough to worry about.* Career, marriage, motherhood – nothing had worked out well for me, and I didn't understand why.

This was my eighth job after college. I'd been a caseworker for the public welfare department, a clerk in the social security office, an administrative assistant for a building company, and now a part-time librarian. I was sort of good at lots of things, but nothing held my interest for long. I was alone and unmoored as a little rowboat on a choppy sea.

While I shampooed my hair, I mentally recited a few affirmations. *You are doing the right thing. All is well. You are in the perfect place today.*

In my car on the way to work, I recited a few more. *Today will be a good day. May I be happy. May I live with ease.* By the time I pulled into the parking lot of the Township Free Library, I felt a little calmer. Giving my dream-catcher a little tap for good luck, I grabbed my purse and headed for the building.

A line of patrons waited while I hurried through the employees' entrance and almost ran straight into Chuck. Oh God. On his way out, briefcase in hand, he nodded curtly, avoiding eye contact.

"Meeting up at the main branch this morning." Big deal. As if I wanted to talk to him anyway. Why, oh why, did I ever flirt with him? Couldn't I see it would wreck my marriage?

About three months earlier, we fell into a habit of chatting over our morning coffee. Alan was deep in his latest project, a screenplay about the Big Bang. I'd come home from work in tears, upset about some angry patron who called me down, and he just gave me a quick hug.

"Let it go," he said and I wanted to punch him. I was raw and bruised emotionally, and he thought I could just let it go. He was nothing like the passionate and devoted lovers in the novels I read. I felt I deserved more. I longed for more. As time went on, Chuck and I joined a group for lunch every Friday. Soon on Mondays, it was just the two of us for breakfast at the nearby diner. After a while, he started calling me at home and the next Friday after work we had a drink that led to one stupid little kiss.

Meanwhile, Alan had grown more and more preoccupied. I shared my hopes and dreams like I always had, from the beginning of our relationship, but he never opened up to me, not the way I wanted. I realized now that just like my dad, he kept to himself. Entire evenings went by without a word between us. That wasn't what I'd signed up for when I married him. He said he loved to travel and I thought he'd be my ticket to adventure. But now here I was, fifty years old with the rest of my life stretched out like a tunnel of colorless days and empty nights. In a panic that I'd never feel truly loved, I thought I'd at least try a mild harmless flirtation.

Then all hell broke loose. Chuck's wife found some notes from me in the trash basket under his desk at home, and jumped to the conclusion that we were having an affair. It was just words, a few hugs and handholding and that one time we kissed, just to see what it would feel like. I should never have put that in a note. But what we had done was not an affair. Was it?

I tried to explain but Alan refused to listen. His first wife really had cheated on him, for years before he found out, and now it looked to him like history was repeating itself. I wished I could erase and rewrite the previous three months. I tried again to explain.

"You don't share yourself with me, Alan! I just needed someone to talk to." The thought of losing him scared me and I started to cry but it had no effect on my husband.

"How stupid do you think I am?" His voice was tight and higher than normal, out of sync with his tall and lanky frame and his usual relaxed demeanor. He was deeply hurt, and I didn't know how to change that, to take back what I had done. I reached out to touch his soft, dark brown hair, but he pushed my hand away. "This is not happening again." He pointed a finger at my nose and used it to punctuate each syllable. "Not. Ever. Again."

"But..."

"No more lies. No more!" He turned his back and ran upstairs to pack a bag, ignoring my pleas for him to wait. I followed him and continued trying to explain as he threw toiletries and underwear, shirts and a few pairs of pants into his suitcase. I walked with him right to the door, still apologizing to no avail. It all happened so fast, it made my head spin. And my heart hurt.

When I tried his cell phone the next day, he had already rented a room in Quakertown, close to the FedEx depot where he parked his truck. He said he would continue his life delivering packages all day and writing screenplays at night, without me.

I hadn't meant for this to happen. I didn't want Chuck, but I wasn't sure about Alan either. What had I been thinking? I needed time. And a secure and stable home. Which was now in my rear-view mirror.

At my desk in the library, I shook my head to stop obsessing over the mess I'd created. At nine o'clock sharp, Nancy, the office manager, unlocked the heavy glass door to the lobby and people streamed in. An elderly couple headed for the stacks, and a woman I recognized waved at me and walked over to the shelves of rental best sellers. A young woman with two toddlers bee-lined for the children's reading nook. I settled into the swivel chair behind the reference desk and flipped the switch to turn on my computer. At least here, for three half-days a week, I knew exactly what to do.

Answering patron's questions kept me busy all morning. Yet every minute I was alone, the face of my mystery woman came back, nagging. Who was she, and what would become of her in police custody?

Once I thought I saw her standing at the circulation desk and got up to take a closer look. The gray-haired woman with her back to me had the same stocky frame. She wore a headscarf and brown boots, and a long brown skirt hung beneath her winter coat. I hoped it was she. I imagined her caregiver stepping up to apologize for letting her get away yesterday when she had wandered into my house. It was a fantasy that might have put my worries to rest but it was only that: a fantasy, a nicely tied up ending like the ones in my favorite books.

The stocky woman turned as I approached and gave me a questioning look, and the image of her unlined face and olive skin came with a sting of disappointment. I smiled at her, and softly said, "I'm sorry. I thought you were someone else."

"No problem," she answered and walked out the door, serenely unaware she had been mistaken for someone who needed a caregiver.

I had concocted a similar fantasy when I was small. Every year on my birthday, a card from my mother arrived in the mail. I began to imagine she would come to my party, and every year, I watched for her at the window. Until I was sixteen, and my best friend, Molly, put her arm around me at my first boy-girl party.

"Kat, I don't think she's coming," Molly said. "Maybe it's time to stop waiting for her." I knew she was right, but that didn't make my heartache less, or ease my shame. Whose mother left and never came back? As far as I knew, only mine. The cards stopped when I was eighteen.

Babcia was my only comfort. Her door was always open to me for cookies and hugs after school and later for tea and girl talk. She told me stories about Mom as a little girl, and how she was smart and loved to read like me. My mother, her only daughter, was always looking for adventure. Maybe it was because her name was Anastasia, like the long-lost Russian princess. She even ran away from home once when she was twelve. *Babcia* said I should never think her leaving was my fault. It was just "her nature." She had taught her to knit and sew, and when she did the same for me, on long winter afternoons, I felt like I was somehow, if only by a thread, connected to my mother.

It was only after I was grown that I realized how painful it must have been for *Babcia* to show me her old photo albums, and to watch me peer at pictures of my mother for hours on end. When I lost my mother, she had lost a daughter. It must have seemed like my questions would never stop, but she was always patient and kind. She always made me feel loved.

Dad never said a word about Mom on my birthdays. He just let me wait and hope and I grew to hate him for it. I hated him for not trying to find her, or bring her back. And I hated him for not making something of his life.

16

"It was hard, Kathy, being married to your mom." That's what he told me, what he told anyone who asked. And just like *Babcia*, he never remembered my new name was Kat.

He was passive and resigned until the day he died of cancer when I was twenty and left me an orphan. The next year, my grandmother had a stroke, and soon after, she was gone as well.

I was a grown woman now, more than capable of taking care of myself. But I still felt like a lonely child waiting at the window.

When my shift at the library ended, I gathered my down jacket and purse and thought of the drive to my empty house. Empty except for Selene my geriatric cat. I waved goodbye to the clerks at the circulation desk but none of them noticed. It was close to two and as I walked to my car, my head held a vision of the previous day, of the frightened woman who was ready to bolt, yet waited when I held up my hand. She had trusted me, only to be hustled off to jail or maybe the psych ward at the local hospital. Maybe there was something I could do for her. *Babcia* would have tried.

I unlocked the door of my Jetta, tossed my purse onto the passenger seat and drove to the police station.

Chapter Three

I HAD DRIVEN BY the white stucco building many times. As newcomers, Alan and I had gone inside for information and even attended a few meetings of the board of supervisors. Originally a one-room schoolhouse, its two added wings housed administrative offices and the police department.

I followed the signs down the walkway to the door marked Police. Inside and down a short hallway, a clear plastic window separated me from the receptionist. I leaned forward and spoke into a slotted metal disc mounted in the window.

"Hello. I'd like to inquire about the woman who was brought in Monday morning."

"The DUI?" Her words sounded far away, though she was right there in front of me filing her nails. I looked around to see if she was talking to someone else but no one stood behind me.

"No!" I shouted into the disc. "She was a Polish lady who broke into my house!"

"I can hear ya. Don't have to yell. Wait a sec." She pushed down on the grey metal desk for leverage and lifted her heavy bottom from the chair. Then she disappeared behind a door in the far wall. She had not looked at me once. It felt familiar, being ignored, and my throat closed.

I stood in the open reception area and wondered how long I would have to wait. There were no chairs and no old magazines, but I was too restless to sit down anyway. I glanced at the clock, out the window, at the walls bearing certificates and proclamations and a photo of the chief. Just as I was about to give up and go home, a door opened to my left. Officer Braun walked a few steps toward me and jammed his thumbs in his belt loops. He looked down at me from his six foot-plus height and I thought of leaving right then.

"You inquirin' 'bout that old lady I picked up at your house the other day, Ms. Kowalski?" His voice told me nothing. I suspected that was the plan. I straightened my shoulders and met his eyes, though it hurt my neck to look up at him.

"Yes, how is she, Officer? Is there anything she needs?" I tried to sound casual and confident while peering up at him like the much shorter grownup I was.

"We got her a temporary placement," he said. "The people at Loaves of Manna will take care of her." I recognized the name of the local Christian group whose mission was to help the needy.

He squinted down at me. "You want to press charges? You said..."

"No, no charges. I just wanted to make sure she was okay." I hesitated but I had to ask. "Did she say why she was in my house?"

He stared at me so closely I squirmed.

"You know, you kinda look like her. No offense."

I couldn't think what to say. Braun looked down at the toes of his shiny black boots and cleared his throat. "So...the language line interpreter said she was from some village... Maui Wonky? Ever hear of it?"

"No, I haven't. Where is it?"

"Well, that's the thing. She seems to think she's near this village but she's scared to death of cars, telephones, all kinds of stuff. She threw up a little in the patrol car, like she was carsick. And there's one other thing. The interpreter said she was speaking Polish, but not the Polish of today. Said it could be an old dialect from like a hundred years ago."

He looked as if he expected me to have an explanation for this. The receptionist, back behind her protective window, gave me a cold stare. The back of my neck prickled with heat.

I looked at Officer Braun. "A hundred years ago? Why would she do that?"

"Beats the heck out of me. But anyway, the Loaves of Manna folks are good people. She'll be all right, if that's what you're worried about." He glanced at the clock on the wall. "Very nice of you to come in and check on her, though. Will there be anything else?"

"No, thank you, Officer." The matter was out of my hands, just as I thought I'd wanted when I called the police from my kitchen phone. But now I felt empty inside. I smiled and nodded and took myself out through the double glass doors to the parking lot.

For the rest of that afternoon, as I drove around town doing errands, the old woman's face swam before me, her dark eyes questioning. I knew she was lost. And I just couldn't let her stay that way.

All my life, I had clung to relationships long after they were over. Friendships ended, people moved away or developed interests I didn't share, yet I kept calling, sending cards, trying to keep the connection going. Alan and I had been drifting apart for years, but no sooner had he moved out than I wanted him back. Or maybe not.

We often fought over his lack of ambition, or rather, I berated and he walked away. When we first got together I loved that he wrote screenplays. It was one of the reasons I fell in love with him. I thought he'd get them produced, but over the years he seemed to care about that less and less. When he wasn't driving around southeastern Pennsylvania delivering packages he was reading up on archaeology or astronomy or zoology or whatever his next play was about. We had no social life but he refused to talk about it. I yelled and he walked away. Frustrating.

Then things went from bad to worse. Our daughter Jessica said I was clingy and controlling, just because I got rid of that horrid death trap on wheels she called a motorcycle. Okay, maybe I shouldn't have done it without asking, but I sold it to save her life. That's what mothers do, who love their children. Didn't that matter to her? And the makeup artist idea? We argued for weeks about that one. I said I would not let her destroy her future that way, that she needed to go to a four-year college like her parents had. Of course, now that it was too late, I realized I'd hurt her by questioning her choice.

Totally by surprise, the day after Alan left, she came home from her community college classes and confronted me. To my horror, Alan had called and told her his side of the story.

"Mom, you are disgusting! You never think of anybody but yourself." She slammed her books down on the kitchen table, her dark eyes fierce with an awful hate aimed directly at me. It struck at my pride and I fought back without thinking.

"You don't know what you're talking about! You don't know anything about your father and me." I couldn't look at her, so I pulled out a chair. "You're jumping to conclusions. Just like your Dad. Let's sit down, so we can talk about it."

"Shut up! Shut Up!" Her harsh cry hurt as if it had come from my own throat. "Stop acting all 'let's talk about it.'" She framed the words with air quotes. "You never appreciated him, just because he's happy driving a truck. Your life is a mess and now you're ruining my life and Daddy's." Her words hit their mark. I had made a mess of my life. She threw me a venomous look and with her long dark hair flying behind her, ran from the room. Alone at the table, I laid my head down on my arms and cried.

Within the week, she had moved to California to live with two girlfriends from high school. They'd been inviting her for months, she said, and now she'd take them up on it. They helped her get a job at the bar in Sausalito where they both worked. I knew this from her Facebook page, but I dared not message her online, for fear she would un-friend me. Or de-friend me. Whatever it was called, I had to know she was all right, even from far away. We might not be close anymore, but I was still her mother. I loved her and I didn't want to lose her. I tried calling but she wouldn't pick up, even left my first ever text messages but it was no use. She never replied.

Still angry with me, Alan was quick to take her side. He said she deserved to find her own happiness, to do what she loved, and not what I thought was best for her. Typical of him,

I thought, the truck driving screenwriter with zero ambition. But now I wondered if I had been too hasty. How had my life come to this? The one thing I was grateful for was his promise to let me know how she was doing when he called her every week.

At home, I gave my daughter's phone another try.

"Hey. Just thinking about you. How was your weekend?" I put a little smiley face icon at the end of the text and touched the little envelope to send it. Maybe today she'd answer me.

I hurried upstairs to the meditation corner of my bedroom, lit my cardamom-scented candle for clarity and placed it on a table draped with a purple satin cloth. Selene padded over and snuggled next to me on the rug. My deck of Goddess cards was in a wooden box on the table, and as I pulled them out and shuffled them, I closed my eyes and inhaled the candle's scent. Taking another deep cleansing breath, I formulated my question: *Why is the old woman in my life?*

I dealt three cards from the deck and turned them face up. Past. Present. Future. A thrill of excitement rippled through my fingers as I touched each card. The first held a picture of two faces within a spiral surrounded by yellow light. Warm memories of my grandmother came to mind, unbidden, and closing my eyes, I let them wash over me. The second card was a human figure with eyes closed and many tendrils coiling from its head. Breathless, I thought of my myriad choices. I closed my eyes again, centering myself like the figure on the card. When I was ready, I looked at the third card. It showed two figures holding hands, their backs pressed together, their open eyes looking out in opposite directions. A warm flush enveloped me in a sense of relief as I envisioned my newfound life's purpose. The old woman was my destiny.

Chapter Four

I HAD THE NEXT DAY OFF from work. As soon as I had showered and fed Selene, I called the number for Loaves of Manna.

The man who answered said they had sent a driver to take my mysterious visitor from the police station to a motel on Route 611 just north of town, a place they used often to provide temporary housing for the homeless.

"You mean you left her alone in a motel room?" I shrieked.

"Well, she didn't have anyone with her, did she? We have funds for a night at the motel..."

"And then what? What if she has nowhere else to go?"

The male volunteer on the line spoke in a calming tone, the same voice we used at the library with certain patrons. *Crap.* The guy thought I was one of those kinds of people.

"Now, please try to understand," he said. "We have limited funds."

"Yes, I do understand." I tried to speak more slowly, in a lower register. "But where will she go now?"

"Don't worry. We had someone go over and check on her this morning. She can't speak English, and she doesn't seem to have a next of kin, so we called Family Services. They said they would find her a place that would take her on an emergency basis."

I thanked the Loaves of Manna guy and hung up quickly, then looked up the number for Family Services. An answering machine picked up.

"You have reached the offices of Bucks County Family Services. Our office hours are..." Too early. I left my name and number after the beep, made a pot of coffee, ate a slice of toast and absently chewed on my thumb. When the kitchen clock showed nine, I called again. This time, I had my story rehearsed and firmly asked to speak to the social worker in charge of the case. The receptionist put me on hold and I listened to an instrumental version of *Bridge over Troubled Water* for what seemed like a week but was probably less than five minutes. Suddenly, a dial tone cut off the music. With a sigh, I dialed the number again.

"Bucks County Family Services. How may I direct your call?"

"I was cut off. You were transferring me to the social worker in charge of the woman the Loaves of Manna..."

"Oops! Sorry. Let me connect you to that office." Holding the portable receiver to my ear, I poured another cup of coffee and sat down at the kitchen table. This could be a long wait. Yanni played the piano in my ear while I closed my eyes and practiced calming yoga breaths. After a much shorter wait, Yanni was gone and the social worker was on the line.

"We don't usually give out information like this," she said. "But since you're the person who turned her in..."

"I'd really appreciate it. I think she might be related to someone I know."

"You do? You should have said so before!" Her eager voice set off alarms in my brain. Why had I said that?

"No, no, what I mean is, she *may* be someone's relative – maybe not. I'm not sure. But I want to find out who, I mean, how she is. You know, see if she's okay." Whew. I leaned back in my chair to keep from going on with this crazy explanation.

"We placed the woman in the local shelter of the County Housing Group. Let me give you the number."

After the woman hung up, I waited for a dial tone. My fingers flew as I punched the numbers she had given me into the keypad. The shelter office answered on the first ring.

"Am I ever glad to hear from you!" a woman's voice exclaimed after I told her who I was. "The elderly lady the

Loaves of Manna volunteer brought in yesterday is quite agitated. We are having a very difficult time with her."

"You are?" I squeaked in a high Minnie Mouse voice. *Deep breath, Kat.* "What seems to be the problem?"

"She's not mean or anything. But she doesn't seem to know about modern conveniences. She went outside to go to the toilet wearing just that old shawl. And she's afraid of the TV. Every little noise makes her jump. And she cries a lot. It's so sad. She just sits on her bunk and whimpers. They said she broke into your house. Where is she from, do you know?"

So she still had my grandmother's shawl. It made a great excuse to go to her.

"I don't know where she came from," I said, "but she stole my grandmother's shawl and I want it back. Could I come get it? Maybe if I talk to her..."

The woman's relief was clear. "Yes, of course. I hope you can help her. Other than providing food and a bed, we sure can't."

With the MapQuest directions on the seat beside me, I turned down a dead-end street. The highway beyond was hidden by a thicket of wild brush, gnarled and brown. In this quiet neighborhood of Sixties-era colonials, the pavement stopped abruptly where the crumbling blacktop gave way to a field of dead weeds. My Jetta fit neatly beside a huge white shed in the parking area.

I grabbed my little Polish dictionary off the car seat, touched my dangling dream-catcher for luck, and stepped out of my car. A rambling brick house loomed before me, alone at the end of a cul-de-sac. I was surprised to find no sign indicating I was in the right place. On the other hand, would you want "Homeless Shelter" on your front lawn?

I walked to a door at the left of the building where a window held a small hand-printed cardboard sign: Office. Inside, a woman sat at a battered wooden desk behind a nameplate: Alecia Brown, Manager. She looked about my age and wore a pale blue cardigan over a white oxford shirt. Her fingers paused over the keyboard of an ancient PC.

"Thanks for coming in so quickly. She's in the women's dorm area. Just go outside and knock on the last door to the right." She peered at me over the top of her half-glasses. "You sure look a lot like her."

Great. The mystery woman was old, tired and dirty and I looked a lot like her.

"OK, thanks, I'll just go and see her," I said, forcing a smile. I had never been inside a homeless shelter and the place made me nervous. A middle-aged woman living alone, I could have some bad luck, maybe lose my job, or Alan could stop giving me money every week, and I might end up there myself. Maybe Jessica was right. I had made a mess of my life. The shelter woman's voice broke through my thoughts.

"Do you know what language she speaks? We haven't been able to get much out of her. I don't think she understands a word of English."

"She speaks Polish," I said, "at least I thought so the other day, but I don't understand much more than 'hello' and 'goodbye.' Does anybody know where she came from?"

"Nope, can't help you there." The woman brushed strands of graying brown hair away from her eyes. "She had to come from somewhere, though. It's not like she dropped out of thin air, now, is it?"

"No, it's not. I'll see what I can find out." I held up the tiny dictionary. Officer Braun had said the woman spoke an old dialect, but I hoped I could piece together enough words to find out who she was and where she'd come from. I turned and stepped out onto the flagstone walk.

The women's dormitory was around the side of the building. A wrought iron number ten hung crookedly on faded bricks beside the door. A few seconds after I knocked, a stern-faced woman somewhere between my age and elderly opened the door. Over her shoulder, I could see a room filled with bunk beds, cots, and a few chairs and tables. A musty mildewed smell stung my nostrils and I forced myself not to recoil.

"Excuse me," I said, pasting on a smile. "I'm here to see a lady, a Polish lady?"

"Right over there," she gestured behind her with a thumb and stepped aside to let me pass. Next to the farthest of the bottom bunks, my mystery woman was on her knees, hands folded in prayer. She was still wearing my grandmother's shawl. The woman who had answered the door stood close behind me.

"She's pretty scared. But we'd appreciate it if she stopped prayin' like that all the time. It's gettin' kinda tiresome."

Her problems were not my concern. I went straight to the poor old woman at the far bunk and used what I hoped was my friendliest voice.

"*Dzień dobry pani.*"

She stopped praying and looked up at me. Then she touched her forehead, heart and each shoulder in the sign of the cross, pushed off on the mattress with one hand and stood before me. She bowed deeply, ducking her head.

Oh, for Pete's sake! I had seen this behavior before and hated it. Women like my mother and grandmother in upstate New York, acting like housemaids to people on Main Street, clerks in department stores, bank tellers. In private, with their own families, they were brave enough. But in public, they turned into submissive women. I never actually saw any of them bow, like this strange lady, but in another time, they might have.

In another time. A buzzing started inside my ears and I thought I might faint. I took a deep centering breath.

"Please, pani, don't bow," I begged. Her face blank, she folded her hands in front of her waist. Short and squat, in kerchief and shawl, she reminded me of a Russian doll with another doll inside, and another and another. "How are you doing? Are you all right? Is there anything you need, anything I can get for you?" While I kept trying to connect, she stood there smiling weakly. I paged through my dictionary until I found the phrase I wanted. "*Czy pani masz pieniądze?*"

The question sounded patronizing the moment it left my lips, as if I believed her having money would solve anything.

She shook her head and looked behind me as though she hoped to see someone else, someone who could really help her. Her darting eyes and hunched body spoke more clearly than any words I knew. The person she needed was not me. And she knew it.

The woman who had let me in bent over a nearby bunk and smoothed out a rough gray blanket. More women sat on chairs and beds or stood around the big room, glancing at me from time to time. In a corner, little kids played with half-naked Barbies and scratched plastic cars, paying me no attention at all.

"I'm sorry for the intrusion," I said to everyone and no one. The air was close and warm. From somewhere I could not place, a cell phone's tinny dance tone broke the awkward silence. The Polish woman walked away from me, head down, still wrapped in my grandmother's shawl. I didn't have the heart to ask for it back. Why couldn't she understand I wanted to help her?

Maybe, Kat, it's because you called the cops to take her away. I unzipped my jacket and looked back at the exit. It was too hot in here. I needed some air.

"Do widzenia!" I called out behind me. Not sure at all that she'd heard me, or even that she cared, I whispered "Good bye."

With a quick wave for whoever might be watching, I hurried away, the rough gravel in the parking lot crunching a reproach under my feet. I fumbled in my purse for my keys and almost walked into the back of a large black SUV. Once inside my own car, I sat in the driver's seat and stared unseeing at the dirt-flecked windshield. It wasn't my fault the old woman was so sad, was it? Why hadn't Family Services found someone who could speak Polish? Maybe they were working on it. The old lady was safe, after all. She would be fed and cared for and eventually returned to wherever she came from. *Wherever it might be, here or across the sea.*

An image of Polish folk dancers leapt into my mind. Years ago, Alan and I attended a Polish festival at a shrine on the outskirts of Doylestown, the county seat five miles from our home. The costumes on the dancers were similar to what the old woman wore. The lace-up boots, the long full skirt, the loose white blouse, and the cotton headscarf tied behind her neck. But the dancers' costumes were far more colorful, ribbons streaming through their hair. And she was far too old to be a dancer. Perhaps she had been separated from a group of historical reenactors. But why had no one come forward to look for her? Surely the police would have known by now.

The roar of the adjacent SUV's engine broke into my daydream. I nodded to the man behind the wheel, started my own car and drove away.

On the highway, I got the idea to hire someone to translate for us, get her address and take her home. Her family would be so relieved. They'd be grateful to me for helping her. Smiling to myself as I pulled in my driveway, I rushed into the kitchen and called the police department again to get the number of the language line. But when their receptionist quoted the fees for interpreting in real time, my plan fell apart. The language line was fine for emergencies, but would cost way too much for a lengthy conversation. Dejected, I hung up and started to walk up the stairs to my bedroom, when a light clicked on inside my brain. The Polish culture festival was held at the Shrine of Our Lady of Częstochowa, just a few miles away, where Alan and I had seen the folk dancing. Maybe someone there could help me.

In my room, I powered up my laptop and found the number for the shrine online, pulled out my cell phone to make the call and shrugged off my jacket as I waited for a machine to answer. I was mentally composing the message I would leave when a voice said:

"Shrine of Częstochowa, how may I help you?"

"Yes, uh, hello," I said, surprised to hear the voice of a real live human being. "By any chance, do you have any Polish folk dancers staying there, at the shrine?"

"Oh, no, we don't get them until our festival in September. It's quite wonderful, you can..."

"Yes, I know. I've been to the festival. I met a woman recently, and she was dressed like one of those dancers."

"Oh, I see. Well, there is no one like that here now. No dancers. Why do you call here? Why not ask her?" Her condescending tone set off my defenses and my reply was curt.

"She doesn't speak *English*."

"I see. Will there be anything else today?"

"Actually, yes. Do you know of any translators? Someone I could hire to interpret for me?"

"Why, yes, absolutely. We have a list. Let me look that up for you. Please hold."

While I waited, a Chopin melody played in my ear, taking me to a peaceful and familiar place. I had never been to Poland. I didn't know much about classical music. Yet this haunting song meant something to my soul. I wanted to hear more of it, but the music cut off abruptly as the woman came back on the line.

"A young woman just called us yesterday. She recently came to the U.S. from Warsaw and wants to be a translator. Let me give you her name and number."

And just like that, Aniela Wegierski entered my life.

Chapter Five

ANIELA AGREED TO MEET ME at the Starbucks in Doylestown on the corner of State and Main. Thirty miles north of Philadelphia, the borough bore signs of city sophistication–chain coffee shops, a Gap store, the movie theater showing indie films–while holding on to its small-town charm. Famous people like James Michener, Margaret Mead and Oscar Hammerstein had once walked its sidewalks. We claimed pop singer Pink and American Idol star Justin Guarini as hometown kids. I liked shopping and dining there, but I loved my little acre in the country, five miles from the center of town. The best of both, town and country: that's what Alan and I always said. It was one thing we agreed on, and the thought brought a pang of regret. Oh well, I had to go on. It was time for my appointment with the translator. I picked up my order at the counter and found two seats in a quiet corner.

An attractive twenty-something woman in a show-stopping outfit walked in the door. I was the only one in the place, so I wasn't hard to find.

She smiled and strode to the armchair where I nursed my cappuccino. "Ms. Kowalski," she said, towering over me. "Thank you for the interview."

I smiled back, and tried for a competent look. "Of course, please, have a seat."

"I am happy to help my people in this country," she said with a smile. Her shiny brown hair fell around her heart-shaped face, accented by a soft black velvet hat with a long curving feather.

We chatted a bit about the weather and the parking situation, always a hot topic in town. When she spoke, her consonants were hard and clearly enunciated. She stumbled over the silent letters in English words so that "height" came out "high-et." She lengthened her vowels: "white" was "why-t." It was a subtle difference, but to me a familiar one, like the speech of my grandmother, and for that reason alone, I trusted her.

"My schedule is pretty much my own," she said, "So I can be flexible."

Luckily, both of us were free in the middle of the day. I worked only three half-days a week and she, a young emigre married to a software engineer, worked only when she felt like it, as a Polish-English translator. Her rates were remarkably low, but at the time I thought nothing of it.

Pleased to have her help, I never questioned her eagerness. Nor did I ask for references. She came recommended by a Catholic shrine. What could be safer than that? I offered her the job and we sealed the deal with a quick, firm handshake that made her laugh. I gave her directions to my house, and the next day, she picked me up in her sporty little BMW and drove me back to the shelter.

With Aniela beside me, I felt more optimistic. We checked in at the office and this time, Alecia stood up at her desk and gave us a wide smile.

"Oh, hi," she breathed, smoothing her skirt with both hands. "Have you brought someone to see our Polish guest? How nice!"

My blue jeans and sweater under a fake leather jacket felt sloppy next to Aniela's haute couture, and my voice turned squeaky. "We thought we should check with you before going over there. Is it all right?"

"Sure, sure, I'll walk you over."

"That won't be necessary." I turned away. Did she think I deserved more attention now because of my well-dressed companion? Well, who needed her? Aniela walked faster to keep up with me, the feathers on her hat fluttering in the breeze.

At the women's dorm, I lifted a hand to knock but the door opened before I could touch it. A young woman with stringy blond hair eyed us up and down.

"Good morning. We're here to see the lady over there, near the back." I pointed at the mystery woman sitting on her bunk, lips moving rapidly, my grandmother's shawl around her shoulders. The woman at the door stepped aside with a little stumble as Aniela pushed past het.

"*Dzień dobry pani!*" Aniela strode toward the woman we were here to see. Her high black boots clicked on the vinyl floor as she reached out her hand. She kissed the old woman lightly on both cheeks and spoke a rapid string of Polish words, and like magic, the woman's face relaxed, the ghost of a smile on her lips. This time she backed away but did not bow.

"What did you say to her?"

"Oh, I just put her at ease, told her we meant no harm." Aniela's warm girlish smile reminded me of Jessica.

"Ask her why she came to my house and where her family is."

"Of course, of course. All in due time. Shall we sit?" With a courtly gesture, Aniela swept a hand from the old woman to the worn sofa in the corner. The woman obediently walked over to it and sat down while Aniela and I sat facing her on faded upholstered chairs. As Aniela translated my questions, the old woman began to speak faster and faster. Aniela leaned forward as if to hear better. Her expression grew serious. She licked her thin red lips and when she looked at me, I shrank back in my chair.

"*What? What is it?*" I whispered. She straightened her spine and motioned to the woman on the couch.

"This lady comes here from far away. Her name is Regina Wrozkowna and she is from village of Mała Łąka in Austrian Empire."

"Then why is she speaking Polish?"

33

"Ms. Kowalski, Austrian Empire? Does that not mean anything to you?"

"Please, call me Kat. It's historic, right? There is no Austrian Empire anymore."

"Correct. Austrian Empire enveloped southern third of Poland in late eighteenth through nineteenth century. She must return there. Her child is very ill."

For a change, I was speechless. And breathless. The old woman sat forward and stared at me, her hands clasped together in her lap.

"You mean she thinks she's living in another century?" I whispered, not taking my eyes off her.

"Looks that way, does it not? What do you want to do now?"

"Jeez." The pressure this gal could put on me was unnerving. "Let me think. At least we know her name."

While we talked, Regina trotted outside, her skirt flying around her legs. The disheveled blonde who had let us in called out from the doorway.

"You better go after her. She's lookin' for the outhouse again."

"What?" Aniela and I said at once.

"She don't like the indoor toilet. Scared 'o the flush. Must of come from a farm somewheres way out. She keeps goin' to pee out there in the bushes."

The door stood ajar and I ran out to find her scrambling through the shrubbery behind the house.

"Regina!" I called. "Come back!" She hurried away from me, heading for the woods at the end of the street. "*Pani,* please come back! Let us help you!"

I caught up with her just as she squatted and lifted her skirt. The cars on the highway were going too fast, I hoped, to see her in the tall weeds. With my back turned, I waited until I heard the dry weeds rustle.

"Please come back inside." She walked behind me as we re-entered the building. "Where's the ladies' room?" I asked the blond standing by her bunk.

"It's down that hallway over there," she said, inclining her head, "but it won't do no good. I already showed her. She don't like the flush."

I led Regina down the hall anyway. Every time I turned to look at her, she stopped walking and gripped her hands together.

"Hey," I said as gently as I could, "I'm not going to hurt you. I'm here to help." She looked down at the toes of her boots as I opened the door to the women's rest room. "Here's where you can wash up." I walked over to a sink mounted on the cinderblock wall, squirted liquid soap into my hands and turned on the faucet. She watched and nodded her head so many times it made me dizzy. "Stop nodding!" She flinched back. "I'm sorry. Come on. Put your hands under here."

I reached for her but she pulled away. Then, very slowly, she mimicked my actions. Pumped some soap into her palms, rubbed them together, turned the faucet on - and screamed. The shawl fell off and landed around her feet.

"Oh, my God!" I shouted. Her hand was an angry red and her screams echoed off the stone walls. I turned the cold-water knob as far as it would go and tried to grab her wrist but she pulled away, screaming and screaming.

"O Jezus! O Jezus!" Her cries of pain, calling on Jesus in Polish like my *Babcia,* brought tears to my eyes and I felt like that little girl again.

The bathroom door flew open. "What's the matter with *her*?" A girl holding a towel stood in the doorway. Her tangled blond hair covered her face and she bit at one of her fingernails. I found my voice through my tears, while Regina continued to scream and call for Jesus.

"She burned herself on the hot water. Can you get some help? Is there a first aid kit?" Guilt rose in my throat. Why, oh why, had I forced her to use the faucet?

"I'll get Miss Alecia." The girl left us and Regina's screaming died down to a whimper as she blew on her burned left hand. This was my fault. I had to make up for it, to show her I could still be trusted to take care of her.

"Look. The water's cold now," I said, and put my own hand under the faucet. "Let me put some cold water on your hand. It will feel better."

The door flew open, hitting the wall with a bang.

"What happened?" In both hands, Alecia carried a blue and white plastic box with a red cross on the outside, and right behind her was Aniela, peering over her shoulder.

"The hot water, she turned it on full force and put her hand under it." I said it all in one breath.

Alecia glared at me then put the box down in the sink and rummaged inside. I fought for control of my voice.

"Do you have any burn ointment in there?" I was desperate to look calm and collected. Aniela stepped closer, straightening her hat with both hands.

"What has happened?" A frown wrinkled her unlined brow.

"She burned herself. She turned on the hot water..." I waved my helpless hands in the air.

Aniela spun around to point a manicured finger at Alecia. "Your water is too hot! You are responsible for this! We may take legal action!"

Alecia's face turned beet red. "Now, now, there's no reason for that."

How quickly everything was falling apart around me. I fought back the panic clouding my mind.

"Can we just take care of her hand?" I took a tube of burn ointment from Alecia and went to Regina. "Here," I said to her. "Give me your hand."

She looked at me through tear-filled eyes.

"*Proszę pani*," I pleaded in a fragment of schoolgirl Polish. "Please." I squeezed a dab of the gold colored ointment onto my own hand and rubbed it in, smiling gamely, then offered her the tube. She held out her uninjured right hand and I let her apply the cream to her own burn, wincing along with her as she smoothed it over her reddened skin. Alecia unwound a length of gauze and wrapped it around Regina's left hand, securing it with a piece of white adhesive tape.

"You'll have to fill out a report. Nothing like this has ever happened here before."

"What?" I stared at Alecia in disbelief.

"An incident report. I *am* sorry, but you have to fill it out. We will be in touch with you about any injury, but it looks like she'll be okay." She motioned me to follow her back to the office.

"You do that," Aniela said, stepping in. "And we will see if indeed she will be okay." She threw the last word at Alecia with disdain. "Meantime, I shall keep my careful eyes on her." "*Proszę pójść ze mną.*" With one arm around Regina's shoulders, she led her out of the washroom.

Twenty minutes later, my report finished and duly signed, I handed it to Alecia in her office. She looked it over with a frown.

"You know, we have a limit here on one person's length of occupancy. And if she has no papers, our policy is to call the immigration officials."

"Well, of course, she has no papers! She doesn't know where she is. She's terrified!" My words came out in a high-pitched squeak. Did this woman have no heart? What was she thinking?

"I'm sorry, we have beds for emergency purposes but if she has no ID..." Alecia pursed her lips and looked away and I wanted to shake her.

"I can't believe this. It's ridiculous." I tried to think. "What will immigration do then?"

"Well, they have detention facilities..."

"Oh, no. You're not sending her to some jail!" I was sweating now, and angry. My nails dug into my palms.

"I am sorry, but there's nothing I can do. If, after two weeks, she has no one to claim her, we have to call the authorities." Her lips pressed together and she turned away from me to open the file cabinet.

Oh, for Pete's sake. This was supposed to be a shelter for the homeless. Regina was a homeless, helpless old woman. And Alecia was just another bureaucrat, following some stupid heartless rules. She didn't care about Regina. I slammed the screen door on the way out of her office and stormed back to the women's dorm where Aniela and Regina sat on wooden chairs next to a round table. I pulled another chair over to them. Because now I knew the burden was mine. The ball was in my court. I was Regina's only hope.

"How's it going?" I tried for a lightness I did not feel.

Aniela crossed and uncrossed her legs. She looked at me then at Regina. "Well, she says her hand does not hurt so bad anymore. She says you can have shawl. She wants to go home to her little girl as soon as possible. The child is quite ill. And she seems to believe it is 1825."

"Well, tell her it's not! Tell her it's *2017*...Wait a minute. This is ridiculous. You know, I wasn't born yesterday." I moved to the edge of my seat, gripping the wood with my fingers.

"Hey, I am only translator." Aniela patted her perfectly styled hair. "She says she is from Mała Łąka. She does not know she is not in Poland, or as it was then, Austrian Empire."

Regina's face registered anxiety as she stared at me, her eyes open wide. My frantic hand gestures and frenzied voice must have told her something was very much amiss. And she didn't even know what I had just learned from Alecia at the office. Strangely, Aniela remained calm, but I was too preoccupied to wonder why.

I walked to the window, collecting my thoughts, then looked back at my translator. She seemed normal, if a bit young for her job. Her English was almost perfect. But what she said was unbelievable. Still, I had hired her to translate the words, as she so calmly reminded me, not to make sense of them. I fired more questions at her.

"Ask her how she got here, what she's doing here, why she was in my kitchen." Regina looked too scared to be a burglar. And too awestruck to be lying. There must be a logical explanation for what she said. A vision of Regina locked in a cell in a detention center swam before me. She'd never be able to handle that. I'd never let it happen.

A rapid sputter of words passed back and forth between Aniela and Regina, and her eyes began to fill with tears. Her hands shook, the white gauze bandage a glaring reminder of my bungled attempt to help her. Then Aniela spoke again, her voice full of sympathy.

"Poor woman, she does not know how she got here. She was praying to Our Lady of Częstochowa, Black Madonna who is Queen of Poland." She cocked her head to one side, eyebrows raised.

"Yes, yes, I know about the Black Madonna. We learned about her in Catholic school."

"Okay. So, while she is praying a bright light comes, and a strong powerful wind. She cannot see anything, and then, as sudden as it came, the wind stops. Everything has become dark, and when her eyes adjust, she is still kneeling, but in cold dead grass behind big white manor house. She gets up and runs around but she cannot find the side road shrine where she prayed. She cannot find her house or her village. So, she cries and she hides in shrubbery and waits for daylight, and then she sees big white machine with wheels next to house. Could be your car?"

"Yeah, I guess... This is too weird." I stood, walked around the table and sat down again. What the hell...? Was she some sort of nut case, too disturbed for me to help?

As if she had read my mind, Regina began to spill out words, phrases, sentences, paragraphs, a steady stream of anxious Polish I could not follow. Aniela nodded now and then until Regina ran out of steam. Then she patted her hand and turned back to me.

"She finds herself in your backyard. She hides there all night; she does not know what to do. It is very noisy. Huge machines go by on road in front of house. She sees them through trees where she hides. In the morning, she is very hungry and goes closer to manor house to look for food. She opens door in back and walks into kitchen, searches and finds big white closet with lots of things to eat. She steals the cheese, for which she would like to apologize." At this point, Aniela said something quick to Regina, who nodded vigorously. "You look nice, and she is tired from hiding. She thinks you look like family. She hopes you will help her."

"Let me get this straight: she thinks she got lost in nineteenth century Poland and decided to walk in my backdoor and eat from my fridge?"

"In a nut case, that is what she says."

"Uh, I think you mean, 'nutshell.'"

"Yes, yes, whatever. The American idiom can be sometimes a bit confused. Anyway, she says she is starving so comes inside during the night, looking for food and finds nothing but paper boxes and metal cylinders - must be your canned goods—in the cupboards. She sees big white box on floor and pulls it open. *Voila!* Cheeses, milk, apples!" Aniela waved her arms to punctuate her words, hitting the feather on her hat so that it fell across her face. She blushed and moved it aside to stare at me but I hardly noticed.

"Why *my* house? Why not my neighbor's?" But the Goddess cards, my grandmother's eyes in the mirror...my stomach clenched. I stole a glance at Regina. *Babcia* had taken care of me when I needed her. She had never let me down. Maybe it was my turn to pay her love forward.

Aniela broke into my thoughts. "There could be many reasons, Kat." She tapped her lips with one gloved hand but offered nothing more.

My logical side worked hard to brush her off, but it was already too late.

"Look at how she's dressed. Who dresses like that?" Still trying for a rational explanation, I knew there would not be one. And I would not let any "officials" take her away to God knows where. She had been through enough.

With barely controlled impatience, Aniela gave a little sigh. "She wants only to get back home, her child has fever and stomach cramps. What do you want to do?"

With Aniela by my side, I felt less alone, and even, for the moment, capable. "That woman in the office, Alecia, says they have to call immigration soon because she has no papers. They might put her in a detention facility." I looked at Regina's wrinkled face. "I think that would be too cruel. And it might kill her."

In the dark airless room, no one moved. I had the odd sensation that time stood still then sped away from us. Regina sat with shoulders curled inward, her arms holding her body tight. I swallowed my fear and made a decision.

"Tell her not to be afraid. We're going to help her. Ask her where her family is."

Aniela exhaled a puff of air. "She says her family is in *Mała Łąka*, Kat. That is real village in Poland near *Kraków*."

This was not going to be easy, I knew that much. But my Goddess cards had meant something. I didn't know exactly what, not in my head. But in my heart, well, that was another story.

Regina's gaze fell to her bandaged hand folded into the fabric of her skirt. She cradled it like a wounded bird and words left my mouth before I realized what I was about to say.

"Please ask her if she wants to come home with me."

Chapter Six

AFTER A BRIEF EXCHANGE with Aniela, Regina agreed to leave with us. No doubt my house seemed better than the shelter, even if I *had* helped her burn herself. At least we tried to speak with her in Polish instead of leaving her in a roomful of women who ignored her and spoke what was to her a foreign language.

Back at the office, Alecia was quite willing to let Regina go. "I'm sure she'll be happier with you. There are so many things she doesn't understand. And I'd really hate to call the authorities on such a sad case." Her look of patronizing pity made me come to the old lady's defense.

"Don't worry, I'll take her off your hands. It's obvious you don't know a thing about taking care of her here. Come on, Regina, let's go." Alecia watched us leave with her mouth half-open, as though she would speak if she knew what to say.

Aniela followed, tossing a regal wave behind her as she went out the door.

"You will hear from our attorney!" I liked her even more for that.

With her eyes shut tight, Regina whispered in the back seat as we drove away. The afternoon was chilly, but when I saw her uninjured hand grip the door handle, warmth wrapped itself around my heart.

"My grandfather used to hold the car door like that." Aniela braked for a red light and gave me a sidelong look. I turned to Regina in the back seat. "He came from Poland, and when my uncle took us for Sunday rides in the country, he sat in the back, just like you are now, and hung onto the door handle, just like that."

Aniela looked into the rearview mirror then ahead again as the light flashed green. I turned to her. "She doesn't understand a word I'm saying, does she?"

Aniela gave me a condescending smile. "She may be sick from riding in the car." When I looked back, Regina's face had taken on a greenish hue. She quietly whispered to herself as we headed north on the highway, past dealerships with hundreds of cars in their lots. Regina covered her mouth, her other hand still gripping the door handle. She'd feel so much better at my house, I thought, away from that dingy shelter. I wanted to tell Aniela that.

"Boy, that place was a real eye-opener. So many women in one bleak room, and I can't believe how hot that water tap was. Who knows what accidents were waiting to happen? At least I can give her a nice warm bed and her own private room, maybe find her family. I don't get what she said about the sick child, though. She looks kind of old to have a little kid."

"Why all this is so important to you?" Aniela's voice was not unkind.

"I don't know. It just feels like something I have to do." I was not yet comfortable telling her about my Goddess cards or Regina's uncanny resemblance to my grandmother. Or that I missed my *Babcia* every time I looked at her with an ache that swelled my throat. *Babcia*: the one who listened to my troubles after Mom left, and held me when I cried. The one who told me I was smart and pretty and strong.

Aniela's stern voice broke through. "Nothing is 'have to do.' She is not your mother, Kat. Maybe other social services know how to handle such cases."

My hackles rose at once. What did this young woman know about my mom? She had quoted back to me the line from my mother's note: "this is something I have to do," as if I was even remotely like her. I shifted in my seat and frowned.

"Cases of old women dressed like Polish peasants who don't speak English or know how to use an indoor toilet? I thought you wanted to help your people in the U.S."

From the back seat came the whispered words of a prayer.

"Zdrowaś Maryjo, łaski pełna." The Polish Hail Mary I learned from nuns at my parochial school. I was determined not to let Aniela see it, but I knew in that moment I had taken on a daunting task. Regina was separated from her family. She needed to find them. What I would never admit, even to myself, was that I needed her, too.

I grew up a lonely child with few friends. After Mom left and Dad withdrew into himself, I tried to be self-reliant. I read for hours on end, and worked out my own little stories with my dolls. When I became a woman, I tried to create a family of my own, but, somehow, I had managed to screw that up. Now, Fate had dropped someone into my kitchen, someone who could be just what I wanted: the mother I had lost long ago.

"Here we are," I said as we pulled into my driveway. I was surprised to see Alan's FedEx truck parked in the turnaround space next to the big maple tree. Regina had stopped praying and I turned in my seat to face her.

"Tutaj," I stammered. *"Jest mój dom."* I was far from bilingual. I didn't know the words for "welcome," or "you'll be all right here," or anything else I wanted to say. I got out of the car and went around to unbuckle Regina's seatbelt, planning my next steps.

"Aniela, can you come by tomorrow and help me talk to her again?" The woman looked half my age, but for some reason I could not name, she intimidated me. I hated to ask but her fee was low and I really needed her to translate. Now her face softened and her voice was quiet.

"Yes, I will come. What time is good for you?"

"I guess we'll be here all morning. Why don't you come around nine?"

"Fine. I come at nine. *Do widzenia.*" At this, Regina brightened. She watched Aniela turn her silver BMW in the

44

driveway. Then she raised a hand and waved at the back of the receding car.

"*Do widzenia,*" she whispered.

"*Proszę,* please come in." I reached for Regina's good hand and with all the gentleness I could muster, guided her through the garage and into my laundry room, my home and my life.

Inside, Alan stood waiting, all six feet of him. His thick black hair hung over the deep frown above his eyebrows and touched the top of his eyeglass frames. He jiggled his house keys in one hand.

"What are *you* doing here?" I wasn't ready to explain Regina and my words came out more harshly than I felt. Behind me, Regina dropped the shawl and whimpered.

"Just came back for a couple things. I still have my key, if that's all right with you. Who's this?" He jerked a thumb at Regina who peered at him from around my shoulder.

"She's from Poland." I put my hands to the sides of my waist. "She got stranded and she needs a place to stay."

"And that would be here?" Alan's hostility hit me hard. Playing unexpected defense, I filled him in on the story of how I found her, called the police and brought her home from the shelter. I left out the part about wanting a mother. Alan already knew that. He had never understood why he and Jessica weren't enough for me.

"Alan, she's Polish. Like my grandparents. I want to help her, maybe learn a little, you know, find out about my heritage." I hated sounding so nervous.

Regina cowered back until she bumped into the washing machine. "You're scaring her," I said, but we both knew it was me who had raised the noise level.

"What are you going to do with her when you go to work, huh? Let the police or one of the county agencies take care of her." He put a large hand on the clothes dryer and scowled at the woman trying to hide behind me.

45

"Alan, she's clueless. She didn't know how to use the toilet or the water faucets. Nobody at that shelter has time to explain things to her."

"Oh, and you do?" His thick eyebrows went up as he stared at me through smudged glasses. His arms were folded in front of his chest in a pose I was quite familiar with, the one that meant the argument was over and I had lost. He glanced behind me and stared at Regina's bandage. "What the hell's wrong with her hand?"

"Oh, she had a little accident." I waved my hand as if I could wave away the white gauze covering hers and heal it in an instant. I tried a different tack. "I know it sounds crazy, Alan, but she looks just like my grandmother."

He peered down at me. "Actually, she looks a lot like *you*, Kat, especially around the eyes." He stared into mine then abruptly dropped his gaze. "I just hope you know what you're getting into." In one quick move, he picked up a bundle of his clothes from the top of the dryer and left.

The door closed behind him. Regina turned her wrinkled face toward mine as if waiting for instructions. Alan had just made it perfectly clear: he was not going to be here for us. Well, so what? Who needed him? I could do this. I pushed back my shoulders and stood a little taller. *Please let this work out for her highest good, and for the highest good of all.*

As I ended my silent prayer, my body felt light, as if lifted by unseen hands. I picked up the shawl from the laundry room floor and brought Regina up the stairs to the kitchen and through to the living room.

"Let's sit down a minute." I patted the sofa cushion beside me. The house was so quiet I could hear the walls creak. "What shall we do next?"

She ignored my invitation and walked into the kitchen, pulled food from the refrigerator and put it on the table. As I followed and watched her, I realized she must have done this the morning I found her. Was she always hungry? Didn't they feed her in the shelter? So many questions I could not ask, because she could not understand.

46

I folded the shawl over the back of a chair and sat, inviting her to do the same. Then I watched her eat cold cuts of ham and slices of cheese as if it would be her only meal for days.

Chapter Seven

THE NEXT MORNING, a hard wind rattled the windowpanes as Aniela, Regina and I settled around my dining room table. It was my day off from work and I was eager to get started.

"*Dzień dobry,*" Aniela greeted us wearing a soft black velvet beret and a gold brocade suit with tall leather boots. Her manner was always formal but I found her costume unusual for a self-assured twenty-something. It seemed more appropriate for an older, out-of-style woman of means.

"*Dzień dobry,*" Regina spoke her part in the little round of Good Mornings.

"So, Aniela," I said, "what did you say your husband did?"

"He is software engineer for TD Bank in the King of Prussia. If I may say it, you have strange names for cities here." She raised her chin.

"Yes, I know, that one's pretty odd. Do you have kids?" She was young, but I wanted to know.

A cloud passed over her face and she brushed at the front of her suit. "No, we do not have children."

"Well, you're young yet..."

She cut me off. "Can we get on with things?"

"Of course. I'm sorry. Didn't mean to get so personal. I'll get the tea things."

While the two women exchanged more pleasantries, I placed a sugar bowl and creamer, spoons, and a plate of chocolate chip cookies on placemats. In the kitchen, I poured hot water from the electric kettle into three cups with tea bags and carried in the cups on a tray.

"So you believe she is who she says?" Aniela asked me, stirring her tea.

"Well, it *is* pretty farfetched, don't you think? Ask her more questions. Try to find out if she's on the level." By now, I almost wished Regina *was* from 1825. That would mean she had no one in the modern world but me. And I might have someone who would stay with me for good. My thoughts were about to take me to a place where everything would be all right, when Aniela's voice broke through.

"Yes, yes, do not pressure me!" Her hands went to her beret. She closed her eyes and took a deep breath. *A deep cleansing breath?* Same thing I did to deal with my stress.

"Breath work is great, isn't it?"

Her eyes flew open. "What is breath work?"

"You know, what you just did. Taking a deep cleansing breath...."

Her dark eyes shot fire. "It is not easy to always do what you, my client, says. So many questions at once. Please, give me a moment." Her cheeks were a bright pink and I worried she might be ill.

"Are you okay...?"

"Stop it, please! I am okay. I am okay!" Her voice was so loud Regina startled in her chair, then blessed herself. Aniela shook her head and reached across to pat Regina's hand.

"Nie bardzo panią rozumiem," she said then turned to me. "She speaks some kind of peasant dialect. It is very different from the Polish I speak as an educated woman. But I will do my best."

She pushed her teacup aside, folded her manicured hands together on the table and began to translate my questions. Regina answered at a fast and nervous clip. Back and forth they went, Aniela's face intent, Regina's agitated.

Finally, Aniela leaned back and gave me another of her dark-eyed stares. "Her child has fever and stomach cramps, she needs to go home and take care of her today. What are you going to do?"

I looked at Regina's lined face, the gray hair sticking out from around the edges of her headscarf, her wrinkled hands. "How old is this child? She has got to be at least seventy, don't you think? Just look at her!"

Aniela threw out another flurry of Polish words, then: "Her child is six years old. She has the name Anna."

Regina bit her lip and twisted her right hand in her skirt. I didn't know what to make of this. How could an old woman have a six-year-old child?

"Is it her grandchild? Is that what she means? She has a grandchild in Poland?"

More words flew back and forth.

"No, no, the child is her daughter, a little 'surprise.'" Aniela's eyebrows rose to the edge of her beret. "Odd that some young women cannot have children and yet this old one..."

"I don't know about this." I looked Regina over, wondering if it was true, and she was really an older mother, or if she suffered from dementia and just imagined herself younger than she was. "Ask her how old she is."

"She does not know for sure, but she thinks around fifty."

"She can't be! I'm fifty!"

"May I say, Kat, you look very good for that age?" Aniela inclined her head with a little smile and I had the uncanny sense she knew more about me than she was letting on. Meanwhile, Regina rocked back and forth in her chair. She wiped at a tear with her good hand. I went to the bathroom for a box of tissues and placed it before her on the table, giving her shoulder a little pat. Poor thing! We would get to the bottom of this. Wherever her family was, we'd get a hold of them, and they'd be so happy and grateful. Have me over for dinner, and holidays...

"Kat! Kat! Did you hear me?" For a second, I didn't know who was speaking. Then I remembered where I was. Aniela frowned at me and leaned forward. "Didn't you hear what I said? I repeat and repeat myself!" Her long red nails reflected the light from the small chandelier above the table.

"Uh, no, sorry, I was thinking about something else. Sorry. What did you say?"

"I *said*, Regina cries for her child! I have asked her again where she lives, and she says the same: Mała Łąka. She does not realize how far away it is."

Regina stared at me unblinking. I tapped at my lips with my fingertips, trying to buy some time.

"Tell her it's too far to go right now. Tell her she has to stay here for a while."

When Regina heard the translation, she started to cry again and raised her bandaged hand to her mouth.

"Poor lady, she did not realize she is in the United States." Aniela faced me squarely. "You must understand: not only is she not in her village, as she believed. She is in what to her is the future."

Aniela looked out the window behind me and I looked there, too, wishing for another answer, preferably something much less freaky. She spoke again.

"Kat, please look at her: *chustka* on head, peasant clothing, and she is unfamiliar with the modern technology. If she is just a crazy woman then why all this? Why does she not know about hot water from faucet, toilet in house?" Aniela pursed her lips and leaned back with arms crossed. "This case reminds me of characters from parallel universe in science fiction." On her side of the table, Regina held her teacup in both hands as if it might keep her from flying off into another century.

"I don't know." I toyed with my teaspoon, thinking. There is more to this world than we know. I had always believed that, even as a little girl. I read a lot then and even now, from fantasy to mystery to New Age and sci fi. Last week on NPR, I heard a quantum physicist say we could be living in a multiverse, with lots of parallel universes. I trusted in my affirmations, my Goddess cards, the objects on my little kitchen shrine, to show me what I could not see with my eyes alone. What if time travel was really possible? A little shiver of excitement ran through me. "See if she knows anything about

Polish history around the time she says she came from, what was it, 1825?"

The two women spoke while I watched and waited, trying to remember to breathe. Regina sniffled quietly but consented to answer more questions. Aniela leaned in closer and stopped to translate only when I tapped her arm.

"Okay, okay, this is what she tells me. Czar fought Prussians to control Małopolska, where she is from. Very dangerous to travel and people disappear." Regina was talking almost as fast as Aniela. "Wait. Oh, too bad. One of them is her best friend, Zofia."

"What happened? *Who* disappeared?" Maybe this was a clue to how Regina got lost. Nothing short of a hurricane could have torn me away.

"Zofia and her husband take crucifixes he carves to sell at market in *Lipinki*," Aniela translated. "They are never seen or heard again. Probably robbed and murdered. She does not know for sure."

"Oh my God!" I placed my hand on Regina's shoulder beside me. She wept without making a sound, and I pushed the box of tissues toward her. She stared at it and pulled one out, holding it up to the light.

"Here." I dabbed at my eyes with one of the tissues to show her what to do. Regina brought it to her nose and smelled it, then wiped her eyes and nose, then tried to put the used one in her shirtsleeve but the bandage on her hand got in the way.

"Give it to me." I held out my hand, took the used tissue into the kitchen and tossed it in the trashcan under the sink. When I came back, I passed Regina the plate of cookies. She gave me a little smile and reached for one, bringing it closer to examine the embedded chips and pick at them with her fingernail.

"It's chocolate." I turned to Aniela. "Tell her it's chocolate."

"Is it so important right now? In middle of possible time travel investigation? Okay, okay," she said when she saw the look in my eyes. *Czekolada,*" she mumbled and gestured at

52

the plate with her amber-ringed hand. "They have chocolate in Poland, even two hundred years ago."

Regina bit off a piece of cookie and chewed. Her eyes still red from crying reminded me of Jessica when she was small, so easily distracted from her tears with a treat, and all at once, I missed my daughter with a pain as sharp as the day she left.

I looked away to collect myself when a stack of books on a chair in the corner caught my eye. I walked over and picked up the one on top, offering it to Aniela.

"I found this yesterday in my old college stuff. It covers the time in Poland when she thinks...when she came from... you know, the early nineteenth century." Talking like this, as if there really was such a thing as time travel, made me stammer. "See if you can condense it. Find out what she knows." Aniela took the book from me and with a deep sigh, opened it where I had placed a post-it note.

"Hmmm...In 1830, the Poles rebelled. Russian troops put down the revolt and the Czar made the Poles adopt the Russian language and culture." She repeated this in Polish, only to have Regina cry again. She thumped the closed book onto the table. "What is point? We are just upsetting her." As the book hit the table, Regina jumped a little in her seat as if to underscore Aniela's words.

"I just thought it might prove she is a time traveler, and maybe connect us to her. We are all three of us Polish, after all."

"Yes, but you were born here, Kat. After, might I add, one of grimmest periods in history of Poland. Would you like me to ask her about Hitler invasion and Holocaust? What about Auschwitz and Birkenau? And after the War, Communist takeover, and Stalin? Exactly how do you think that will help you to connect?" The fire in her eyes took me by surprise. For a woman so young, she scared me. I would never have taken this from my daughter.

"You're right," I said, backing off. "Maybe it's not such a good idea." A sudden gust of wind threw a dead branch against the house. Regina sat up straight and blessed herself with her right hand. A knot began to form in the pit of my stomach. "Do you think she's on the level?" I whispered. "I mean, about coming here from the past?"

Aniela gave an exasperated sigh. "You pay me to translate her words, not make existential judgment." She tapped her foot against the table leg. "I care what is best for her and for you. Do you not see it? What is all the arguing and questioning for? Can you not hear what I say to you, the words I am translating?"

With each question, her color deepened. Finally, she blew a puff of air that fluttered the hair above her brow. Her questions sounded like a test meant only for me. Time was passing, carrying us along as Regina whispered her prayer and the winter wind howled outside my window.

Chapter Eight

AFTER ANIELA LEFT for the day, Regina sat in my favorite chair near the living room window as if she was waiting for someone to come and take her home. She turned at the sound of my footsteps on the hardwood floor, and my mother's eyes, as they were in the days before she left, looked back at me.

Often, I had found Mom staring out the window just like this. I had always believed that if I had only known how unhappy she was, I might have done something to help, to keep her from leaving. But I didn't know what that was. Today, in my house, there was someone I *could* help. Someone who needed me like my mom. Maybe.

Regina watched me, her eyes sad, her mouth downturned, and waited. I tried on what I hoped was a reassuring smile and turned on the TV, my back to her. Colorful scenes flashed across the screen as I flipped through the channels with the remote. *Come on, there's got to be something on she would like.* Impatient, I accidentally hit the volume instead of the channel finder. Regina screamed so loudly I dropped the remote. She stood pointing at the screen, her little fist covering her mouth. For the first time, I was glad we hadn't opted for the big flat screen. Ours was a 24-inch table model, and that was, apparently, realistic enough to be frightening.

"It's okay. It's just the TV..." *Hah! Just the TV.* She obviously had no idea what it was. "Look. It's just a box." I turned the revolving stand around so she could see the cord running from the back to the wall. "You can watch a story."

55

On the screen, Mel Gibson ran headlong in front of an army through the hills of ancient Scotland. Regina backed away and fell against the couch. Her hand shook as she made the sign of the cross over her forehead, heart and shoulders. I muted Mel's war cry and carried the remote control over to her.

"See, you can make it quiet or loud, even change the picture." Regina cowered deeper into the couch.

"Okay, maybe TV is not such a good idea." I was all too aware of my ineptitude. She could not understand a word I said. I flicked off the power and tossed the remote onto the coffee table where it skidded to the floor.

Regina huddled on the couch with her arms around herself in a lonely embrace. I wanted to curl up into a ball myself, on the cushion right beside her. But that would never do. I tried to pat her shoulder but she flinched and turned away, and something came loose inside me, a hurt and wounded broken thing. No use to her now, perhaps ever, I left her there alone.

Upstairs in my room, I let my own tears flow. I lay down across the quilt covering my bed, a familiar pose these days, and cried. Whatever I did, I seemed to mess things up. I was desperate to make the right choices, but there were so many. The first time Chuck and I flirted played across my mind. I had felt trapped and lonely then and made the wrong choice. I was trapped and lonely now, but I didn't want Alan back. Not yet. Not until I was sure. Nor did I want Chuck, who spoke to me at work only when necessary. My daughter wouldn't take my calls, and I only wanted to help her. Now I'd taken in a strange old woman who depended on me, and I couldn't even talk to her without a translator. Why wasn't anything working for me? I pounded my fist into the pillow. It didn't help. Nothing helped. But I couldn't just lie there. Just like the day Mom left, just like always when my heart was breaking, I had to go on. I sat up, ran my hands through my hair and went to the bathroom to wash my face.

At dinner, Regina ate with tears falling onto her plate. My throat tightened as I witnessed again, in her slumped posture, my mother's sadness and my father's stoic defeatism. I put down my fork and tried to think of something to say in her language to comfort her, but I was still hurting, too, and the words would not come. She went on chewing, and cut her fish with her knife and fork ...with her bandaged hand! What was this? She acted like it didn't hurt at all.

"When you're finished, let's take a look at that burn." She nodded with no change of expression, still focused on her plate. I tapped my foot against my chair rung until she put down her fork and wiped her mouth with her sleeve. "Come on." I took her upstairs to the bathroom. With long narrow scissors, I cut the tape and gauze from her hand. When I took them off, she didn't even wince. I dropped the scissors onto the floor.

The burn was gone. She let me turn her hand over, searching for a mark I had missed. There was no evidence of any injury on her skin, not even a blemish. Open-mouthed, she pulled her hand away and blessed herself.

"You heal fast, don't you?" Unnerved, I wondered if she had special powers, like the crystals on my altar. I held them sometimes, for good luck, but never to achieve something like this, something so real, so visible. She fell to her knees, her lips moving, and folded her hands in front of her chest with her head bowed.

Of course. She believed in miracles. In prayers answered. I wanted to believe it, too, but I was rocked to my core and my rational mind fought for an explanation. Maybe the burn wasn't as bad as I'd thought. Maybe she had some special kind of Polish immunity. Maybe...

Regina blessed herself again, stood and smiled a little smile. Okay, I'd deal with it. I had to, for her sake. And maybe for my own sanity. She followed me back to the kitchen and watched me load cups and saucers into the dishwasher. After a while she touched my shoulder, picked up a dishcloth, and used it to cover her hand as she gingerly turned on the faucet over the sink. Smart lady, I thought. She won't get burned again. She smiled at me over her shoulder, a small thing I grabbed and ran with toward a fantasy of our life together. *She'd learn to like it here. I'd make sure of that.* I squirted dishwashing liquid into the sink, and laughed with her at the suds forming in her hands.

Regina washed every dish and scrubbed every fork and knife until it shone. The dishwasher behind us was half-empty, the door hanging open. We could have filled it, and let the machine do the work, but she looked so content, I picked up a towel and dried. Working beside her, a comfortable peace wrapped me and my kitchen in a soft warm glow.

That night, I stopped in the doorway of the guest room as Regina prepared for bed. Her clothes lay over the back of a wicker chair. Though we'd washed them with my laundry, I was tired of looking at them. Tomorrow, I would find something else for her to wear. Wearing only a plain muslin slip, she walked to the window and looked out on my back garden, where moonlight bathed the flowers and herbs. Regina gazed down at them, her hands gripping the wooden sill like a medieval princess trapped in a tower.

How could I have thought that a walk through European history would prove anything, or help us understand her plight? Even worse, I had exposed her to a violent movie. She obviously didn't watch TV in her normal life, wherever that might be. Aniela would help us at our next meeting. But tonight, it was all up to me. And I couldn't give up now. I knew I could make her like it here.

We would start with personal hygiene. Her small teeth were brownish yellow, but we could fix that. In the bathroom, I took a new toothbrush, embossed with my dentist's name, from the medicine cabinet, squeezed out a line of toothpaste and held it up to her face.

"Toothbrush!" She backed away. "Sorry. Look, I'll show you." I loaded my electric toothbrush with mint green paste and pushed the start button, making it vibrate with a loud hum. She jumped and held her hands behind her back.

"Okay, you don't have to brush tonight. Here, let me show you how to wash up." I plugged the sink and demonstrated the faucet handles, gesturing at the steam rising from the water in the basin. "Just like the one in the kitchen, which you already know." I sounded like a lecturer, tiresome even to myself. Maybe I should just wash her face like a child's. Like Jessica's. Another pang of loss moved through me but I shook it off.

Regina stepped closer and took a bar of rose-scented soap from the dish, held it to her nose and inhaled deeply. She dipped a face cloth into the water, rubbed the soap against it and brought it to her face.

"Good! Good! You know how to wash your face!" She looked at me as if I had two heads. She rinsed the face cloth, and proceeded to rub it over her teeth. Then she wiped her wet face and hands on her slip.

"Oops. Sorry." I moved away from the towel rod, and handed her a fluffy white one. "*Dziękuję.*" She finished drying herself and hung the damp towel back on the rod, smoothing out the wrinkles. When I touched the light switch, she gasped and jumped against me in the sudden darkness.

"Sorry!" I demonstrated flipping the little plastic switch and she nodded. I waved for her to come closer and try it herself, but she shook her head and walked back into the guest room murmuring either another prayer or a question about my sanity. I couldn't tell which.

"That's enough new stuff for tonight." It was a declaration to myself as much as to her. "Good night, Regina! *Dobranoc!*"

"*Dobranoc,*" she echoed, already climbing into bed.

Chapter Nine

THE NEXT MORNING, we were up with the sun. I found Regina sitting on the living room couch with a blanket pulled up to her shoulders. She gazed out the window at the fog-shrouded field through darkly circled eyes. My own head felt as foggy as the field.

In the kitchen, I measured coffee into the filter basket. Regina walked in and huddled into a chair, her blanket still wrapped around her. It was the same chair she had been sitting in the first time I saw her. And she was wearing the same long skirt and blouse.

As the coffee's pungent aroma filled the room, I went back upstairs to find her some fresh clothes. From the back of my closet, I pulled a pair of baggy grey sweatpants and a selection of large sweatshirts. They looked large enough to fit her stocky frame, and they were warm enough for this chilly day.

"Here you go." I walked back into the kitchen with the pile of clothing in my arms. "You can wear these."

Regina smiled at me but made no move to take the clothing from my arms, so I placed them on the empty chair next to her. She reached out a tentative hand to touch the logo on Jessica's Penn State sweatshirt.

"Here, let me help you try it on." She moved her chair back and shook her head.

"*Nie, nie, dziękuję.*" She blinked rapidly, still clutching the blanket around her shoulders.

60

"You can wear these. It's okay. Come on, try them on." She stood up and shook her head once more, then hurried upstairs, the blanket trailing behind her. The morning was not off to a good start.

I ate my oatmeal alone and took the clothes back to my closet, repeating another empowering affirmation. *I always know what to do, in every situation.*

Aniela was due to come over at nine, and I hurried to get dressed before she arrived. My shift at the library would start late that afternoon, so we'd have plenty of time. When I heard her car in the driveway, I went to the door.

"Maybe if we can get Regina to tell us more about her family, we can figure out how to help her," I said as I led her to the dining room. Regina was already seated with her hands folded on the table before her.

The furnace kicked on with a roar. I pulled Babcia's shawl from its usual place on the back of a chair and wrapped it around my shoulders. In an instant, the flowered cloth enveloped me in a warm and comforting glow. Across from me, Regina looked so small and wan. I pulled another shawl from a basket on the floor and gently placed it around her. I had knitted this one myself, and it pleased me to see her stroke its soft white folds as she talked to Aniela, her voice low and even. After every few sentences, Aniela stopped to translate, rattling off the facts in a hurry, as if she knew we would reach a point when I would know enough.

Regina said she lived with her husband Pawel and six of their twelve children. I covered a gasp with my hand. *TWELVE children.* My foot tapped on the wooden chair slats so fast Aniela gave me a frown. I smiled at her, uncrossed my legs and returned my attention to Regina.

Her family lived in house number 19. She said it was much smaller than mine. Her church was St. Bartholomew. Her pastor was Father Marek. Whatever we wanted to know, she said, she'd be happy to tell us, if only we would take her back home as soon as possible. She had to take care of Anna, who was only six and very ill.

The back of my throat ached. She was so obviously homesick, and maybe she really did have a sick child, though she looked far too old. The name of the church didn't sound familiar. I wanted to give her some ease and comfort while the police continued to search for her family. And if I found out, as I hoped, that she was part of mine... My heart did a little dance. She might be a woman a lot like me.

"Ask her what she likes to do to de-stress."

Aniela tilted her head and peered at me. "I beg your pardon. This is a word I do not know. De-stress?"

"Relax, calm down, you know, center herself..." I waved my hands in the air.

Aniela rolled her eyes. "Okay, I get."

A puzzled look came over Regina's face as she listened to the translation, then gave her answer.

"She does not know what you mean. She cooks, she cleans, she feeds the animals. Sometimes there is holiday, and for this, she also cooks, cleans."

"But what does she do in her spare time?" Aniela gave me another look. "Oh, I get it. No spare time. Hmmm. Ask her what makes her happy."

More words tumbled back and forth. "She likes to pray to Black Madonna, Queen of Poland, at her shrine, and to have big holiday dinners with her married children and their families coming to visit."

The holiday dinners sounded good to me too. I had wanted a big family as far back as I could remember, but it hadn't worked out. Could I still make that happen? How could I find House 19 in Mała Łąka? Or St. Bartholomew's Church?

Aniela's imperious voice broke through my excited mental plans.

"She wants to go back to her family! She does not care to talk about what makes her happy right now. Little girl is sick. Would you not too, in her situation, want to go home?" She clicked her fingernails against the table top.

Of course, I would. If Jessica were sick, I would certainly want to take care of her. I would move heaven and earth to be by her side. How could I even think Regina would abandon her child? I knew what it felt like to be on the receiving end of that, and I didn't wish it on anyone.

"Didn't she say she was praying for help just before she ended up here?"

"Yes, absolutely." Aniela pulled her fur-trimmed cardigan close around her shoulders.

"A fat lot of good that did her!" I put a sheltering arm around Regina's shoulders. Aniela frowned, and the two women spoke in rapid short sentences while I waited. Finally, Aniela shook her head and sighed.

"She asked for Blessed Mother's help with her husband. He hits her when he gets drunk, quite often."

A cold like ice water shot through my veins and my mouth fell open.

"Oh, my God! As if she doesn't have enough problems, now we add domestic violence to the mix?" I tightened my arm around the poor old woman, a reflex to protect her. What a mess! She needed to get back to her sick child, but her husband would probably be there waiting to beat her up. No wonder she looked like seventy but claimed to be only fifty. No wonder she fell to her knees and prayed at the drop of a hat.

My thoughts crashed into each other as they danced through my mind. Then the biggest blackest crow I had ever seen flew into the window across from us. Aniela and I recoiled in our chairs at the sight. Regina screamed.

"It's okay, it's okay." I tried to comfort her, stroking her hand, as tears spilled from her eyes. "Please tell her it's okay, Aniela. It's just a crow."

The two of them jabbered a hurricane of words, ignoring me. When I tried to interrupt them, Aniela waved me off. I begged her to tell me what was going on. When I couldn't wait any longer, I pulled at her arm. She pulled it back, smoothing the blue cashmere sleeve.

"The crow reminds her of bad time," Aniela said without taking her eyes off Regina's sad face.

"What happened?" Regina lifted her trembling hands and straightened her headscarf. But said not a word, merely stealing a glance at me from the corner of her eye.

"She was working in the field, cutting hay with *kosa*, big knife." Aniela made a chopping motion.

"You mean a scythe?"

She nodded and waved her fingers in the air. "Big curvy knife, very long, very sharp."

"Yes, it's a scythe in English." I mentally kicked myself for interrupting. "It doesn't matter what it's called. Go on. Please."

"Nobody was near. Her friends each had field to cut. It was busy time, so they were all spread out. On the other side of hill nearby, children gathered cut hay into bundles. It was end of summer. Crow flew over her head, and came down to look for seeds in the dirt. Then, on big black horse, came Jurek, son of landowner. He is *szlachta,* so she put down her knife for respect. She could hear children laughing but could not see them. She was afraid he might hurt them. He is not right in the head."

I didn't want to hear this but I couldn't move. My legs, my arms, my whole body was pinned to the chair. Aniela went on.

After Regina put down the scythe, she stood up and straightened her skirt, intending to check on the children, but Jurek jumped from his horse. He held the bridle with one hand and grabbed Regina's long brown hair with the other, pulling her close. His face was inches from hers.

"His breath smelled like wódka," Aniela said with a shudder. "He is very strong man. "Not one sound,' he said. He threw horse reins over tree branch and tied them in tight loop. He twisted her arms behind her back and pushed her between rows and into little barn where tools are kept."

Aniela's cheeks colored. My ears hurt because I knew what was coming, what had happened to this poor little soul sitting here in my home. I wanted to stop it, but it was already too late. It was done and could never be undone. I reached out and put my hand over hers, squeezing. Aniela's voice dropped so low I could barely hear her.

"He did a very bad thing, the worst thing, with his hand over her mouth. She was crying whole time." Tears welled in her eyes and mine. "Crows in field called the whole time but nobody came."

"Oh my God." I put my arm around Regina's shoulders. She hung her head and pulled at her scarf as if to bring it over her face. Aniela went on.

"After, he took little knife from his boot. It was very sharp, and he waved and pointed it and touched her breast here." Aniela touched her own left breast in the cashmere sweater. "She was so afraid he would cut her, but he took knife away then and spit on her instead."

I stood up and went to Regina, putting my arms around her from behind and laying my cheek on top of her head. She didn't move, but kept her gaze on her hands in her lap.

Aniela said that Regina lay in the little barn until long after the sound of the horse's hooves receded. Her body hurt all over, but she had to go home and make dinner. Later, when she pushed up her sleeves to wash the dishes, her husband Pawel saw the big purple marks on her arms. At last, justice.

"Did he go after Jurek?"

Aniela sighed. "Peasants would not go after noble son. It is not done. Never. And Pawel, he said it was her fault."

"What?" I screeched, too loud, startling Regina who pulled herself smaller in her chair, wrapping her arms around herself. "Tell her that's wrong, no way, she can't think that!" My sense of outrage clouded my empathy for this poor old woman, and seeing how it frightened her, I dialed it down. I took a slow deep breath and smiled at her but she was looking at the door.

Aniela shook her head, her lips pursed. "Everyone knows Jurek is not right in head. She was in wrong place at wrong time. But she cannot forgive herself. She feels shame. Many women do, you know, in these circumstances."

How little had changed in two centuries.

65

I left Regina alone that day except for bringing a plate of food to her room at supper time. My anger at the way she'd been treated by Pawel had frightened her, and I wasn't sure how to handle this new development. What if she had post-traumatic stress disorder, and that was why she thought she was in the wrong century? But no, that didn't make sense. All that stuff about mowing hay, and the scythe, and horses. Did anyone still do that?

The next morning at breakfast, I pulled out a postcard of the Black Madonna I had kept from a woman at a religious retreat and held it out to Regina. She took it from me with a little smile and stroked the scarred face of the Madonna. Did she bear a scar herself, in a place I could not see? Aniela would be back in an hour, and I knew I needed her help more than ever.

When the doorbell rang, I sprang to let her in. Regina greeted her warmly and we took our places again at the dining room table. Regina placed the Madonna postcard on the table before her.

While the two women spoke in Polish, I stared sideways at the picture. The dark-skinned figure, her azure robes painted with gold *fleur de lis,* held the infant Jesus with her left arm. Her face was marked with two dark scars caused by Hussite warriors in the fifteenth century. I knew that the icon had rested in a monastery at Częstochowa, Poland for over six hundred years, and was credited with saving the monastery from Swedish invasion in the 17th century, after which the King declared the Black Madonna of Częstochowa Queen and Protector of Poland. But when had I known these things? And how had I learned them? The walls around me moved closer... but no. Of course, they didn't. What was happening?

Was I remembering or ...was this the "channeling" I had read about on metaphysical websites? The air filled with the scent of roses. But that couldn't be. There were no roses here, in the dead of winter.

"Do you smell that?"

"What?" said Aniela, frowning.

"It's a floral smell, like roses."

66

"Only thing I smell is coffee I would like to be having." She shrugged and readjusted the pearls at her neck. On her finger, a gold ring inset with a large amber stone caught a beam of sunlight from my window.

"Wow, that's really beautiful. Is that Baltic amber?"

"Yes, it is." She put both hands in the pockets of her black velvet trousers, concealing the ring. "Might we have some coffee now?" Looking at her, I wondered if young women in Poland really dressed like this, even the rich ones.

Regina watched me bring out a bag of coffee beans. She flinched when I turned on the electric grinder, then relaxed and inhaled deeply as the fresh aroma filled the room. I took a deep breath myself, enjoying the moment. Finally, I had done something that made us all feel good.

"Does everyone want coffee?" I set mugs on the table with a carton of milk, a bowl of sugar, and three spoons.

"Yes, please. Regina would like it too." Aniela stood close beside me, her hands still in her pockets. I stared at the coffee maker, watching the liquid drip into the glass pot below. I could swear I had smelled roses a moment ago. *What was going on?*

"Regina is very devoted to the Blessed Mother." Aniela nodded at the old woman. "And also to the famous and saintly Jadwiga." She fluffed her hair with both hands.

"Who? Oh yeah, I remember her. We had a procession for her feast day at St. Hedwig's, my elementary school. Hedwig is the English translation for Jadwiga, the queen of Poland back in the Middle Ages. A girl would dress up as Queen Jadwiga and ride on a float down the street to the church..."

Aniela interrupted.

"How nice that you do that here. Do you know her story?" She tilted her head.

"Whose story? Queen Jadwiga's?"

"Why, yes. Although she was also king. To show clearly that she was ruler and not consort. There were no queens in Europe then. So, Jadwiga was king." She pursed her lips and held her hands behind her tall straight back.

"Hmmm. Interesting. Kind of a feminist thing, wasn't it?"

Aniela dismissed this with a wave of her hand. "Whatever. I shall tell Regina about my...I mean, about the Queen." A few sentences passed back and forth, then this: "Yes, she likes Queen Jadwiga very much. Many women in Poland, including her sister, name daughters after this great woman." She cleared her throat and rocked back on her heels. "Jadwiga became king back in 1300s, you know. Exact year was 1384." She gave me a smug smile and adjusted an imaginary crown on her head.

"Okay." I tucked my arms in at my sides. Aniela seemed unusually fond of Jadwiga, and what was that about? I sat down and listened while fresh coffee dripped into the pot on the counter.

"King, or if you prefer *Queen* Jadwiga, as they say today, she married Jagiello, duke of pagan Lithuania, when she was only twelve, and brought his entire country to Catholic Church." Aniela threw her arms out wide and Regina smiled at her, so rapt I wondered if she understood.

"Jadwiga performed miracles. After she visited stonemason, her footprint was left in cement which had hardened before she ..."

"Oh, for Pete's sake. You don't really believe these old superstitions, do you?"

Aniela frowned. "They are not superstitions, Kat. I am supposed to translate, why are you interrupting me all the time? How am I to do my work for her?"

"What do you mean, 'her?' Aren't you working for me?"

"Okay, sorry. Sorry. Many pardons. I mean for you." A little glimmer of sweat shone above her lip. "I do not have much experience in this job." She looked down at her toes. "Actually, you are my first mission."

"Mission?"

"Sorry, my English. I mean you are my first client. But I will do very good job, I guarantee it." Her smile was forced and I pitied her. I knew what it was like to feel incompetent at nearly everything I tried. But I was beginning to see that if you stuck with it, you did develop a certain amount of skill.

"I'm sorry," I said. "Please go on. I'll be quiet." I folded my arms against my chest. I needed this annoying young woman for now. Even if my life had no room for dusty tales about saintly women, if this was important to Regina, I had better listen to what she said.

From all the arm waving and hair patting going on, it was apparent this medieval queen was pretty important to Aniela too. The coffee was done, and I poured us each a mug, then sat down at the table. Word by word, the story soon had me in its spell. Jadwiga spoke six languages, was a patron of the arts, led two military expeditions and negotiated with the Teutonic Knights. Quite the woman. Maybe there was another way to look at this.

"Hey, tell Regina I appreciate what a powerful woman Jadwiga was. Tell her women have played an important role in history, little known..."

Aniela sat up even straighter in her chair, which I would not have thought possible until I actually saw her do it. She held up a hand and translated my words. Regina looked at me wide-eyed. "She does not get it, Kat, the feminist information. She is peasant woman." Aniela adjusted the pearls at her throat. "But I myself appreciate your intentions."

"Okay. Sorry. I just thought if she could see how much better life is for women today she wouldn't be in such a hurry to go back in time. Uh, I mean, if she did come from another time. Which it looks like maybe she did." I stared at the black liquid in my cup.

"Regina is devoted to the Blessed Mother and to Jadwiga, two great female saints. She is not what you call feminist, but does it matter?" Her dark eyes sparkled.

The Blessed Mother. Mary, model of female gentility when I was a girl. My prayers to her had ended sometime in junior high. When I was in college, I learned there are hundreds of Black Madonna icons all over the world, their dark skin the color of ancient goddesses. I was eager to enlighten Regina. Aniela, however, discouraged me.

"You are just going to confuse her. What is the point of that?" Her face clouded as she fondled the gold band of her watch.

"Okay, we can leave it for later." I had just thought of a much better idea.

Chapter Ten

IN REGINA'S POLAND, the parish church was likely the center of everything. I knew exactly what that was like. In the Mohawk River Valley of central New York State, where I was born and raised, each ethnic group–Italian, Lithuanian, Ukrainian, German, Irish and Polish – had its own Catholic church with Mass on Sunday in the language of the immigrants who founded them. On weekends and holidays, in hard times and in celebration, the church was the center of activity. You made friends there, worshipped God together in familiar ways, and found the practical help you needed: a carpenter, plumber, pharmacist or shopkeeper who understood your language and customs. In a sometimes strange and hostile land, you could trust the people who went to your church. They were people like you.

I would take Regina to the Shrine of Częstochowa, the very same place that referred Aniela to me. She would feel more at ease there, among Polish American people, relaxed and at home. I would buy her a set of rosary beads at the gift shop. Excited, I turned to Aniela, interrupting what she was saying. "We should take her to the Shrine. To Częstochowa," I said. "Would this weekend work for you?"

On Sunday morning, Aniela arrived promptly at nine, wearing yet another velvet suit, this one royal blue, and a matching hat complete with a long feather that appeared to have once belonged to a pheasant. I asked if her husband minded her working on a Sunday.

"No, he is off shooting somewhere," she said, waving her hand at somewhere in the distance. I was surprised and pleased when she didn't ask for more money than the weekly stipend we'd agreed upon. Regina clasped her hands together as we walked out the front door and mumbled an aside to Aniela.

"She says, why go everywhere in moving machine," Aniela translated. "Why not walk to church? Does nobody have horse and wagon?"

"Tell her I'm sorry. I don't like driving everyplace either, but it's just not safe to walk on these roads, and no, we don't have horses or wagons. Hasn't she noticed that?"

Regina listened, waved her arms as if she were shooing flies, and with a disgusted look on her face, bustled down the walk to Aniela's car. In my best jeans and a light jacket, I followed, my steps slowing as I realized what had come out of my mouth. *Horse and wagons. For the love of the Goddess and all that is holy, it must be true. She is from another century.*

I hurried to catch up as we climbed into Aniela's BMW. After I buckled Regina into the back seat, we headed for the Shrine. As before, Regina clutched the inside door handle and stared out the window. I imagined the scene through her eyes: Developments of newer homes, perhaps as huge as mansions in Poland; a strip mall with a chain drug store, nail salon and pizza parlor. Typical scenes of central Bucks County, so familiar to me I hardly saw them as I drove past every day. We were only thirty miles or so north of Philadelphia, but for Regina, the scene might as well have been a landscape on the planet Mars. I glanced at her in the back seat. Her face was as gray as her hair and a film of sweat had formed on her upper lip.

"Aniela, can you step on it? I think she's feeling car sick again."

"I am going ten miles over speed limit. She will be all right. She has been through much worse. I will not get ticket for speeding to church." Her dark eyes shot me a sideways glance then returned to the highway ahead.

"Okay, just warning you." I stretched an arm back and gently patted Regina's brown skirt at her knee, the only part of her I could reach. Thankfully, we were almost there. Aniela signaled a right at the entrance to the Shrine, where a larger than life gold painted statue of the Madonna loomed above us, her right arm bent at the elbow, finger pointing to the sky. Regina craned her head around to stare until it was out of sight. A few seconds later, we crested the hill and pulled into a large parking lot in front of a massive stone building.

After I'd gone around to the backseat and helped Regina unbuckle her seatbelt, we looked up at the church a hundred yards away. Another larger than life statue, this one of the Madonna and Child in granite, filled a recess high on the front of the starkly modern building. Stained glass windows shone in the wings on either side. Beside the church, a freestanding bell tower with more stained glass rose toward the sky. Regina quivered at the sight, her eyes filled with wonder, her mouth open but void of speech. What was I thinking, bringing her here? This huge structure with its ultramodern design was nothing like her village church, I was sure of that. But we were here now and I would make the best of it.

Aniela stood with arms folded, one foot tapping on the blacktop. "Ready?" she demanded. More imperious with each passing day, she seemed oblivious to Regina's hesitancy.

"I want to buy her a rosary. Isn't there a gift shop here?"

"In Visitor Center. Follow me." Aniela strode ahead, leaving me and Regina to scurry behind her. What a stupid question. Of course, she knew her way around this place. The Shrine receptionist had referred her to me just a week ago, though it seemed like much longer. And anyway, I'd been here before myself, though it was years since Alan and I attended the festival. I knew a few things too. I glared at the back of her glossy brown hair and took Regina's hand.

We caught up and walked beside her deep in thought, Regina probably marveling at the scene, and me, recalling the moment Regina told us she was from another time. I had freaked out at the story, scared by the very idea, but now it didn't seem so strange. In fact, it was beginning to work its way into my consciousness. I whispered an affirmation. *All is well and all shall be well and all manner of things shall be well.*

A little gust of wind blew my hair into my face, bringing me back to the task at hand. Aniela and Regina were way ahead of me now, walking into another futuristic building behind the church. I followed them inside and down a wide corridor echoing with footsteps.

Around us, people spoke Polish in soft voices, and Regina's face brightened. We were in a large room with floor-to-ceiling glass windows looking out on the wide hallway. Glass counters held every type of Catholic paraphernalia I had ever seen. Hundreds of rosaries glinted in locked cases between four evenly spaced cash registers. Two sales women with permed gray hair waited stone-faced while a few other customers milled around the shop. Suddenly uncomfortable among all the relics of my past, I nudged Aniela.

"Tell her to just pick one."

Words flew between Aniela and Regina until at last, Regina pointed to a sparkly set of crystal beads with a shiny silver cross. The price was far more than I had planned to spend but I paid the clerk in cash, told her we did not need a bag, and held out the beads to Regina.

"*Dziękuję bardzo,*" she whispered and clutched them close to her heart.

"Nice of you," Aniela muttered. "I notice no pictures or statues of Queen Jadwiga. I shall speak to the manager."

"Oh, please, can we skip it this time," I pleaded. "You can come back later, on your own."

She huffed with her nose in the air but headed for the door.

We walked across a courtyard and into the cavernous building where Mass was about to begin. The sanctuary was filling up fast and we settled into a pew near the center of the crowd. With wide eyes and parted lips, Regina sat on my left and gazed at the altar. A gigantic bronze sculpture of a crowned bearded man with open arms and below him, a figure of Jesus, also open-armed, hung high above, along with a square icon of the Black Madonna of Poland. Below, angels pointed long necked trumpets at the Madonna's feet.

"Well, *she's* impressed," I whispered. I tilted my head toward Regina, staring at the sculpture, the icons, and the people around us. On my right, Aniela leaned close to my ear.

"Her church at home would be much smaller, and you must admit, this is a beautiful place."

That it was. I smiled and settled back in my seat.

We had timed our arrival for the ten o'clock Mass, because the Shrine website said it would be entirely in Polish. I recognized very few words, but I remembered enough of the ritual to stand, sit and kneel at the appropriate times, taking my cues from the crowd. Regina followed the priest's every move. She looked at ease and maybe, I fervently hoped, closer to happy.

When it was time to receive communion, people moved slowly down the aisle. I sat back, lulled by the shuffling sound of hundreds of pairs of shoes. Somewhere above us, a soloist in the choir loft sang a mournful Polish hymn. To me, they all sounded mournful.

Aniela gestured from Regina to the priest with an upturned hand, but the old woman shrank back in her seat. Aniela leaned over me and whispered loudly in Polish. Regina whispered back.

"What's the problem?" I hissed.

"She says she can't receive Communion because she has not been to confession. And she does not like how people touch the Host."

"Oh, for Pete's sake. Tell her it's okay, these days anyone can receive. And they can touch the Host."

Aniela bristled. "That cannot be true." She straightened her shoulders and faced the altar. Light from the ornate lanterns overhead turned her dark chestnut hair into a perfect ad for shampoo and conditioner.

"Oh, *excuse me*," I shot back. "I guess what I see before me, people holding the Host in their hands, is not really happening. Got any better ideas?"

"I am not priest, Kat. I do not hear the confession." She gave me a scornful sideways glance. A few more prayers, standing up, sitting down, Signs of the Cross all around and we were done. Fine with me. I had had enough of this rigmarole.

Outside, the sun was warmer and high in the sky. "Let's take Regina to the cafeteria, if they still have one. Alan and I ate here once. She'll like the Polish food and we can have lunch. My treat!"

Aniela guided us toward the dining hall entrance on the other side of the building. Beside the open door, piles of red silk roses lay atop a long table. Two elderly men in gray suits stood behind the table looking as solemn as undertakers.

"One dollar each," said a gravelly voice. A sign hanging from the front of the table read "Pennsylvanians for Life." Regina walked up to the table and touched the rose petals with her fingertips. *"Dzień dobry pani."*

Regina smiled at his greeting, lifted a rose off the table and sniffed it.

I grabbed her arm. "Come on, let's get lunch." Another minute here would require an explanation and it would not be about artificial roses.

"Dzień dobry pani." The other man repeated the greeting offered by the first, and jabbered at Regina in rapid-fire Polish. She raised her fingers to her lips.

"Aniela, what is he telling her?"

"He is just explaining pro-life. Because of her clothes, he thinks she is from Old Country. Which, actually, she is." She turned to me with dawning comprehension. "Are you not pro-life?"

"I believe in a woman's right to choose," I said evenly.

"I *see*." Aniela stared at me as I mentally turned over alternatives. Should I stand up for my views? Or would it be best to let it go, just this once? I glanced at Regina. Chimes rang out from the bell tower in a hymn that clamored against my eardrums.

"Come on, time to go." I turned away.

"She wants the fake rose. I too love the roses. Why not get her one?"

"And support those old..." I stopped. Hadn't I just decided to let it go? I spun around and walked off toward the cafeteria.

Our lunch was a mostly silent affair, but Regina didn't seem to mind. She focused on her plate of pierogi, stabbing each little pillow of dough with her plastic fork and transferring it to her mouth with a little sigh. A silk rose rested on the table beside her plate. I had lost my appetite.

Chapter Eleven

I LEFT HER CAR as soon as Aniela pulled up to my house, and with Regina close behind me clutching her rose, headed for the front door. Aniela turned around in the driveway and peeled out onto the road as if she couldn't wait to get away from us. *Good riddance. Who needs your haughty attitude, anyway?* We would be fine without her. Inside, I grabbed my little Polish dictionary from a bookcase and went into the kitchen. I took a piece of scrap paper from the basket on my cookbook shelf. Slowly, painstakingly, I found and wrote in piecemeal Polish the words I wanted to say.

Do not be afraid. I will help you. Unfortunately for me, I couldn't find words in the dictionary to say, "I think you might have time traveled here and I don't know how to get you back. Plus, I want you to stay."

When I handed the paper to Regina, I smiled, leaned closer, and nodded my head to encourage her. She looked at the paper and smiled but handed it right back to me. It hit me like a slap to the forehead: illiterate, like most women of what she said was her time. With her one simple gesture, I felt the weight of the responsibility I had taken on. I felt the strain of my mother's sadness, my grandmother's self-effacing love, and an uncanny sense that all my female ancestors were counting on me to redeem their lives.

Regina's eyes were as openly pleading as a child's, but I needed comfort too. My grandmother's shawl around my shoulders, a cup of tea. Somebody else to take over here. But I had made another bad choice. I had sent that someone away.

Without Aniela, it was impossible to communicate with Regina. When I powered up my laptop at the kitchen table and looked online, I found the language line Officer Braun used was too expensive and the online translation sites or even the new handheld devices I found on Amazon still required you to type and read. She picked up my white knitted shawl and wrapped herself in it, mimicking me as I rubbed my arms. So, there we were: two women alone in a kitchen with comfort shawls and teacups. For her sake, and for my mother and grandmother, I pushed back my doubts and led her to the couch in my living room.

"Okay, we can do this. Even if you can't read, we can learn to talk to each other."

Of course, she did not understand a word I said. Digging into the dictionary, I pieced together phrases and spoke them in Polish. When she flinched, I realized I had been standing over her, yelling. I tried again in a normal tone of voice, but she gave me a weird and puzzled look. *We were going to need a bigger dictionary.* I had bought my little phrasebook years ago for a "someday" trip to Poland, but Regina and I would need a lot more than "Where is the train station?"

I dropped into an overstuffed chair. Surely there was an easier way. Back to the kitchen for my laptop. I opened it on the coffee table in front of me and Googled translators. A list of language schools appeared, and lucky for me, there was one right in the heart of Doylestown. I called the number on their web page and made an appointment for private lessons.

"Soon, we'll talk without a book or Aniela," I told Regina as I hung up the phone. Pleased with myself, I imagined us chatting together like girlfriends. She watched me closely and mirrored my body language, even putting on a smile: my grandmother's smile. I felt as though *Babcia* was here in the room with me. I didn't know that while I pictured us happy together in my world, Regina believed I was planning to get her back home.

Our teacher at the International School of Languages was a tall, blond woman with a round face and large hazel eyes. Tekla was eager to help me learn to speak with my "Aunt Regina" as quickly as possible. And she knew Aniela. Both of them had answered an ad for interpreters the Shrine had placed in a Polish language newspaper, and they met at the recruitment interview.

"Aniela is good person," Tekla said, "but you want to talk woman to woman with no middle person. I understand this." She arranged for an English-as-a-Second-Language teacher to work with Regina while, in the next room, she would drill me in basic Polish phrases like hello, how are you, see you later.

Like everything else, however, nothing worked out as I had planned. Every few minutes, Tekla stopped the lesson with another question about Regina. Her knitted brows and puzzled expression made me nervous. I was afraid to tell anyone what I now suspected—that Regina really had time traveled here —for fear they would think me a lunatic. A woman living alone, with no real career—they would pity me at the very least, or call the mental health hotline. Even worse, they might report Regina as an illegal immigrant, which she was: without papers, displaced and definitely undocumented. From there, things could only go from shaky to a full collapse. I crossed and uncrossed my legs and bit at my thumbnail.

A knock sounded on the door. It opened to reveal a frowning middle-aged woman with Regina hovering close behind her.

"Is there a problem?" Tekla asked.

"This woman has a *big* problem." The ESL teacher jerked a thumb toward Regina standing in the doorway behind her. "She doesn't *want* to learn English. She keeps babbling to me, in what is it, Polish? She's terribly upset. I think you should talk to her, because I can't do a thing with her." She gave me a rueful smile and a shake of her head.

"Oh, dear, I'm so sorry." I wanted to find a hole to crawl into and disappear. Heat crept up the back of my neck and spread across my face. To distract the curious women, I stepped over to Regina and put a protective arm around her

80

shoulders. "My aunt sometimes gets confused. Maybe this wasn't a good idea."

"What's the matter with her?" Tekla said, wrinkling her brow. "Did she react this way with Aniela?"

"Actually, yes, she did." I ran a hand through my hair. "She seems to think she's in the wrong place, or lost, or, oh, I don't know. Look, let me just pay you for the session, and I'll take her home now. I'll call you about setting something up later."

A desperate image of Regina and me fleeing down the stairs took hold of me and it was all I could do to keep my composure. Somehow, we managed to make a somewhat dignified exit while the two teachers darted worried looks at each other.

Shit. I had messed this up royally. On that odd note, Aniela's face swam into my mind. Maybe she wasn't so bad after all. If I could just overlook her condescending attitude, she might be a bigger help than I had thought.

Chapter Twelve

I CALLED ANIELA as soon as we got home and apologized for my rudeness at the Shrine. She quite easily agreed to come over the next day, so easily, in fact, that I wondered if she was also caught up in our drama, and if this was now more than just a job to her. When she arrived at my house, she had on the same black velvet trousers she had worn before, this time topped by a long silky white tunic. We took our places in my living room and tried again, only to realize we were not getting anywhere. Regina said the same thing over and over through her tears. Her child was sick. Could we please take her back home? And over and over again, we told her we didn't know how. I didn't like feeling so helpless.

"Aniela, maybe we should look into this, you know, research time travel, find out how it's supposed to be done." Had I just said that out loud? I gripped the edges of my seat. And hoped she wouldn't think I was crazy. Because I wasn't. No, I was just a woman whose mind was open to the metaphysical world, that's all. I was totally and completely sane, and took a deep cleansing breath to prove it. To myself.

Aniela rolled her eyes to the heavens. Her loud exhale sounded a lot like relief. My hunch had been right: she believed Regina, too. Her dark eyes met mine and held them. When she lifted her dark brown eyebrows I knew were on the same page. She was waiting for something from me. I jumped up from the couch.

"Let's Google it," I said, and ran to the spare bedroom that served as my office. I brought my laptop back to the living room and placed it on the coffee table, while Regina watched, her hands clasped tightly in her lap. Aniela watched me, too, but unlike Regina, she knew what to expect. She tapped the toe of her knee-length leather boots and played with a pair of matching gloves while I powered up the machine.

We all stared at the image on the screen. In place of the word Google, an animated flying saucer bobbed over the search box. I moved the mouse over it and words appeared: 50th anniversary of UFO sighting over Poland. I blinked my eyes a few times. It was still there. I looked at Aniela. She raised her eyebrows, a smile playing at the corners of her full red lips.

"No," I said. "No, no, no, no. She did not come here on a flying saucer, and she won't be going back on one either." A nervous giggle escaped my lips. I reached for my mug of coffee. Could three people lose their sanity at once, a sort of psychological suggestion?

I took a heartening sip of the hazelnut brew and typed the words: time travel. At the top of the list of results, the words of Albert Einstein glowed: "... we physicists believe the separation between past, present, and future is only an illusion, although a convincing one." Next was a reference to Richard Feynman's theory that other worlds are just other directions in space. I gripped the edges of my laptop with both hands. Farther down the screen, a long list of web sites ranging from Wikipedia to How Stuff Works. Black holes, wormholes, time warps, star gates. I clicked on a few but soon realized there was just too much information. So much to read, so many credible sources: why did scientists write so much about time travel unless... *it was real.*

As soon as I let the thought sink into my mind, my whole body relaxed. What I knew in my heart was true, real and so very right. The Goddess cards. Two women figures looking back and ahead. My skin tingled as if the Black Madonna had touched me herself with her slender hand. I laid my fingers on Aniela's arm and leaned my head toward Regina.

"We have to tell her. Explain that we suspect she came here from another time."

Aniela's dark eyes shone and her cheeks took on a rosy glow.

"As you wish."

What? So, she was buying it too. I wasn't alone in this, and I wasn't crazy. She spoke to Regina in a low voice as the poor lady's eyes opened wide in horror. Her hands shook as she blessed herself, then wrapped her arms around her body and rocked back and forth, keening. Her low moans brought a dull pain to the back of my throat.

"Tell her it will be okay. Tell her I'll take care of her." I moved closer and put a tentative hand on Regina's shoulder. Her voice went down in volume but despair etched her face and filled her eyes.

Aniela remained calm and focused while I jumped up and brought a box of tissues from the bathroom, placed it on the coffee table in front of Regina and gently rubbed her back. She and Aniela talked so long I began to feel left out. When I asked, Aniela said Regina repeated the same words she had translated before: Please take me home.

I took a deep cleansing breath. *All is well, all shall be well, and all manner of things shall be well.* But the familiar words of Julian of Norwich, female mystic, failed in their promise.

"Kat." Aniela tapped me on the shoulder. "Did you forget we are still here?"

"No, no." I rubbed my fingertips up and down my forehead. "My head feels like it's about to explode."

Aniela stood and gripped her huge leather purse to her side. "We have done much work and you are tired. I shall go now." She pulled on her gloves, licked her upper lip and turned to Regina.

"*Do widzenia,*" she said, and marched out the door.

I glanced over at the TV in the corner. A friend at the library once said that when her mother came to the U.S. from Russia, she practiced English by watching soap operas. The characters spoke slowly and clearly, and their body language conveyed their meaning. That could work. I decided to

84

introduce Regina to the TV again. I sat close beside her and kept the volume muted until she relaxed. There were no soap operas this late in the day, but after a half hour of Virgin Property Owners on HGTV, her body leaned back against the sofa and her hands rested loosely in her lap.

That night, a cold winter rain pelted my roof and windows as Regina knelt in prayer beside the guest room bed. I knew she was praying for a way back home. Again and again, night after night. My shoulders ached as I turned away, my footsteps on the wooden floor a slow drumbeat of worry all the way to my own room. This house felt empty since Alan moved out last month. I hadn't heard from Jessica in weeks. Though I texted her every day, and followed her on Facebook, she still didn't respond. My few distant cousins were scattered all over the country and I hadn't spoken to any of them in years.

With Regina here, I felt connected to someone and something besides myself. Out of all the places in the modern world, this Babcia had landed in my backyard. And she needed me. Maybe, way back when, we were related somehow.

After her bedroom door closed, I turned on my laptop, logged into Ancestors.com and typed her full name, the one she had given Aniela and me at the shelter: Regina Wrozkowna. I held my breath and clicked on the symbol of a little magnifying glass. In an instant, my search came back empty. "No records listed in our database." Okay, I told myself, the Internet does not have the answers to everything. There must be a record of her family somewhere and I knew just the people who could help me find it.

In the morning, as soon as the library opened, I called Donna, the reference librarian and told her what I needed.

"I'll get right on it," she said, as I knew she would. "We're not busy yet, and my schedule is clear, for once."

"Thanks, Donna. I really appreciate it." She was friendly and cheerful and I wished I had tried to get to know her better. Maybe now I would.

"No problem! Always glad to help. Talk to you later!" The click of her receiver transmitted to my ear, blunt and matter of fact. Now I had to wait. It didn't take long but it felt like days when two hours later, Donna called back.

"Sorry. I came up with nada. Empty. Zilch. Nobody by that name in any European databases."

I didn't try to hide my disappointment. "Do you have any other ideas?"

"You could try LC," she said, referring to the Library of Congress. "But I have to tell you, we access the same databases they do. The only other thing I'd suggest is the LDS files, or maybe a trip to Poland to check the church records." Her deep-throated chuckle unnerved me.

"I don't think so. Not today, anyway."

"Just kidding. You could call or write the parish church."

"Good idea. See you at work next Tuesday." How would I find the address of St. Bartholomew's, Regina's village church, if it still existed, or its present-day phone number? This would take work, but I couldn't quit now. I spent the next couple of hours on the phone, calling directory assistance for numbers of libraries in Poland and trying to make my feeble Polish language skills work to get someone there who could access church records. Meanwhile, Regina prayed on her new rosary and watched real estate shows on HGTV.

No one could help me at the numbers I called, unless I was willing to send in a request and wait. But I was not willing. I was driven to find out who this poor old woman was and where she belonged. I wanted her to belong to me, and I couldn't wait.

I tried calling the LDS people in Utah. I knew these dedicated Mormons made it their mission in life to collect birth and death information on everybody everywhere, but the ones I spoke to wanted to teach me how to access their records online. And none of them knew for sure if they had what I wanted. Then a thought occurred to me: why not ask Aniela? She was from Poland, after all, and apparently well-educated. She might know how to get this information. I called her that same night.

Unfortunately, her answer was disappointing. "I would like to help you," she said, "but so many records were destroyed in wars. And if her family was illiterate, I don't know what we could find. But I do have one other idea."

"What's that?" I latched onto her last sentence. If there was any proof we were related, I wanted it.

"Why not try a DNA test? You have heard of these, have you not?"

"You mean where you send in a saliva sample and they tell you what part of the world you came from? Sure, I've seen them on TV... but what would that prove? We pretty much accept that she's from the part of Europe that is now Poland, right? She could still be off her rocker." But somewhere behind my words, a part of me wanted to stop the defensive questions. Aniela got that right away.

"Come now, Kat, I know you don't believe she is crazy. And neither are you. DNA can tell if you are from same ancestry. You could both send your samples and know for sure."

I tapped the back of my cell phone with a finger. Why not? What was I waiting for?

"Okay, I'll do it. Thanks for bringing it up." I swear I could hear her exhale of relief.

"Very good. Call me anytime. I am glad to help."

I ran to my laptop, typed "DNA testing" into Google, and found several companies who promised results in six weeks. Soon we'd know the truth.

When Aniela came over at lunchtime, I asked her to tell Regina but as she translated the details, a frown appeared on Regina's face.

"She says how can spit tell you are from same family?"

Regina bit into her ham sandwich as I tried to explain.

"You know this, right? Everybody from the same family has the same thing in all the cells of their body. Little strands you can't see with the naked eye. If our saliva has the same strands, we'll know we are related. Doesn't she want to find out?" I sat back and waved a hurry-up-and-tell-her hand motion.

"*You* want to find out, Kasia," she said, using my Polish nickname. "She just wants to get back home and take care of her daughter. As would you, am I correct? You have a daughter?"

How did she know? "I don't remember telling you that." And why was she calling me Kasia?

"Well, surely you must have told me. How else would I know?" She gave me one of her forced little smiles.

"My daughter is not in trouble, as far as I know. She lives on the West Coast."

"Ah, but if she were ill like Regina's child, you would want to be with her."

"Of course." I nibbled at a ragged cuticle. Aniela gave a satisfied nod and did as I asked and when she was done, patted my shoulder. "She says, okay, Kasia, if it makes you happy she will give you her spit."

My heart warmed at her words, and not just the ones she translated. She called me Kasia, the same affectionate nickname my grandmother used. She must like me, if only a little. And soon Regina would too, I just knew it. I ordered our DNA test kits from a website and later in the week, sent our samples to the test lab in their specially provided mailer.

That afternoon, Alan stopped by to pick up more of his gear and spied Regina watching TV in the living room.

"You know, she's not your mother, Kat. You don't have to take care of her." He looked downright sulky, and I wondered if he was jealous of Regina. I knew better than to ask him but instead sprang to justify myself.

"We could be related."

"What, because she sort of looks like you, now you think she's some long lost relative?"

"For your information, I'm getting a DNA test. You may be surprised when you see the results." I jabbed at the air in front of his face.

"Okay, okay, calm down. Geez." Alan put a hand on my shoulder then jerked it away. "Just be careful." His gray eyes and arched brows gave his face a worried look, one I remembered and appreciated before all our problems started.

Now, everything was different. The house was mine to use as I pleased. That included having my own guests. I opened my mouth to point this out, but the warm feeling on my shoulder where he had touched it distracted me.

"Right," I said. "I'll figure something out." His face was so familiar, I let down my guard. "Remember that book by Stephen Hawking, where he talks about time warps?"

"What does that have to do with...whoa! Are you spending too much time with your altar crystals?" He squinted at me and little wrinkles radiated out from the corners of his eyes. I had forgotten how attractive they were, and for a second, I lost track of his question. "Kat? Earth to Kat!" I straightened my spine and met his eyes with a sharp look of my own.

"It's possible, Alan. I mean, what else could bring her here?"

"Well, she could be one of those wandering seniors. What if her real family is looking for her?" He glanced out the big bay window at the front yard. Beyond the trees, a police car sped down the highway with its roof lights whirling and siren blaring. I shivered and looked away.

"If someone's missing her, they'll find her eventually, won't they? What do you want me to do? Take out an ad in the newspaper?" My voice rose with my indignation. Our local paper had run a story just the other day about an elderly man found walking down the road miles away from his nursing home. That wasn't Regina. She was not some stereotypical senile person. She was special, and she was my family. Soon I would have proof.

The following week, March arrived and rainy days underscored the sadness pervading my home and following me at my part time job at the library. Donna asked me how it was going with Regina, the "aunt from Poland" I had told her about. She was a good friend but I kept her at a distance, fearing she'd probe for information I wasn't ready to divulge. And fearing she'd think I was crazy. Cory, my boss, was kind and solicitous after I told her Alan and Jessica had left. Chuck totally ignored me, which was fine. I couldn't look at him without feeling embarrassed.

Despite my high hopes for bonding with her, Regina continued to wander from room to room of my house, praying and weeping. I worried about her when I was at work, though she was always fine when I got home a few hours later. I hated waiting and wondering what to do next, and I could tell it was killing her too.

Aniela came over almost every day, but we weren't making progress. On Wednesday morning, I greeted her at the door. Regina stood behind me, clutching a hankie.

"Poor lady," she said, shaking her head. "What shall we try today?" Her penetrating look made me squirm.

"Uh, I know you're very good at what you do, but we don't seem to be getting anywhere. Let's see if we can teach her some English. Or teach me some Polish. I don't know." Rain ran down the windows in sheets, closing us in together. "What do you think?"

"Well, I can teach her, but I do not think she is interested. Wait...perhaps if I tell her that learning English will help her get home." She straightened in her chair, turned the amber ring on her finger, and stroked it with her thumb. The stone sparkled with tiny yellow lights. I felt hypnotized by its glow, and caught in a comforting spell. Aniela cleared her throat, and the sound drew Regina's attention. She leaned forward on the sofa as Aniela spoke to her in a quiet, serious tone. Regina nodded and rearranged her skirt over her knees.

"Okay, she agrees. We will do this." Aniela looked around my living room and returned her gaze to me. "I have it. She is hardworking woman. We can show her things around your home, tasks a woman would do, and teach her those words. Have you any chores?"

"Chores...sure, I guess...we can do the dishes. She seems to like that." And that was how we started. Aniela taught Regina the words for dishes, soap, washing, water, and whatever else caught her eye, all the while stroking the amber ring on her finger. The simple objects in my home became dear to me that day, with the three of us completing a little world I wanted to last forever.

At first, it was just "repeat after me," like my high school French class. Even though it was hard going, Regina literally pushed up her sleeves and went to work. After a few days, she began to use new words in phrases and even sentences. "Good morning, Kasia," "May I have coffee?" "Have a nice day!" and of course, "I want to go home."

"I can't believe it!" I said, a little bit frightened. "How can she pick it up so fast? Do you think she knew English all along and suppressed it after some kind of trauma, like a stroke or something?"

My voice was shaking by the end, and I put my hand to my heart as if I might have a stroke myself. *Get a grip, Kat. Calm yourself.* I inhaled and closed my eyes for a second, then opened them and looked to Aniela standing beside Regina in the kitchen. Again, the scent of roses. Must be her perfume.

"No, Kat, her trauma is rape and flying off to 21st century. I thought you had accepted her story. Why do you not trust beyond yourself?"

The raindrops on the window behind her sparkled. The sun was coming out. There was no sound but the ringing in my ears and soon even that was gone. Why not, I thought. A new lightness came to me, traveling deep into my every cell. What harm could it do, just this once, to surrender and believe?

That night, I took Regina upstairs to show her my box of keepsakes and the photo album from my childhood. I showed her the pictures of my grandparents, aunts and uncles, and the few of me with my mother and father.

"Look, my mother and my grandmother have the same nose and mouth as you."

She gave me a noncommittal nod.

"Haven't you seen it when you look at yourself in the mirror?"

"What is to see, Kasia? Looking glass is for young girls. You have looking glass in bathroom, bedroom, even in what you call living room, which by the way is all one room in *Mała Łąka*. Here cannot go anywhere without looking at my face. So much looking is sin of vanity. I try not to look. So many wrinkles anyway..." She shook her head and smoothed her skirt in her lap.

Wow. That was the most English I'd ever heard come out of her mouth. Aniela's lessons were working miracles. And Regina was so calm about it, like she learned a new language every day. I leaned close to her and peered into her eyes. She was the same old woman I'd found cowering in my kitchen just a few months ago, and yet...something about her was different. A new confidence, maybe, a way of holding herself, erect and unbowed. My admiration for her grew. I wanted her to stay in my life.

"I just want you to see how much we look alike. We could be from the same family, but different times. Since you are from another time..." I mumbled the last part and looked out the window at darkness. I got up and pulled the drapes closed. When I turned back, Regina was still on the sofa, touching the album pages and licking her lip.

"Which is Mama and which is *Babcia?*" Seated beside her again, I pointed to a photo of my mother and grandmother wearing their Easter finery, complete with little white corsages pinned to their cloth coats. "Look like nice ladies."

"Thanks. My *Babcia* helped raise me after my mother left." When I gave her the short version of my story, Regina reached out to touch my forearm. "Poor Kasia! Mother should not leave her child!"

"There's a lot I don't know about her. I haven't seen or heard from her since I was ten, except for a birthday card every year until I turned eighteen. That was the last one."

"O, Kasia, it is very bad. How can she do this?" Her worried voice and puzzled frown touched a spot deep inside me, a place I'd worked long and hard to hide. Tears pricked at the inner corners of my eyes.

"Yeah, well, that was a long time ago," I said with a wave of my hand, surprised at how much it still hurt to remember.

Regina stared at me, then at the photos on her lap, and gave a slow nod of her head. She broke the silence with a voice so soft it was almost a whisper.

"Let us pray for her." She knelt on the floor and blessed herself, and I almost knelt down beside her just to see how it would feel, but I couldn't do it. In a minute, she was standing again, ready to go on. I envied her. None of my affirmations, yoga poses, or meditation CDs had done for me what a simple prayer did for her, over and over again. Maybe someday I would try it.

A few weeks later we were coming back from ShopRite after one of our dizzying walks through the overflowing aisles of American plenty. Regina got a touch of vertigo every time I took her to the supermarket, and I totally understood. Who needed to choose between forty kinds of toothpaste?

When we rounded the curve in the road a few houses from mine, the mail truck was just leaving my driveway. I pulled in, went to the mailbox and took out a handful of what appeared to be junk mail. A long white envelope slipped from the pile and landed on the driveway. The return address for Gene Testing Inc. and its bright blue logo marked the upper left corner.

"Our DNA test results!" I waved the envelope at Regina, got back into the car and pulled up to the garage. Oh please, let it say what I hope it does. I yanked the emergency brake up hard and tore the envelope open. Then I leaned back against the headrest.

"Take letter out. See if spit alike or not." She hid her mouth behind her hand but her eyes had crinkled in a smile. I took a deep breath and unfolded the printed pages.

The letter was formal and concise. Regina and I had matching segments of mitochondrial DNA. We shared a "maternal line," meaning we were directly related through one of her daughters down to my mother's family. A warm glow washed over me. This had to be the reason she came to my house that cold winter day. It was no coincidence.

"So." Regina tapped an index finger on her knee. "My daughter has daughter and so on, some child come here to America, and become your grandmother. Or something."

"Right. We don't know exactly who. But someone. And that makes you my ancestor." Her matter of fact attitude left me deflated. "You don't believe this, do you?"

"*Tak, tak, tak,* believe." She patted my hand. "We have same looks, both using left hands. Pictures of your family, some of them look like my family. I pray and Matka Boska send me to you. How do you say it: Make sense?" She looked out the car window at my yard, wet from a quick spring shower.

"But you're so calm! Aren't you glad to know..." My voice trailed off. The test results were exactly what I had hoped for. Before this moment, all I had in the world was Alan and Jessica, and for all I knew, I had screwed that up forever.

I had wanted this result so much, but to Regina, it was no big deal. I was a fool. I had loved my mother, and it hadn't mattered to her, either. I tossed the envelope onto the dashboard. Regina sighed and took my hand in hers, but I pulled it away. She sighed and began to speak softly.

"I am glad we are family, Kasia. Matka Boska work many ways. Not big surprise, correct?" She gave my hand a squeeze. When I looked at her face, I remembered the faces in my mirror. A long line of women led from her to me. She was my place in the Universe, my anchor and refuge. A little hard to understand, but hey. I could extend myself more.

"Regina, what did you say your family name was, before you got married?"

"Wrozkowna." She unbuckled her seat belt. "Can we go in house now?"

I tried the name on for size: "My name would be Katherine Wrozkowna Kowalski – wait, there must be some other names in between there. Oh, and they would be the father's last names. We'll have to go back and trace them all."

"If you wish, Kasia, but why it is important?" Her voice was kind, though not as thrilled about all this as I'd hoped. It was okay. She was still here, beside me. She hadn't left.

She opened her arms then and hugged me long and hard. For a change, I put aside my worries and fears, and let myself feel the strength of her, the warm yeasty softness of her body. And for just a moment, I allowed myself to pretend we would always be this way.

As more time passed, Regina's English skills grew. I couldn't explain it and I didn't try. Instead, I tried to make her comfortable until I figured out what to do next. I got the idea to call Jessica and ask her what she suggested but my calls went right to voice mail. I thought of asking Alan. He was coming by less often for his mail and for things he'd left behind. But I knew what he'd say: She's not your problem.

One April afternoon, after Aniela went home, I asked Regina to help me move some things into the attic: gift-wrap paper and ribbons, rolls of unused drapery fabric from a project I had long since abandoned, a couple of decades of Christmas decorations. Arms loaded with my stuff, she stopped at the top of the attic stairs and peered into the dim, chilly space. Bits of fuzzy pink insulation hung from the walls through rips in the brown paper covering. Sounds from outside drifted in through the tiny window at the far end of the attic: trucks on the highway, the cawing of crows, a branch scraping the roof. Regina set a box of Christmas decorations down on the dusty wooden floor. Her mouth half open, her eyes wide, she took in the clutter around us.

"So many books! And papers! What child has so many playthings? Your baby dies?" Her face softened and her eyes grew round.

"No, no, nobody died. The toys were Jessica's when she was little. She lives in California now. We never got around to giving her baby stuff away." A shadow passed across Regina's face and her eyes looked beyond me at a place I could not see.

95

"We have play things. First child go to heaven, I put doll under bed. Save for next baby. But for me, too." She met my eyes with a shy little smile. "Hold doll at night. Not same as baby," she finished in a whisper.

"I'm so sorry." Even as the words left my lips, I knew how inadequate they were. I wanted to say something more, something that might help. "How awful for you!" I sat on the attic steps and reached out a hand to her.

"Father Marek say God's will." She took my hand and lowered herself to sit beside me. "Be good wife, he say, get new baby." Her voice was louder now, and higher. "But next child, she dies same way. Fever high and cannot keep food in stomach. Throw up everything."

"Oh, no. I am so, so sorry." We sat together, lost in a mother's thoughts while the house creaked in the wind, its gentle sound our witness and companion. After a while, Regina spoke again.

"Very hard. Give her name, that baby. Call her *Zosia*."

"Tell me about her." I hugged my own waist. Regina's reply was abrupt.

"Not today." She stood and brushed her hands down the front of her long skirt, and the longing filled me again. If I could just keep her here, everything would be all right. I followed her down the attic stairs, went to the linen closet and brought out clean sheets for her bed.

"Pretty color." She took them from my hands and stroked the pink and rose pattern with her finger. "Like roses men sell after Mass." My spine stiffened, but what she said next surprised me. "Men do not understand what mothers go through."

"No, they don't," I said, not sure where this was going.

She sat on the bed and stroked the rose-printed quilt spread over the top. "Mothers can be very sick when expecting. Some do not want so many children. In bad harvest, they starve. There is woman in Lipinki who helps."

What was she saying? I had to find out more. "I understand how losing your own babies might make you feel that ending a pregnancy is wrong."

96

Regina shook her head. "Because my child dies, does not mean other woman must have baby. Different woman, different story."

You could have knocked me over with a feather. "Did you ever..." but I couldn't. It was none of my business.

When I took the folded sheets from her arms and went to fit them onto her mattress, she watched me for a moment then stepped around the bed and helped me tuck them in. Then she stood facing me.

"Your baby, Jessica, who has toys in attic, you don't want to see her?"

"Well, yes, actually, I do. But she went away angry and I can't get her to talk to me. You know, on the phone?"

"*Tak, tak.* Phone on wall and little black one for hand." She sighed. "If I could talk to Anna on phone...but no phone in Mała Łąka. Make me so happy to hear her voice."

I imagined the little girl wondering where her mother had gone, unable to understand. And I thought of myself as a child, waiting for the call from my mom that never came. I was not that kind of mom to Jessica. No, I was not. She was the one who had left our home.

We worked slowly, as though the serious topic made us both pensive and respectful. When we were done, I offered Regina some things I'd picked up for her from the thrift shop after work but she refused. Okay, maybe they didn't suit her. But I was tired of looking at her in the same outfit, and tired of tossing her stuff into the laundry with my own clothes every week. I slapped my hands against my jean-clad thighs.

"Let's go shopping. You need some new clothes, all your own."

"Shop in Lipinki, take wagon and..." Her face fell as she remembered. She hadn't seen a horse and wagon in months. Or a hundred years.

"We'll take the car." Her eyes widened. She still hated riding in my Jetta. But that would change. My grandfather learned to ride in a car, and she could too. I gave her a reassuring smile. "You'll be all right."

Regina closed her eyes for a second, moved her lips in a prayer then opened them again. "Okay, let us go." She patted my shoulder and followed me downstairs.

Chapter Thirteen

THE MALL WAS FIFTEEN MILES AWAY, but the magic of all the different specialty stores would surely cheer her up. I could hardly wait for her to see the two levels, the glass elevator, the escalators at each end, and the colorful clothing on display. The store entirely devoted to scented candles, the ice cream counter, the cookie shop.

Traffic was heavy as we turned onto the highway and headed south. When we entered the bypass, Regina covered her mouth with her hands. Her face was as gray as the sky outside. I wished I had thought to give her something for motion sickness. At County Line Road, waiting for the light to change, I turned on the radio. The smooth sounds of Kenny G floated from the speakers on either side of the dash and behind the back seats. Regina's head snapped around to see where the music was coming from. Then she looked accusingly at me.

"It's not a trick. It's the radio. Didn't they have one in the shelter?" So much explaining when I needed to concentrate. The light turned green. "Look. Press these buttons." I demonstrated on the dash but she held her clenched fists close to her sides. "Go on, try it." I stepped on the gas pedal and drove into the intersection.

Regina reached out her left hand and pressed a button with her index finger. A loud drum beat blasted from the speakers all around us. My foot hit the brake when she screamed.

"Bor-r-n in the USAyyyy!" The sound pushed her back against her seat as if Springsteen himself had reached out of the dashboard. Lucky for us, there were no other cars in the intersection. Shaken, I pressed the gas pedal and continued across.

"Don't be afraid. Look, you can turn it off." I pressed the Power button and like magic, Bruce was gone. I touched my dream catcher dangling from the rearview mirror and whispered a thank you for our safety to the Universe. We rode on in welcome silence, with only the soft hum of the wheels on the road.

After a while, Regina reached a hand out to the radio and gave the nearest button a gingerly push. She flinched when the music came on again, but she kept poking the buttons. Jazz gave way to rock and roll, to a talk show, sports news, rap, hip-hop, more jazz, then classical. I could not believe my eyes – and ears. She had gone from scared rabbit to investigator of technology, in less than fifteen minutes. By the time I pulled into a space at the mall, I was feeling nauseous myself from the jangle of music in my brain.

It was two o'clock on a Wednesday afternoon and only a few shoppers wandered among the stores. The sprawling two-level building held a Macy's at one end and J.C. Penney at the other, with Sears in the section at the middle where we had come in. Skylights high above us gave the only natural light. Along the walkways between stores, open kiosks displayed cases of cell phones, watches, or gold jewelry, staffed by young people who could have represented India, Africa, Mexico or South America with a bit of the Caucasian Midwest thrown in.

Despite the United Nations of salespeople, Regina attracted a few stares herself. An elderly couple holding hands peered at us while a peppy instrumental of a Foreigner tune played overhead. *I've been way-ting for a girl like you to come in-to my life...* My face felt hot.

"Come on." When I put my arm around her shoulders and nudged her along, the woman gave me a frown but they went on their way. I led Regina toward Penney's as more people stared at her long brown skirt, boots and headscarf.

She stopped short as a tall black teenager walked by swinging a white plastic bag. His ears were plugged with white ear buds trailing long wires into his pants pocket. Next, a giggling group of Asian girls ran past and she pointed a finger at them.

"Stop staring! It's not polite." My mind flashed to Jessica and her high school girlfriends, laughing as they walked from my car on Friday nights, eager to shop for clothes and see who else would show up at the food court.

"Why not look at them? Maybe visitors from other country like me!"

One of the girls looked back over her shoulder, popped her gum and grinned at us, then ran to keep up with her friends. Ran away from me. Jess...I shook myself.

"No, they're not. They are not from another country. They live here. I mean, I think they do." There was so much she didn't know, so much I had to teach her. But I didn't want to do it now, in the middle of the mall. "We can talk about them later. Meanwhile, don't stare."

She stood her ground. "But..."

"Look, their ancestors came from a place far away, just like you did." *Some of them against their will.* Racism, genocide, slavery: how would I explain it all? Pressure in my forehead threatened the start of a headache when Regina stopped short at the front window of Victoria's Secret. A cloying sweet smell drifted from the open door.

"*Matka Boska.*" She blushed to the edge of her headscarf. The manikins in the storefront wore sexy underwear in cotton candy colors. They struck very sexy poses. My headache was getting worse.

"Come on." I grabbed her hand and pulled her toward Penney's, where just inside the store, a perfume counter glittered with small shiny glass bottles. Tall attractive women with perfectly applied makeup stood in the aisle and offered us samples. Regina collected the tiny flasks, tucking them into the sleeves of her blouse and beaming.

"That's nice. I'm glad you like them." I headed for Women's Casuals off the aisle to our right, guessed at her size, pulled a few tops and skirts off a shiny metal rack and led her to the dressing room. Her head moved from side to side as I pulled her into a booth. When she realized I meant her to take off her clothes and try the new ones on, she folded her arms in front of her.

"Strangers can come in."

"I'll stand out here and make sure nobody can see you." The dressing room smelled of the perfume samples. I heard her move behind me amid the rustle of clothing. "Let me know if you need any help." Hangers dropped to the floor. Long pants flew out of the booth over the top of the curtain. "What's wrong with these?"

"Metals like teeth inside."

"What? Oh, the zipper! It holds the pants up. Want me to show you how to work it?"

"*Nie, nie*, no zip her. And no man pants."

I went back for an armload of skirts with elastic waistbands. Soft fabrics won out. Knits were a big hit, as were pretty colors: pink, blue, green, yellow, and red, the brighter, the better. I shoved a pair of dark pull-on trousers through the gap in the curtain.

"No man pants!" She stuck her head through the part in the curtains and scowled at me.

"They're not man pants, I mean men's pants. They're for women, and they're very comfortable. Haven't you noticed that most women here wear pants every day? Like me?"

"*Tak,* Kasia, okay for you. But not for me." Her voice was stern but her eyes were kind. And she had called me Kasia, like *Babcia*. With her, I felt safe. It was a strange thing. We had a secret between us, the secret of who she was and where she came from. If the wrong people knew, that secret could tear us apart. But no one except Aniela knew, and she'd never tell. She had called me Kasia, too. I had two friends who liked me. I didn't have to do everything alone.

"Okay, you don't have to wear pants if you don't want to. But can we get rid of this for now?" I reached for her headscarf and she let me take it off, then fluff her curly gray hair with my hands. In that moment, I wanted to give her anything she desired. "Come on, let's pay for these and go."

"Take off new clothes?" She walked out of the booth caressing the red flowered skirt she wore. A sunny yellow tunic top hung from her round shoulders. I had grabbed them in a rush from the sale rack but Regina looked as though she had fallen in love with them. For the time being, she was pleased, and not talking about going back home. The shopping expedition had been a success.

"Leave them on. It's okay," I said. "You can wear them out of the store." She smiled while I explained to the sales clerk that "my friend" would be wearing the outfit she had on. The clerk cut the tags off with a pair of scissors from under the counter as Regina watched, fascinated. "Don't they have scissors..." The clerk looked up. "My friend is from Europe," I told her, covering my mistake. Not good enough. The woman stared at me, scissors raised. "Eastern Europe."

"Uh huh," she muttered, shook her head and continued snipping. She threw the tags into a large white plastic bag with Regina's other new skirts and tops and the headscarf and clothes she had on when she first arrived in this century.

Outside the store, no one gave us a glance. Regina looked like any other older woman at the mall in the middle of a weekday afternoon.

"Let's go to the Food Court." If she was going to experience a suburban mall, she had to have an Orange Julius. And maybe a Cinnabon.

Riding the escalator with her was like being at a theme park. She bit her lip, held on to my arm with a vise grip, and hopped off at the top as if she were jumping over rocks in a stream. As she walked beside me, I tried to remove her hand from my arm, which was losing its circulation. She finally let go when loud voices caught our attention.

"Ow! Stop, you're hurting me!" A young woman twisted away from a tall skinny male of about the same age. "Let go of me!"

"Shut up!" He growled and pulled on her arm. Other shoppers stared at the couple and each other, but then looked away. I couldn't believe what I was seeing. The place wasn't crowded, but still. Nobody intervened to help. Nobody, that is, but Regina. Before I could stop her, she had released my arm and trotted over to the young man.

"Get away!" She waved her arms in his face. "Leave her now!"

"Mind your own business, old lady," he snarled. That was enough to wake up a couple of men in business suits at a nearby café table.

"Hey, what's going on?" one of them asked as they walked over to us.

"Do we need to call security?" the other man asked the young woman. She wiped at her nose with one hand, shook her head and looked down at her feet.

"It's not your problem," the young bully mumbled. He turned to his girlfriend. "Are you coming or not?" She nodded and followed him to the escalator. The rest of us stood there wondering what to do.

"Can't do much if she just goes along with him," one of the businessmen said. They shook their heads and went back to their burgers.

Regina stood straight as a post. Her hands were bunched into fists though her arms hung at her sides. I put an arm around her.

"I'm proud of you. You did the right thing."

"But still she goes with him." Her fists opened and she looked in the direction they had gone.

"Yes, for now. We don't know what she'll do later. At least she saw what he was doing is not okay, thanks to you."

Her face was blank, as if she didn't understand, and I was too tired and shaken to explain.

"Let's go home."

That night, I called Alan. I needed to know where he kept the income tax records but when I went on to tell him about our excursion, he was amused.

"I can just see it," he said. "Two little *Babcia's* go to the mall..."

"Shut up," I chided. Still, I had to smile and I'm sure he could hear it in my voice. "They probably thought she was a dancer in costume, or that she was visiting America from another country."

"Right. Try another planet." He chuckled softly in my ear, through the phone, and for a second or two I remembered how things had been with us in the beginning, years before my imaginary affair with Chuck. Would we ever get back there again? We were so much younger, so much in love. Before I began to feel trapped. I shook my head to clear the memories. "Hey, earth to Kat! Are you still there?" Alan's deep voice called me back.

"It may as well *be* another planet with all the new things she has to deal with every day."

"*She* doesn't have to deal with anything. *You* deal with it for her."

"Well, somebody has to help her. You know, Aniela thinks she may have traveled here from another time and, crazy as it sounded at first, I have to say, it makes a lot of sense to me too."

"Now I know you're losing it. All those crystals and candles and cards you're always looking at. They're messing with your head."

"Oh, so that's it. You think I'm fooling myself." My right hand flew up and down as I talked but he could not see. All he heard was the anger in my voice.

"Whoa, whoa! Calm down. I think *you* believe her, and that's all that matters. It's nice of you to take care of her. But sooner or later..." He paused.

"What? Come on, say it! Sooner or later, what?" I was angry enough to spit. Or cry, but I'd be damned if I'd let that happen now.

"I'm just saying, sooner or later, somebody will come for her and take her back where she came from. Maybe she wandered away from her Alzheimer's unit. Have you thought about that?"

"Yes, actually, I *have*. But it's been months since the cops checked the Missing Persons database. They said they would call all the nursing homes and hospitals in the tri-state area. So far, nothing. *Nada.* What am I supposed to do, put her on a plane to Poland?"

"Okay, calm down, you know that's not what I meant. Geez."

"Well, it's better than doing nothing, like some people." A second later, I wanted to bite my tongue. It was the worst possible thing to say. Alan's lack of ambition had been a sore spot between us for years. A click sounded in my ear, then the hum of the dial tone. *Shit. I'd meant to ask him what he'd heard from Jess. But I couldn't call him back now.* Why did talking with Alan always end up this way? I called him often because I needed to know things: How to get oil for the furnace. How to find last year's tax return. Stuff like that. I wasn't the one who had asked him to leave. He just took off in a huff when he found out about me and Chuck, when there was really nothing to find out. He wouldn't listen. Not then. And not now.

Regina stood in the doorway, a sympathetic smile on her lips.

"Not good with husband?"

"No, not good. We always end up arguing."

"Why arguing?" Her eyes were kind and she looked as though she really did want to know. Although she said she was fifty like me, she looked much older, like she could be my aunt. Or my mother. I lowered myself onto the couch with a dejected thump. Regina sat beside me, and for the first time, I told her *my* story.

I knew I was the one at fault. I had messed up and hurt my husband, a nice guy who had done nothing wrong. When I mentioned Alan's first wife had cheated on him, Regina winced. I couldn't meet her eyes. I just kept talking and picked up the pace, my words tumbling out like water from a faucet. I told her about Jessica, too, how she had left in a huff right after her dad.

"I didn't want Alan or Jessica to find out like that. It wasn't supposed to go as far as it did, and Chuck was supposed to destroy my note, not put it in his home wastebasket, where his wife could find it."

I brushed a speck of dirt from the toe of my shoe. The silence between us grew until it was a deep gulf fraught with the unspoken words I read on her face. Whether or not I called it an affair, what Chuck and I had done was still cheating and I was ashamed. It hurt, having her see me like this. And seeing myself for who I really was. It had taken this, her appearance in my life, to bring the truth home to me. I needed time to process it all but it was getting late. I wished her good night and left her sitting on the couch while I went up to bed.

After breakfast the next morning, I walked through the trees to my meditation bench of weathered gray wood, and sat in the dappled sunlight. A stone Buddha rested on an old stump and a bell dangled from a tree where a soft breeze could start it ringing. I often came here in mild weather to center myself, to lean back and look up at the undersides of leaves high above or watch a hawk slow dance across the sky.

Sleep had come late last night. Trying to mentally justify what I'd done kept me awake with no one to listen but my wild mind. I knew my behavior with Chuck was wrong. But even if I could make Alan understand and forgive me, I'd be going back to the dull unfulfilling life we had together. At least that's how it was for me. He wasn't exactly the most attentive husband. Often, he put me down for my New Age beliefs. I was stuck, unable to move forward or back or decide which way I wanted to go. Regina's plight, at least, gave me something to focus on besides my empty life.

By now, spring had taken my world in its gentle embrace. Snowdrops and crocuses popped up on my lawn overnight. Jonquils opened their yellow eyes in the herb garden outside my kitchen, and the tiny white faces of spring beauties carpeted the floor of the woods where I sat a hundred yards behind the house.

Dry leaves rustled on the ground behind me and I looked over my shoulder. Regina took heavy slow steps through the trees and stood, arms folded, squarely before me.

"*Kasia*, very nice here in America," she said. "but not *Mała Łąka,* not home. Anna, she is very sick, need Mama. Pray and pray but no help comes. Can you find help? Maybe Alan can find?" She depended on and trusted me, and I was glad. We were close friends, and even knew we were related, thanks to the DNA test. Seeing her standing there brought all we had been through together to the forefront of my mind. I loved her, this short stocky peasant woman. She was my family, and I wanted her here, with me, where she was safe. But that didn't make her happy. Just like it didn't make my mother happy.

I was torn. Her husband *Paweł* beat her. If I helped her go back, I would be doing what my self-help books called enabling. I told her again that she didn't have to go back to a man who hurt her but she brushed me off. She looked so bereft, and if her little girl was as ill as she said, she must be sick herself with worry. I ached to ease Regina's pain. She had been away from home for months. For all we knew, her child could be well by now. Part of me knew it was wrong, but I wanted her to stay here, where life was better, to be *my* family. To replace my mother. Eager to do something to distract her, I jumped at the first idea that popped into my head.

"Hey, Easter is coming. We can go to the Shrine for *święconka*. Wouldn't you like that?"

"*Święconka* help to go home? People at Shrine know how to go to *Mała Łąka*?"

"I don't know if we can count on that." I stood up from the bench. "They might know where it is, but probably not about how to do time travel."

Regina kept her arms folded in front of her waist. Her voice was strong and steady. "Kasia, you are good woman. *Matka Boska* answer prayer, I think she send me to you for rest." Her eyes filled with hope. "Maybe rest soon will be over."

Was she right? Would her time here soon come to an end? My knees turned soft and I had to sit down again. What if the Madonna *did* answer her daily prayers? If she had sent Regina here, couldn't she just as easily send her back home again? Fear caught in my throat. That couldn't be right. I couldn't lose her, too, like I'd lost my mom. There had to be more to this for me.

Regina stood smiling in my direction, a question on her face. I rose and put my arm around her shoulder.

"Let's go back to the Shrine and find out." Together we turned back toward the house, trampling hundreds of spring beauties beneath our feet.

Chapter Fourteen

THE NEXT DAY was Holy Saturday, the day before Easter. Regina calmly went along with my plan to visit the Shrine again on this holy day, hoping she'd meet someone there who could show her the way back home. She talked about it as we prepared food for the priest to bless in the Polish ritual and I didn't try to dissuade her. I had nothing else to offer, and a part of me still hoped she'd learn to like it here, especially if I kept taking her to Polish-linked events.

When she tried to show me how to make a traditional butter lamb, she got frustrated by the hard sticks of butter, but after I softened them for a few seconds in the microwave, she stood part of one stick atop the end of a horizontal one and cut tiny ears, shaping the lamb's head and reclined body, with cloves from my pantry for eyes. We boiled eggs and dyed them with food coloring, and bought sweet smelling ham, pungent kielbasa and dark chocolate bunnies at the gourmet supermarket on Route 309.

Regina hummed to herself as we assembled our basket on my kitchen table. I told her it was the same basket my parents had given to me long ago, filled with cellophane grass. A few straws stuck out here and there, but it held together remarkably well. I had kept it all these years because of the fond memories it held. Memories of the time before my mother left. I blinked my tears away. Regina's mind was already working on something else.

"Forget it is Lent," she said with a frown. "Lent is time for Mass and fasting, and now almost over."

"Sorry, I didn't think of it. I'm out of touch with the church calendar these days. But it's not your fault. Hey, I can take you to Mass every Sunday if you like."

"No, no, no," she fluttered her hands at me like she was shooing chickens. "You are how you say, busy, busy. Pray *Matka Boska* every day here in house."

"Fine with me." I tucked fake grass around the dyed eggs in our basket in a futile attempt to make it perfect. Always futile, that was me. Mom never told me what was wrong until the day she left for good. I wished I had known. A little bit of resentment crept into my words. "You know all you have to do is ask. I'm not a mind reader."

Regina's look was cold. "Fine, I ask."

"What's the matter, now? I can see you want to say something else."

She folded her arms across her chest and she shot my words back at me. "Not true what you say, 'all you have to do is ask.' Ask and ask and ask *Matka Boska* bring me to home. But no. Still here. In *Mała Łąka*, pray every day. One day, angry and crying, go to side road shrine to pray." She flung her arms out as if to fling stones into a moving stream, filled with rushing water that was passing her by. "Cry and look to heaven. 'Please, help me from Pawel,' I say. And what happen?" She shook a fist at me. "Wake up in other country, other time! So, all have to do is ask? No. It is not so." She recrossed her arms and glared at me. I didn't know where to look.

"You're right. I'm sorry. We'll figure something out." I tried to put my arm around her, but she stepped out of my reach and stuck out her lower lip. Her face was as pink as the flowers on her new skirt. "We don't have any answers right now, that's true. But I'll help you. I promise. For now, let's just go to the *święconka*." What else could we do but go on with our plans? Make that my plans.

At the Shrine high on a hill, the morning chill in the air reminded me of Amsterdam, New York, the small town where I was born and raised, "in the foothills of the Adirondacks," as my father used to say.

"Cold like spring in *Mała Łąka*." Regina gave me a tentative smile.

"I was just thinking the weather feels like spring in *my* hometown."

"We have some things same." She lifted our basket from the trunk of the car.

I took it from her hands. "Something in common."

"*Tak, tak, tak*, some things in common." She wasn't mad at me anymore. Maybe things would work out.

Around us, the parking lot filled up fast. SUV and car doors flew open and people of all ages and sizes climbed out, loaded down with huge wicker baskets piled with whole hams, rings of *kielbasa,* and clusters of colored eggs. Regina and I joined the crowd filing into the glass-walled cafeteria. The room was still cold from the night before, when temperatures had fallen to freezing. The furnace rumbled on and warm air reached my feet.

Regina whispered in my ear. "Like your house. Heat from floor."

How different my world must seem to her, how disorienting. No wonder she blew up at me now and then. Yet here she was, gamely trying to get along. I put my right arm around her as we stood at the table behind our basket and waited for the priest to enter the room. She smiled up at me and slowly placed her left arm around my waist.

On the ride back home, Regina was talkative. "So much food in *święconka* baskets! Big ham! Dozen eggs! And so much chocolate!"

"Yes, Americans sometimes get carried away with food." I flicked on the turn signal as we reached Route 611.

"Carry away?" A look of recognition came over her face. "Oh! People we see today are *szlachta?* Kasia and Alan are nobles? Where is church for peasants?"

"No, no, we are definitely not nobles. We are middle class. Alan and I never went to that church anyway. There are no special churches for nobles here."

But what was I saying? Churches in poor inner-city neighborhoods had closed for lack of funds, while just a few miles from my house, Our Lady of Perpetual Help, in its brand new multi-million-dollar building, served as a house of worship for affluent suburbanites. An uneasy feeling grew in the pit of my stomach. Best to drop the subject.

As we traveled down the Pike near my home, I remembered our plan to ask at the Shrine about travel to Poland. Regina must have forgotten. Too late now, I thought but didn't say. Maybe we'd ask someone tomorrow.

The following morning, we went back to the Shrine for Easter Mass. The sanctuary was crowded with people and the clean fresh scent of lilies permeated the air. I took Regina to a waiting priest at a side aisle who heard her confession in Polish and, cleansed of her sins, she happily joined the line for Holy Communion. After Mass, we headed back to the gift shop to ask about trips to Poland. I felt like a charlatan, or at best, a fool.

A sixtyish female clerk waved at an aisle of books near the back where I spotted some travel guides. Regina eagerly paged through them, looking for scenes of *Mała Łąka*. The photos of "big metal machines" on the streets of Warsaw and Gdansk puzzled her. She stared at the many pictures of John Paul, the Polish Pope, on a counter next to the books.

"The pope a few years ago was Polish. Just so you know."

"Nice. Look like good man." She blessed herself, then shook her head and headed for the counter. "Excuse, can you say how to go to *Mała Łąka*?"

The sales woman took a step back and pursed her lips. I moved closer to Regina. "She's from the Old Country and she doesn't like to fly."

"Well, good luck, then." The woman coldly turned her back. Regina's face fell and I put my hand on her arm.

"Let's go home. We'll find a way." I said it only to comfort her. I still had no idea what to do. Part of me still wanted to keep her here, safe from Pawel. My higher, better Self wanted to return a mother to her child. Even though no one had done the same for me. That Easter morning, I felt like a child myself, the little girl who hid her sorrow and loneliness behind the covers of books. The woman I was now had no such option, and truth be told, I didn't want to hide anymore. I wanted to do something good with my life, to redeem myself and, perhaps, my mother.

Rather than leave Regina home alone on Monday afternoon, I took her to the library with me. Cory said she could sit in the reading lounge, after I introduced her as my great aunt from Poland and explained that it would be a temporary arrangement. I settled Regina with a stack of food magazines on a big couch near a window. For the time being, she put up with me and offered no resistance. When my break time came, I walked to her, poring over the slick colorful pages on her lap. She turned her face to me with a sad little smile.

"In *Mała Łąka*," she said as she slowly turned the pages, "not so many kinds of food. Winter always hard." When the stored-up wheat and rye were gone, she said, women pounded acorns into flour for bread, sometimes even adding sawdust to thicken it. I couldn't move.

"You eat *sawdust*?" She kept talking. Meat like the beautiful roast in the magazine on her lap was only for holidays, if then. At Christmas, the older boys might have permission from the landlord to kill a pig, but for most of the year, everyone lived on cabbage, beets and beans, plus a concoction of porridge or soup made from whatever was available in winter.

"Mix and turn and put bread in bake oven, all day long, to fill stomach, not so hungry." She patted her own midriff with a satisfied nod.

114

The intercom broke into our conversation: "Reference, you have a call on line 3. Reference, you have a call on line 3." I glanced at the line of people waiting at my desk.

"Okay, I have to get back to work."

"Yes, work." Regina waved me away, her head bent over the colorful pages in her lap.

I hurried to my desk. When I took a quick look back across the room at her, the irony of what I had done slapped me in the face. I had taken a woman who could not read to a place full of books.

The next morning, Regina and I were folding laundry still warm from the dryer when Alan parked his delivery truck in the driveway and walked in through the garage. I snapped a towel in the air, keeping my back to him as I folded and added it to the stack on the counter. What did he want now? My heart did an annoying little tap dance in my chest.

"There was a show last night on the Discovery Channel," he said, ignoring my pique, "about worm holes. The guy they had on, a scientist from Berkeley, said people might time travel that way." I leaned on the pile of towels to keep from spinning around to face him. What did he just say?

Regina held a fresh warm towel up to her face. The rhythmic hum of the machine as it washed our next load always soothed her. She would have done laundry every day if I let her. But as soon as Alan said "worm holes," she put the towel down on the counter and shook her head.

"Say many times: Pray to *Matka Boska,* strong wind and big light and I am here. No hole for worms." She grabbed a pile of folded clothes and with her head high, marched up the stairs.

"Boy, she picked up English really fast!" Alan said. "Are you sure she didn't know it and just forgot, you know, like when you have a stroke..."

"No, I'm not sure of anything right now, including whether she had a stroke, which is just what I needed to hear:

something else to add to my list of problems!" I ran to the hall and called up the stairs to Regina.

"Will you please come back down here? You can't run away every time somebody says something you don't like!" When I had reached the doorway of her room, still shouting, Regina was standing at the window. She whirled toward me.

"Please!" She wagged a finger in my face. "You know no things about *me, my life. Your* idea. *Your* question. Tired of you, *your* house. Want *my* house." She plopped down on the bed as far away from me as she could get, her arms wrapped tight around her waist.

A masculine cough broke the tense silence. Alan's tall frame filled the doorway. "I'm sorry. I just thought maybe..." He scratched his head.

I turned on him. "So now you are interested in 'worm holes?' All of a sudden, you believe us? That's a first!" My angry words took him by surprise.

"Hey, I'm just tryin' to help here." Something inside made me stop and think. I could stay angry. Or I could trust that he was on our side. Maybe Alan and I didn't have to argue every time we met. But I didn't like having Regina mad at me either. I missed the closeness we had built up over the Easter weekend. My arms reached out to her.

"Okay. I hear you. If you want to go back, I will do everything I can to help you."

"*If* want to go back? What is *wrong* with you people?" I had to smile at the last sentence. I knew she had heard it on *One Life to Live* and at the rate she was picking up American idioms, she would probably use it again.

Less than a minute later, I heard the growl of Alan's truck engine as it backed down the driveway. Regina and I went to the window and watched him go. Then she turned to me and with an exasperated sigh, looked back at the now empty road.

"Your husband Alan, he is not bad man. He does not shout, he does not get drunk, he does not hit you. He gives you money. Why always fight?"

"I don't know. Maybe because it's not enough, what he *doesn't* do. I want a man who will talk to me about important things. He never shares how he feels." Pretty lame, I know. *He doesn't share.* Did I really think my life should be like a romance novel? I looked away.

"Men *show* how they feel, not always *talking*, Kasia. That is for women. Look to how he *behaves*."

"Talking about personal stuff is not just for women anymore, not like the old days. But you're right. He does good things. I just don't know yet if I want to try living with him again." I walked away from the window. "Let's go back to your predicament. Maybe I can ..."

"No! No more *what you will do.* Not *idiotka*," she said, pointing a finger at her chest. "Work together in house. Work together to get me home. And call Aniela. She wanted to help." She clamped her mouth shut so tightly her lips turned pale.

"Okay. You're right. I'm sorry." Sorry for making her upset with me, that was true, but I still didn't want to lose her. I still thought I could figure out a way for both of us to get what we wanted.

What Aniela was supposed to do was another question. Now that we understood each other, and Regina miraculously spoke English. When exactly had that happened? After one of our sessions with Aniela, the one where she kept rubbing her amber ring? While my mind worked its tortured path, Regina nodded her head once, then turned away from me and climbed the stairs to her room.

Chapter Fifteen

THE NEXT MORNING, I went downstairs to put on the coffee maker. I had to work a morning shift at the library, and I'd been taking more time off than Cory liked. The last time she saw me, she called me into her office and suggested I take a leave of absence.

"Just until your life settles down," she said. "I really need someone I can count on to come in when they're scheduled." The job was pleasant enough, but I'd never given my whole self to it, and it was even less of a priority right now. Today I'd take Cory up on her offer. A few weeks off would let me focus all my energy on Regina.

My house seemed more quiet than usual that morning, but I figured she wanted to sleep in, after her upset the day before. After an hour, I had a funny feeling that things were not right. I went upstairs to knock on her door but there was no answer. When I pushed it open, my heart froze in my chest. Her bed was made, not slept in. In the center of the smooth untouched quilt was a piece of paper. On it were two words, squarely in the center, printed in block letters with a shaky hand. GOOD BYE.

For a second, I told myself it wasn't her. She didn't know how to write. But I couldn't escape the truth. She had obviously learned a few words somewhere, in her church, in her home, or even here in the modern world. She had learned enough to tell me goodbye.

My tears were sudden and familiar. I collapsed onto the bed, clutching the note. Like a child, I wept and clenched my fist around the crumpled paper, holding it as if my strength could hold her here. But it was too late. She was gone.

Time had no meaning for me as I lay across her bed and cried, just like the day my mother left me with another note her only farewell. Though it had been forty years ago, the pain came back as if it were yesterday and the similarity made me wonder what I was doing wrong to make both these women leave me. I wanted Regina back with an ache that went to the bone. And this time, I would go after her. I would find her. But I needed help.

My muscles were stiff when I finally got up off the bed, reminding me I wasn't as young as I used to be. Time was changing my world, passing me by. I was too embarrassed to call Aniela. Maybe I'd get a hold of her later. Right now, I thought of Alan.

"She can't have gone far," he said when I called. "Have you even looked outside?"

I ran to the window but the yard and the road beyond were empty. "Yes, I looked. She's not there."

"How long ago did she leave? Do you know?"

"No, but her bed wasn't slept in." I started to cry again.

Alan's voice was gentle. "Kat, just call the police and give them her description. They'll pick her up." He paused for a beat. "I can take the afternoon off. Want me to come over and help you look for her?"

I sniffled and wiped my nose on my arm. "I guess. That would be good."

Alan said he'd be by in about 20 minutes. After he hung up, I called the Plumstead Police Department. The quaver in my voice surprised me. After taking down my description of Regina, the desk sergeant had a question. "Aren't you the lady who called back in February about that old woman who couldn't speak English? Polish, wasn't she? "

"Yes, that was me. I'm sorry to bother you again but she seems to have run away and I'm worried about her."

119

"Okay, we'll put out a Missing and Endangered Person Advisory. You say she was on foot?"

"Yes, she would have to be. My car is still here and she doesn't drive." My voice broke and I could hardly speak the next words. "She gets carsick."

"Okay, we'll get on it, Ms. Kowalski. We'll let you know as soon as we spot her."

I thanked the officer and ended the call just as Alan's truck stopped outside.

He let himself in through the side door next to the garage just as I was about to open it. Still wearing his FedEx uniform, he appeared to have more wrinkles on his forehead, and more gray strands in his dark hair. When had that happened? It was as if time was speeding up around us, making us older. He pulled at the skin on his throat.

"Anything yet?"

"No, I called the Plumstead cops though." My hand still clutched a wet tissue and his face softened when he saw it. I couldn't meet his eyes but when he held out his arms I stepped into their shelter without a moment's hesitation. His hands patted my back for a short while before he stepped away, releasing me. He cleared his throat.

"Okay, let's not get too excited. She can't have gone far on foot. What if we drive around for a while, see if there's any sign of her?"

For lack of a better idea, and because I didn't want to give him a reason to leave again, I grabbed my car keys and opened the garage. The FedEx truck had only one seat, so we both got into my Jetta, with me driving. Alan may have been a passive sort of guy but he never criticized the way I drove, and this time I really appreciated that.

We traveled west on the Pike toward Doylestown for a few miles, then I turned down one after another of the narrow roads that ran past farm fields and a variety of homes spaced far apart. The beautiful Bucks County countryside, so often soothing to my spirit, was now an endless warren of trees and high grass, with endless places for a wandering Regina to hide. My fear for her grew with every mile.

After half an hour or so, Alan made a suggestion. "Maybe we should try going back toward the river." Oh my god, the river! I shot him a worried look but turned around in the wide dirt driveway of a farm on Moyer Road. The Delaware River was about two miles east of our house, down a steep hill that ran past a noisy stone quarry. Surely, she wouldn't have gone this far.

"She'd be afraid of those dump trucks," I shouted. Clouds of dust rose around the huge tires of the vehicles exiting onto the road in front of us. I had to slow down to let them go. "You know, I think she'd try to go back to the homeless shelter. And that's the other way, back towards town."

Alan was not convinced. "How would she know which way is town? She doesn't have a compass, does she?"

My hackles rose. "No, she does not have a compass. But she is a very smart woman who knows how to follow signs in nature, like the angle of the sun, stuff like that. She might be able to figure it out."

Waiting for the trucks to pass, I touched my dreamcatcher, closed my eyes and asked for clarity. *Where is she? Which way did she go? Please help us find her!* Once the dump trucks were in my rearview mirror, I kept driving east, toward the river. I had no idea which way she'd gone and there was no place to turn around again as the road went downhill and into the forest. I had to concentrate with both hands steady on the wheel. The road was narrow with no shoulders and a massive tractor trailer climbed the road toward us, half its eighteen wheels across the yellow line in the middle. As soon as it passed us, I caught a glimpse of water through the trees.

"What's that?" Alan pointed through the windshield and shaded his eyes with his other hand. A flash of red and yellow moved among the rocks in the little park at the base of the hill. I slowed the car, put on my left turn signal, and pulled into a space in the small gravel lot.

"I see her!" Alan opened his door before I came to a stop. He skidded across the rocks and made for the water with me behind him, calling her name.

"Regina! Please wait!" My voice sounded like a child's, a little girl afraid, but I couldn't stop now. I clambered over the rocks to where Alan stood balanced on a boulder, surrounded by the rushing river. *Oh my God.* She was on her side in the water about ten feet away from us, struggling to get back on her feet. Her face was red and her clothes were wet and weighing her down. Panic filled her face when she saw us and I read her decision in real time. She was caught but she needed our help to survive. It couldn't have taken more than a split second to make up her mind. The current pulled at her as she screamed and stretched a hand out toward Alan.

"It's okay, I got you!" He was close to her now, his shoes sinking in the mud. "Grab onto my hand!" With slow deliberate steps, he made his way toward her. I held my breath and tried to think of a way to help. I saw a sturdy branch on the loose stones at the river's edge, picked it up and held it out toward my husband.

"Alan, take this!" I screamed. He turned to me and grabbed one end of the long piece of wood. Wet leaves still clung to its sides. He stepped further into the river and held the branch toward Regina. She grabbed it with both hands and sobbing, let him pull her to shore.

Chapter Sixteen

I COULD HAVE LOST HER. The whole time we were getting her into the car and driving up the hill toward home, my mind raced. I could have lost her. Fear rushed through me like the river's current. I had been there before. At ten, when my mother left. Six months ago, when Alan left. Two days later, when Jessica left.

Left, again and again, alone with my fear and my pain. There must be something wrong with me. I wanted it to stop. A sob escaped from deep within me as I guided my car across the intersection at Wismer Road. I couldn't lose her now. Alan's head turned sharply toward me, his eyes squinting behind his smudged glasses.

"Are you all right?" His voice was concerned but distant, as if I were someone he knew but was not particularly close to. Not anymore. The rattle of machinery as we climbed the hill past the quarry again made it hard for me to hear my own words. I told him I was fine, just scared for a minute, but really okay. Really.

"What about you?" I asked. "Your feet must be cold in those wet boots! You could have fallen in yourself!"

"I'm okay," he said, staring out the side window. "I can clean up when I get back to my place." Right. His place, not ours.

Regina huddled in the back seat, shivering. "Thank you," she said. "Both. I am sorry for being cause of your trouble." Alan and I glanced at each other.

123

"It's okay," I said. "We're glad you're all right now."

Back home, I led Regina upstairs and turned on the warm water in the shower. Then I left her in the bathroom while I got out some of the clothes we'd bought her at the mall. Alan stood in the hall.

"I'll call the Plumstead PD and let 'em know we found her. And then, if you're okay, I'll get going." A half smile curved his thin lips. His body was half-turned away from me. On the way out.

"Sure. Thank you *so* much. I never could have gotten to her in time." My voice shook. "You saved her life." It was true. I never could have pulled her out of the river. I wasn't strong enough. If not for Alan, Regina would have drowned.

He nodded once, told me he was glad to help and headed down the stairs. I stood in the hall holding Regina's new flowered skirt and yellow blouse. I would have liked to give her underpants but she still refused to wear them. Nobody wore panties in *Mała Łąka*. The shock of what we'd just been through took away my sense of the way things should be. All I wanted was for her to like me, to forgive me. So, no underwear. I left the clothes outside the bathroom door and called Cory to tell her I was ready to take that leave of absence. How could I go to work at a time like this? She wasn't in, and I had to leave a message on her voice mail. It might be the end of my job, but I couldn't have cared less.

In the kitchen, I brewed a pot of jasmine tea, Regina's new favorite, and put some fresh chocolate chip cookies on a plate, for me as much as for her. Then I called Aniela.

When she answered, my voice broke as I told her what happened.

"I shall be right over," she said. As I ended the call, a glimmer of hope landed in my soul. This mysterious, sometimes haughty young woman felt like a friend. I couldn't wait to see her again.

When Regina came downstairs, she looked clean but shaken. I saw no cuts or bruises on her exposed skin but I still wanted to take her in my arms, protect and comfort her and never let her go. And I was afraid she would not let me touch her.

At first, she stood in the doorway and hung her head. Her mouth opened but no words came out. Her shoulders hunched over and when I took a step toward her, she let out a wrenching sob. In an instant, we were holding each other and crying as the full impact of what had happened coursed through us.

"Sorry, sorry," she said against my shoulder.

I told her it was all right, that everything would be all right.

"Have to go back to Anna." Her wet eyes pleaded and tore at my heart.

"Of course, you do," I said. I led her to the kitchen table, poured a cup of hot tea and when she was seated, placed her shaking hands around it. Then I covered them with both of mine. "I'm sorry for trying to keep you here. You belong with Anna. Aniela is coming over. We'll find a way to get you back home."

Our translator arrived, hatless and with her hair disheveled. Her face was pale. "This is what I feared," she said.

"But it's not your fault!" Regina and I both cried.

"Come on in," I said, taking her arm. Regina and I took her into the dining room where we'd spent so much time getting to know each other. It seemed like years ago but it had only been four months. Now it was June. We needed to make faster progress. I didn't want to lose either Regina or Aniela again. I looked at her, the elegant young woman drinking her tea, pulling at her hair, straightening her skirt. She reminded me of a more mature Jessica. I would call my daughter tonight, and make her understand how much I loved her. After pouring my own cup of tea, I sat down and reached both hands across the table. Aniela and Regina took my hands in theirs. We squeezed hard and nodded. Stronger together, we would do this.

"I run away, but not your fault," Regina said to us both.

Aniela shook her head. "I stood too far back and you could have lost your life. I am sorry for this. Please accept my apology. I will try harder." She clutched her amber necklace and with a little cough settled back in her chair.

We ate the cookies and drank the tea, and slowly our strength returned. The time for endless talking was over. I had to do the right thing. I would get Regina back home to her child. Then I would reconnect with mine. And Aniela would help me.

When I asked Regina what she thought, I expected her to suggest more prayers to the Black Madonna, or maybe another Old Country superstition. To my surprise, she told me, instead, that we should look on the computer.

We all three headed for my office upstairs. I sat at my desk and powered up my laptop as Regina pulled at my arm. "*No* worm hole. Father Marek say pagan worship worm before Christ. Mortal sin!" She pulled up a chair and sat beside me while Aniela stood alongside us both.

"Don't worry. There's probably another way. Wait a minute. What am I saying? A wormhole does not have real worms in it. It's a scientific term."

Regina's brow furrowed. She was thinking hard, but in a different direction.

"Cross ocean on boat!" She looked so excited I think she might have left that day if only she knew where to find the harbor. I turned away from the glowing screen.

"No, no, people don't do that anymore. Now everyone flies to Europe. In planes, you know, like I showed you, in the sky."

"No plane. Take boat." She clenched her hands together in her lap.

"Regina, it would take a very long time, weeks, and you could get seasick, like you get sick riding in the car. And it's very expensive." Plus, I had no idea how to book a transatlantic voyage.

"Boat better than car." She stole a glance at the little TV in the corner of the room.

"Regina, the people on *Love Boat* aren't real. It's a story. And even if we do get you back to Mała Łąka by plane or by boat, time has passed. Lots of time, like a couple of centuries. You won't find Pawel or your kids there. They're long gone."

The words were barely out of my mouth before I wanted to eat them. Regina's face clouded as tears filled her eyes and traveled down her softly lined cheeks. What was wrong with me? I had no idea where and when another time travel journey would take her, yet I acted like an authority. I didn't know what I was talking about. Aniela glared as I struggled to fix things.

"Take a moment, Kat," she said. "Go within. You must succeed or I will...never mind." Her hands were trembling. She was more invested in this project than I'd realized.

"Um, okay, wait a minute." I scoured my mind for the words. I tried to access my intuition. We needed Guidance, not logic. I took a deep cleansing breath. And sure enough, it came to me: remembered scenes from movies about time travel. There was always a special place, a car or a bridge or a doorway, that whooshed people backward or forward. A portal in time. "You want to go back to the exact time and place where your family lives, so...you have to go through the same portal you used to come here!" My ears buzzed like an alarm clock. "Come on! We have to find the portal you came through in the backyard!"

Regina ran behind me through the open door of my garage while Aniela walked at a more dignified pace. We crossed the driveway and slowed down where the asphalt met the grass. Above our heads, a cardinal twittered from a branch in the maple at the edge of my property, as if it wanted to join the little party. Regina walked in circles on the grass, moving farther and farther from the house.

"Can you tell me where it is? Can you find the spot?"

"Over there," she pointed, and walked slowly toward my herb garden near the back door. She stopped next to the chives and tapped her foot on the ground. "Over here, I am sitting on ground at night with dizzy head."

"Great! The portal has got to be here." I knelt beside her foot and she crouched beside me. We moved our hands over the grass and combed it with our fingers. Dirt, weeds, scurrying ants and a couple of spiders.

"Not finding hole." Regina sighed and wrinkled her forehead.

I sat back on my heels. "I thought there would be something, I don't know, some kind of little door or tunnel..." I peered up at Aniela. She bit her lip then spoke.

"Keep trying, you will get there."

"Maybe door is closed." Regina pressed a hand into her stomach. "Because I was selfish."

"You are *not* selfish. Maybe we just don't know what to look for." I stood up and brushed my hands on my jeans. "Come on. Let's check the Internet again."

We entered through the back porch but once inside, I had a spell of vertigo. My head swam at the thought of wading through all those online sources again. I sat down in a chair at the kitchen table and tried to breathe slowly. Aniela put a trembling hand on my shoulder.

"I am going away now," she said.

"What? You can't! You have to help us!" Panic fed my words. Aniela smiled sadly.

"I will be back," she said. "But now I need some space."

"Space?! What the..." But she was out the door, and the sound of her BMW's engine retreating left me again with that empty feeling.

Regina could not sit still. She stood and poked at my side with her finger.

"Feel okay? Take little rest, go on internet for ideas!"

"All right. Just let me get centered here. I feel a little dizzy." I walked over to my corner altar, touched the purple cloth and picked up a soft flat stone. As always, its coolness soothed me as I stroked its surface with my thumb. Regina scurried upstairs and came back carrying my laptop in front of her like a serving tray.

"Go on internet, please! Need more ideas!" I took it from her with a sigh and set it on the table.

This time when I searched, a link at the bottom of the screen caught my attention: *Marvels, Mechanics and*

Mysteries of Life on Earth. Clicking on the title, I browsed through the strangest combination of subjects I had ever encountered online or in print: Aviation, Contradictions, Fantasy, Spiritual Beings, Unicorns...and Time Slips.

"Hmmm, time slips could mean time travel..." Regina leaned in closer and stared wide-eyed at the screen she could not read. "Listen to this." I read aloud. "'Persons might travel through time by means of a portal.' Okay, we got that right." I went on. "'These places of extreme high energy exist all over the earth. To travel to the same portal at different times in history one must find a place very similar to the place left behind.'"

Regina's gaze went to my altar shelf on the wall. I pictured tiny wheels turning inside her head as she thought for several minutes in silence. Then she spoke.

"Altar in here same idea as my shrine, yes? But Kasia backyard not same as *Mała Łąka* shrine, except grass and trees." After another minute, she threw her hands in the air. "Ask people from big church. Find porthole in those people village!"

"It's 'portal,' not 'porthole...never mind." Even if she *was* picking up words from *Love Boat* reruns, she was on the right track. I didn't need to correct her every minute. "Regina, the people we saw at the Shrine don't live in a village. They live all over Bucks County, in houses like this one." Where would I find a place that resembled her *Mała Łąka*?

Wait a minute. I did indeed know of a place that just might fit the bill. It wasn't a village, but it *was* a close-knit community filled with Polish people: The Port Richmond neighborhood in Philadelphia.

We took the quickest route to the city, straight down I-95. Regina covered her eyes with one hand and peeked between her fingers as cars and trucks whizzed by. She wore the garish red skirt and yellow tunic from our trip to the mall. While I drove, she whispered *"Święta Maryjo"* and scrabbled in her skirt pocket for the crystal rosary from the Shrine gift shop.

She always seemed to direct her pleas to the Virgin. Maybe Regina was more of a feminist than she knew. I smiled to myself at the thought.

My parallel parking skills were rusty, but I managed to jockey the car into a space on a side street off Allegheny Avenue, the main commercial thoroughfare. When I opened her door, Regina stepped onto the sidewalk but immediately cowered against my car. Busy shoppers passed us by without a second glance. Why weren't we attracting stares the way we had in the mall? I looked around us: mostly white people in blue-collar clothing. A fair number of older women in babushkas like Regina's. Young men and women in jeans and t-shirts. Tired-looking adult males in forgettable clothing.

"Don't be afraid. No one here will hurt you." Just then, a group of teenaged boys shouldered us aside and continued down the sidewalk. Regina's hands flew to her chest. The boys crossed the street, laughing back at us. I was angry, but the dirty look I gave them was a waste of time. They weren't malicious, just young and arrogant. I looked around for a place to escape the crowd. A block ahead, the glass front of the Syrenka Luncheonette gleamed in the sunlight.

"Come on, let's get a bite to eat." I guided Regina to a spot where we could cross at the corner of Richmond Avenue and enter the haven of the quiet café. A middle-aged waitress with a round face and ponytail served us iced tea and cookies on heavy white plates. On the wall beside our table hung a mermaid in gold-painted plaster, above a white index card. I leaned close to the card and read that she was the symbol of Warsaw. "Did you know that?" Regina gave me a little nod, still shaky from our encounter on the street.

"Lots of teenagers out today," I remarked to our waitress. "They scared my friend."

"Those kids, they are always causing trouble. Decent people cannot go out anymore. Street is only for them, the spoiled boys." She shook her head and glanced out the glass storefront.

Regina nibbled at a sugar cookie. I looked again at the mermaid on the wall, and as I did, an idea came to me, like a gentle nudge from my cat's nose, so soft and quiet I might have missed it altogether.

"Do you know where there's a picture of the Black Madonna around here?"

"Why, yes, actually. I have one in my wallet." She gave me a puzzled look.

"I mean, is there a big one, like that?" I pointed at the mermaid.

"Yes, sure. St. Adalbert's on Allegheny, two blocks up on right."

"Thanks. Come on," I said to Regina. "Let's go."

"I will write up your check." The waitress reached for the pad in her skirt pocket.

"Don't bother, this should cover it." I threw some cash on the table, told her to keep the change and pulled Regina outside.

"*Czekaj,* Kasia! What happens now?" Regina had stopped on the edge of the curb.

"I have an idea."

"*Tell.*" She stomped one foot like Jessica when she was two. She was right. I was leading her around like a child again, instead of telling her what I was doing.

"Sorry." I forced myself to stand still. "I think if we can get you to a picture of the Black Madonna, *Matka Boska Częstochowska*, it might be a portal. Didn't you say you were *praying before a picture* of her before you got thrown into the future?"

"Okay." She nodded once. "That is true, it was her painted picture." With that, we headed down the street.

Tall metal spires on either side of the main entrance of St. Adalbert's Church pierced the sky, and high on the roof's apex, a plain gold crucifix glimmered in the sun. Inside the building, we shifted from foot to foot as we waited for our eyes to adjust to the dark. Regina saw it before I did: the side altar and a huge painting of the famous Black Madonna, Queen of Poland.

She looked the same to me as she always had. *Fleur de lis* on a dark robe, her dark face scarred on one cheek with two long lines like the tracks of tears. Around her head and that of the Christ Child, gold haloes gleamed. Quiet filled the sanctuary with a presence I could not name and my breath caught in my throat. Regina knelt at the side altar rail and whispered a prayer, her gaze pinned to the Madonna's face. I wanted to kneel beside her, and for once, I gave in to the impulse. What happened next took me completely by surprise.

The two haloes shimmered as if they were molten gold, and wind blew my hair into my face. I felt my body rock back and forth. Beside me, Regina seemed to be doing the same, but I could not look at her. I could not take my eyes off the painting. The wind grew stronger and a door slammed with a loud crack in the church behind us.

"O Jezus Maryo!"

"Oh my God!"

We jumped up and threw our arms around each other. When my heart stopped beating in my ears, I realized the wind had stilled. The haloes in the painting were as before, no longer shimmering.

"What the hell?" I whispered and a scary shiver ran through me. "I mean, heck. What the heck?" I blinked up at the Madonna. "Did you see that?"

Regina wrung her hands and whispered. "What happens?" She glanced up at the icon and blessed herself. A voice spoke from the shadows at the entrance.

"What is the problem, ladies?" The deep silky tone was familiar. Aniela stepped out from behind a marble pillar. Regina and I froze.

"What are *you* doing here?" My voice shook with anger and fear. I was still mad at her for leaving us so abruptly the day before, for needing her "space."

"Lucky for you I came along, is it not?" She tilted her head and gave me a cocky smile.

"Why are you here?" I repeated. "Don't you still need some 'space?' Have you been following us?"

"My friend lives around here." She waved her arms outward like wings. She stood tall in her shiny high-heeled boots, her amber ring twinkling in a beam of sunlight. "Port

Richmond is my friend's neighborhood." She stepped closer. Unnerved, I put my arm around Regina.

"Where have you been? I called your cell to tell you we were coming here but there was no answer, not even a voice mail box." I had thought she was my friend, but now she was again a mystery.

Aniela leveled her gaze at the two of us. "I have other matters to attend to. And I am here now, am I not?"

Chapter Seventeen

ANIELA WAS FAR MORE self-assured than most young women I'd met, and this time her manner had me completely flustered. My face and arms felt hot as I searched for words and came up empty. Quickly, Regina chimed in, excitement filling her voice.

"Try porthole here, at *Matka Boska Częstochowska*." She moved her arms up and down to punctuate each word. "Big light and wind like when I am praying in *Mała Łąka*!"

"You try so hard," Aniela murmured, shaking her head. "It is a pity to see."

"Of course, she does." I threw up my hands. "We don't know what else to do. And instead of your pity, why don't you help us?" There. I had said it. We needed help. Even if Aniela's condescending attitude did give me a pain in the neck.

She tilted her head and gave me a bemused look. "Perhaps your ideas are indeed good ones but they cannot work as yet. There may be a reason."

"What are you talking about?" Despite my annoyance, her words aroused my curiosity. She knew more than she was saying and I wanted to hear it. Now.

Aniela raised one hand in a call for patience. "Perhaps if *Matka Boska* sent Regina to this time, she had a reason. Perhaps, instead of running all over the place to find portals, Regina needs to learn something before she goes back home. Then portal will be no problem." Regina stood mesmerized as Aniela looked from her to me. "Just think about it." She turned on her shiny high heel and tossed her final words over her shoulder. "You too, Kat. Perhaps you have something to learn as well."

"What about you?" Both Regina and I spoke at once. I pointed a finger at the younger woman. "What's in all this for you? If you have 'other matters to attend to,' why show up now? When you couldn't be bothered to answer my call?" I crossed my arms and glared at her. Some friend she was. Plus, she was still my employee. "Aren't I paying you to be available?"

For a change, Aniela looked flustered. She licked her lips. She swallowed. "Fine, I come to check on you but I see you have everything under control. Hah!" She spun around and stalked out of the church, letting the huge door slam behind her with a bang.

"What the..." I whispered. All at once the towering sanctuary seemed to close in on me. I fanned the air in front of my face and took Regina's arm. "Come on. Let's go outside for some air."

By the time we opened the heavy wooden door and looked outside, Aniela was nowhere in sight. Around the corner on Richmond Street, another glass storefront glinted in the hot afternoon sun. As my eyes adjusted to the light, I made out the words Bakery and *Piekarnia* in white block letters against the red painted wall. They actually glowed. And shimmered. Regina looked at me. I looked at her.

"There's something about this place...I'm going with my gut this time. Let's check it out." I grabbed her hand.

"*Tak, tak, tak.* Check out." She looked back over her shoulder. "Aniela not coming?"

"Apparently not." I glanced up and down the street. "Do we really need her?"

"Maybe not at moment, but she is good woman."

Her wise words made me think again. I didn't like Aniela's superior attitude but she did seem to know something about this time travel business. More than I did, anyway. And she did get Regina to learn English awfully fast. Miraculously

135

fast, one might say. And just now she had suggested Regina was sent to me for a reason. I liked that idea. I liked it a lot. After all, I read all kinds of metaphysical books, consulted my Goddess cards, and was drawn to feminist spirituality in a big way. What if this was another step on my path: looking to a female figure for guidance? So what if Aniela was young enough to be my daughter? The more I thought about it, the more I liked it.

"You're right," I said. "We should give Aniela a call when we get home. I mean when we get back to my house. Meanwhile, let's check out that bakery."

Regina flashed me a happy grin. We hurried down the front steps of the church until we reached the curb and stopped to look left and right. When a gap in the traffic opened up, we crossed the street and headed straight for the bakery. A little bell jangled when I opened the door and as we stepped into the sales room, the rich aroma of freshly baked bread made my mouth water.

"Something here," Regina whispered, taking in the room. I felt it too, a warm and welcoming energy, gentle as my *Babcia*'s caress. Regina walked with a light step toward the back of the store. "Here," she whispered, then lifted her hand and walked through the open doorway without a backward glance.

From behind the counter, a pretty blonde woman moved to go after her. I held up my hand. "*Proszę pani,* my aunt is visiting from Poland. Is it all right if she takes a look around?"

The woman stopped and smiled, resting her hands on the top of the pastry-filled case. "Sure. But please to be careful back there. Ovens are hot." There were no other customers. She lifted her long white apron over her head. "We are closing soon. I should come with you." She dropped the apron on a wooden stool, came around the counter and flipped the sign on the door to Closed.

Outside the back door, Regina was halfway across a courtyard and headed toward another building of faded red brick at the end of a long narrow lot. She walked as if she knew exactly where to go. As if she was following something.

As the bakery clerk and I entered the old building, more yeasty warmth engulfed me.

"This bakery has been here since 1922," the shopkeeper said. "We have original yeast brought here on ship from Poland." She pointed to a bathtub-like container on the floor. Regina was already standing on the other side of the metal tub. When she looked up, our eyes met and locked, and I knew in my Polish bones we were meant to be right here, right now. All the prior weeks of struggle and wonder had led us to this very spot. Regina nodded her head and I nodded back. *Yes. Yes.*

As the bakery lady talked about the room's history, Regina and I walked around gazing at timeworn tools – flat wooden bread trays, shelves of ceramic bowls, and against one wall, a huge black oven, its door covered by an iron wheel about the size of my car. At the top, in crusted black iron, I read the date aloud: "1825." Regina gasped. *1825.* The year she had left *Mała Łąka*. Before I could stop her, she reached for the wheel.

"Wait! That's hot!" I grabbed her arm. Instantly, the oven door opened and the glow of the fire inside flared into a blinding flash. My eyes squeezed shut in reflex as a hot wind blew around my head.

In the very next heartbeat, the wind was gone and I heard the sound of water rippling nearby. When I opened my eyes, Regina was standing beside me, her arm still in my grip. She was laughing so hard I had to let her go. My legs refused to hold me and I collapsed in the wet grass beside a noisy little stream. We were not in Philadelphia anymore.

PART II

Chapter Eighteen

"DOM! DOM! HOME!"* Regina laughed and twirled, her flowered red skirt flaring around her. When she saw me sitting on the ground, she held out her hand, but I could only sit there with my mouth open. Regina hopped from foot to foot and pointed up the hill to a little wooden shrine perched atop a bark-covered branch.

Breathe. Just breathe. All is well. All is well. Slowly, very slowly, my shoulders released, and my stomach unclenched itself.

When Regina stopped laughing and hopping, the sound of chirping reached my ears. Chocolate brown sparrows and red-breasted robins flew low across the sky while a chalk white stork descended onto the top of a tall linden tree. The air was filled with a pungent mix of new mown hay and manure.

I drew more calming breaths as my heartbeat slowed to a steady hammering inside my chest. Regina pulled me up to stand. I brushed at my jeans with both hands. She said she was home, but I would have recognized it without her. She'd talked about it often enough. Could it really be this easy, after all our struggle, stumbling by accident into another time?

139

"Come." She led me up the hill to the shrine where she blessed herself and motioned me closer. A painted image of the Black Madonna and the infant Jesus decorated the front, both wearing shiny gold crowns like the ones in St. Adalbert's and the Shrine of *Częstochowa*. The Madonna's right hand touched her blue gown just below her heart, and peace descended over me like a soft cloak. I breathed deeply of the warm and fragrant air.

"Pray here." Regina's voice, in English, came deep and soft over my shoulder.

"Is this where, that day?"

"Yes, here." She moved her weight from foot to foot. "All right now, Kasia?" Her hand was a light touch on my shoulder. I was still lightheaded, but she looked so happy it warmed my entire being. We had actually found a portal that worked. And we had done it by accident. We had dropped back in time to the very place Regina left.

A sudden thought froze me in place. How would I get back home? What if I couldn't...and I never saw Jessica...or Alan... ever again? I wasn't ready for this!

Regina pulled on my hand. I remembered how she had grown to trust me. If she could handle this time travel stuff, so could I. Maybe now that we'd done it, we could do it again. Shakily, I followed her up the gently rising slope.

As we crested the hill, Regina quickened her pace. I stopped short at the sight. About a hundred yards away, little girls in long muslin dresses raced along the road, laughing in the squealing way of little girls everywhere in every time. Boys carried white geese in their arms, one girl led two goats by ropes around their necks, and a group of smaller boys in short dark pants shouldered long sheaves of grain.

We moved toward a row of log houses, where women dug in garden plots fenced with roughly cut limbs. Three old men sat on a wooden bench outside a cottage with whitewashed window frames, puffing on long pipes. A couple of elderly women scattered corn before a flock of chickens in another fenced yard farther down the road.

"Where are the men? I only see old guys and little kids."

"Working in field for Zalewski, noble landowner," Regina said. She grinned as one of the old women spotted us and pointed with one hand, made a quick sign of the cross and pulled on the arm of the woman beside her in the chicken yard. They each pointed a finger at us and stared. Uh oh. Regina had on her skirt and blouse outfit from the mall and I was wearing jeans and a Gap shirt. She still had her old boots on but I was wearing Reeboks.

A blond girl let out a shout and broke away from the other children to throw her arms around Regina's waist. Regina held the girl close and kissed the top of her head. The child wore dusty black boots and a blouse made of rough white cloth speckled with dark threads. Over her brown skirt, a muslin apron was tied around her waist.

Right behind her, a boy and girl who looked about seven or eight pushed close to Regina and I backed away to give them room. She looked old enough to be their grandmother, but they called her Mama. The older girl reminded me of Jessica. She pulled at Regina's new skirt and yellow tunic, laying her cheek on the sleeve.

Regina looked over the tops of the children's heads. "*Gdzie jest Anna?*"

The two older women from the garden eyed me with unfriendly looks. I felt alone and conspicuous in my jeans and shirt. Regina was supposed to go back to *Mała Łąka*, not me. My mind scrambled and came up with nothing.

She motioned me to her side and spoke to the women in Polish so fast I couldn't catch more than a few of the words. *Wdowa. Bieda. Las.* I didn't know what any of them meant. Regina turned and whispered in my ear.

"If we say you come from future, they will curse you for witch. I say you are poor widow I find lost in forest. You dressed in husband's clothes because you are crazy from grief. We always help widows. You will be all right." It was obvious my jeans and sneakers were a problem. They shook their hands and chattered and pointed and stared. These people were not used to strangers, and I was one of the strangest, a woman in snug denim. How would they treat me here?

I didn't have time to worry. In the next moment, all eyes turned to a figure moving down the road. A middle-aged priest in a long brown cassock took hasty steps toward us. As he drew near, his eyes glittered like bits of pale blue ice. I gave him a weak smile and shrugged my shoulders, hoping to look innocuous. I knew I looked nothing like a poor Polish widow, grief-crazed or not.

The priest put his hands into opposite sleeves of his cassock and gave me a piercing glare. Holy Mother of God, what had I gotten myself into? Thankfully, Regina showed none of the fear that had taken up residence in my breastbone. She spoke with serene confidence, and so clear was her Polish I understood every word.

"Father, I pray to *Matka Boska Częstochowska* and find this poor widow wandering in woods."

I struggled to keep my whole body from trembling. My admiration for Regina grew as she stood in the dirt road, her eyes on the priest. I took shallow nervous breaths while she talked on as if our lives depended on it, and for all I knew, they did.

The priest glared at me from under his thick gray eyebrows but said not a word. Regina turned and headed down the road with her children close behind.

I was about to follow when a noise like thunder stopped me in my tracks. A horse and rider headed straight for us, kicking up a cloud of dirt and dust. Screaming people and honking geese scattered across the road in every direction, knocking against each other in terror.

The black-haired bearded rider rode like a hurricane, a leather whip raised high above his head. Regina grabbed my arm and pulled me away, hard. I screamed at the pain in my shoulder but she began to run. My feet barely touched the ground. I saw a blue headscarf flying through the air before everything went black.

My head felt like the top of my skull was about to come off. The light hurt my eyes so I squeezed them shut.

Something was missing in the air. No smell of manure. I opened my eyes again the tiniest crack. And saw my Pennsylvania backyard. Regina lay in the grass beside me, weeping.

"Why, why back to here?"

I pressed one hand into the wet grass and struggled to sit up. My head throbbed with every move. "Are you all right?"

"No, not all right! How can be all right? *Psia krew*, dammit to hell ..." She pounded the ground with her fists.

"Hey, don't blame me. I didn't ask for this. Ow! My head is killing me." I pushed my palms hard against my forehead. "Who was that guy on the horse? And what was the idea with the whip?"

"Jurek, son of Zalewski. Ride around estate and village, mean to peasants...what you call billy."

"What? *Oh*, you mean he's a *bully*! Wait a minute! Isn't that the name of the guy who raped you?" Horror coursed through my veins.

"*Tak, tak, tak.*" she nodded in an undertone, waving me off with one hand as we sat exhausted in my backyard.

I pondered the enormity of what had just happened. Our search for a portal to 1825 had worked. But for only a few minutes. Our mission had suddenly aborted. And frankly, I was relieved. When crazy Jurek came at us with that whip, and Regina yanked my arm, I had never run so fast in my life. I reached up and massaged my left shoulder with my right hand. *It was fine.* No pain, no wrenching. The rose bushes swam before my eyes.

"Hey, Regina. My shoulder doesn't hurt." My voice was weak and shaky.

She yanked up handfuls of grass with both hands. "You scream like pig when I am pulling your arm!"

"I know, it hurt a lot...a *pig*?"

"Yes, Kasia, you scream like pigs in pen on market day!" She wiped at her tears with one hand.

"Huh. Whatever. I can move it all around. It doesn't hurt at all. How is that possible?"

"Miracle, Kasia. Who care? Anna sick and I cannot go to her." She pulled up still more handfuls of grass and tossed them into the air.

I didn't try to stop her. *Let it out. I don't blame you.*

After a while, she stopped throwing grass and just cried. I put my hand on her back and left it there until she sighed and lifted her head to give me a weak smile. Her headscarf was cockeyed and I straightened it for her.

"Come on. Let's go inside. I'll make you some tea. And then we'll figure out what to do next."

"Kasia, where is white car?" She pointed to my empty driveway.

"Huh?"

"Car we go to Polish streets in, where it is now?"

"Oh, no, my car! It must be still parked in Port Richmond. I hope." *Why hadn't we been tossed back to Allegheny Avenue instead of my backyard?* I was tired of trying to figure everything out. My shoulder was fine but my head hurt like crazy.

I helped Regina up and together we walked through the open garage. The door that opened into the laundry room was unlocked. "I must have forgotten to close the garage when we left. All this is making me so distracted." I called Alan for a ride back to Port Richmond, where, lucky for me, my car was right where I'd left it.

"Too bad time travelers can't take their cars with them." Alan's smirk made me regret telling him about our adventure. It was clear he didn't believe me. He was quick to give us a lift so why did he have to put me down this way? And why did I care? Next time I'd call someone else to give us a ride, if we ever needed one again.

On Allegheny Avenue, I yelled a quick "thanks" and jumped out of his truck as soon as he turned off the engine. As we buckled ourselves into my Jetta, Regina gave Szypula's Bakery a wistful look. I was having no more of it.

"Not today. We've been through enough for now. We could have been killed back there! Let's try again another time." I turned the ignition key and made for the I95 northbound ramp. Regina twisted in her seat and watched the bakery until it was out of sight.

Back home in Plumstead Township, I retrieved Aniela's number from the bulletin board on the wall. This time, she answered on the first ring. When I told her what we'd just been through, she gasped.

"It is too much. What am I supposed to do with you? Stay put. Do not go anywhere. I will be right over." The call clicked off, and I turned to Regina, stunned.

"She's pretty upset. Now she wants to come over. Where the hell was she when I tried to call her before?"

Regina just shrugged and sat down at the table, looking tired. I was more confused than ever.

"Alan was right., even though I don't like the way he said it. Why didn't we get thrown back to the bakery?"

"Kasia, we are lucky to be alive. Cannot always have everything we want. We go back and try again tomorrow."

I don't think so. I am not in a hurry to go back to the land of crazy Jurek. I took my time putting teabags into mugs and placing them on the table, as I had done so many times before. But this time, Regina was petulant.

"Why not put tea into pot?" The little white teabag dangled by its string from her chubby hand.

"We could do that, but this is easier."

"Always 'easier, easier!' No little tea paper in Mała Łąka. Put tea in pot, hot water on top. Not hard to do." Frustration etched little frown lines across her forehead. "And by the way, no special room in *Mała Łąka* for eating and cooking. Only *szlachta* have big kitchen. Most people eat and sleep in one room."

By the way. For *Pete's sake.* She copied my expressions more and more. I liked that.

"So, you see it's much better for you here." Oops. What was I thinking? How great it was to have a separate room for sleeping, and a bag for tea, while her daughter Anna was still sick, for all we knew, and needed her mother. I should have kept my mouth shut, but it was too late.

"Bigger house not better for me without family. Not better sit in car every day, running around to do what next. What I have to do so you understand?" Regina's chair scraped across the floor as she pushed away from the table and stomped up the stairs to her bedroom. She refused to come down when Aniela arrived, no matter how the young woman pleaded outside her closed door. Finally, she came back downstairs to talk to me.

"What am I supposed to do? I try to help you. But she does not cooperate." Aniela's once proud posture slumped and she seemed to grow shorter before my eyes.

"I don't know," I said. "But we'll think of something. You look like you could use some rest. I'll give you a call tomorrow."

The next morning, dawn was nothing more than the graying of the black night sky. It matched my mood and Regina's as well. After a desultory breakfast, we emptied the dishwasher, working side by side, but I couldn't enjoy it. My plan to make my life appealing was crumbling around me by the minute. But the thought of losing her to an abusive husband frightened me. Didn't I have a responsibility to protect her from him?

"We didn't see Pawel in *Mała Łąka*. Won't he be angry that you left? Again? Won't he find out you were back?"

Regina snorted loudly through her nose and bent her head. "He is always angry, what is new? Strong woman does not mind this."

I replaced the empty cutlery basket in the dishwasher while I composed a persuasive argument in my head.

"I know you think it's strong to put up with abuse. And I understand you need to get back to your kids, especially Anna. But I don't want him to hurt you again. If you go back, you have to do something to stop him. For her sake, as well as your own."

Regina kept her head down so I didn't see her reaction. I wiped my hands on a dishtowel, poured the rest of the morning's coffee into a mug and gave it to her. She gripped it in both hands and inhaled the fragrant brew.

"One thing good here is *kawa*."

It was hazelnut, my favorite blend, but before I could tell her that, she placed the mug back on the counter with a little thump. When she raised her head, the look on her face was so direct I couldn't move a muscle.

"Not always good to be doing something, changing something." She took a deep breath and blew it out so hard her wiry gray hairs lifted off her forehead. "So hard for you here, always having to do something." She reached out and put both hands on my shoulders. "Computer, TV, car, job, so many things can make you crazy like Jurek." She pulled one hand away and pointed to the side of her head.

"You can't possibly understand." I turned away. "My life is nothing like yours."

"True. And I do not want Kasia's life. I want life God has given me! Why not mind your business, find your own daughter?"

My mouth opened but no words came out. Heat spread down my face and over my shoulders. I couldn't look her in the eye. Regina gathered the mugs from the counter and placed them in the dishwasher. She grabbed a dishcloth and carefully wiped the table, the counter, and all the flat surfaces in my kitchen. When she was done, she folded the cloth neatly and with a little nod, placed it squarely next to the sink. She left me there, standing alone, tongue-tied. I watched her go up the stairs until her worn flat-heeled boots disappeared at the top.

In my own room, I sank, heavy-hearted, onto my meditation cushion. My Goddess cards lay neatly stacked on a low table. Candles, incense and matches were lined up beside them, ready for my fingers. But this time, I left them where they were. I closed my eyes and inhaled deeply.

May I be safe. May I be strong. May I be happy.

Could I be happy if I kept Regina here, away from her family? Would she ever learn to like my world? The answer came in no time. Perhaps I had already known it before I sat down. To both questions. *Not very likely.*

But without my help and Aniela's, she was stuck here. And she was right about my daughter. Even though she'd left me in a huff, I was her mother. Whatever my mistakes, I needed to make amends. But she was a young woman, healthy and strong, and time away from me might help her gain confidence. First things first. Regina's child was only six, and she was ill.

I made an appointment with Aniela for that evening. She arrived early, her self-assurance on full display once more.

"Don't give up, ladies," she said. "You will get there. I am sure of it."

But Regina didn't look convinced. She frowned, standing with hands folded at her waist.

Aniela gave her a wide smile and waved an amber-jeweled hand in my direction. "Kat, do computer searching again."

It was a lovely evening, so I took my laptop out to the front porch, sat down on one of the wooden rockers and looked up the website I had bookmarked earlier. After a minute, I felt Regina's eyes boring a hole into the back of my head.

"Come out here, both of you, and sit down. Listen to this: *If a subject is not completely ready to leave a place in time, and tries to force it, the time warp can become very unstable. A sudden movement or physical violence can instantly return the subject back to the starting place and time.*" Regina lowered herself into the chair beside me as I pointed at the screen. "That is *exactly* what happened to us. It says 'physical violence!' Crazy Jurek ran us down in *Mała Łąka* and we got thrown back here because we were not ready!"

Regina slapped her hands on the arms of the rocker and pushed off so hard it hit the wall of the house behind her. I hurried to explain.

"Okay, okay, wait a minute. Maybe it was me who was not ready and I slipped through the portal with you, which screwed things up. Please, sit down. I'm sorry.".

148

Mollified, she again took her seat. "Why send *me* back here too? I am ready." She closed her eyes and rocked back and forth. Aniela sat beside her and covered her hand with her own.

I scrunched up my forehead and pressed my fists to either side of my head, thinking hard. After a minute, it came to me. "Okay, maybe you weren't supposed to use that portal in the bakery. That was an accident. We didn't know what we were doing, right? Maybe you have to go back through the same portal you used to come here....in the backyard...if we could only find it."

Regina gave me a withering look and scuffed her boots against the cement floor of the porch. She had done nothing wrong yet here she was, stranded. It was so unfair. But if this website—and Aniela—were right and I was the one who was not ready...the lights turned on inside my brain.

"Is there something you'd like me to know? Maybe there's some message you're supposed to give me before you can leave." I tried to catch Aniela's eye but she was looking at Regina, whose face was tomato red.

"Here is message for you, Kat." Her words flew out in a burst that struck me squarely in the middle of my chest. "Regina not *belong* here!"

Chapter Nineteen

I GOT THE MESSAGE, loud and clear. And I had finally accepted it. Regina didn't belong here, in the 21st century. But what exactly was I supposed to do about it? Go back to the bakery and try again? Keep looking for the portal in my backyard? The weeks were flying by and we were getting nowhere. It was the middle of summer already. Was my not being "ready" holding Regina back? And how exactly did one get ready to send another person back in time?

All the next day, options whirled around my head until I felt a spell of vertigo coming on. In the silence of my house, while Regina prayed, I stood at my altar and wished for a simple answer. It was so quiet I could hear the walls creak. In the living room, I walked to the sofa and leaned down to stroke Selene's soft warm fur. She re-crossed her paws but kept her eyes closed as if engrossed in a dream. I wondered how she would have fared in 19th century Poland. Would she be a barn cat or a pet of the aristocracy? She stirred a little beneath my hand and let out a soft exhalation that ended in a low-pitched sigh. Regina came downstairs, sat beside her and scratched her furry ears.

I settled in a spot next to them on the sofa and opened my laptop. "Let me see..." I clicked on the search engine and found the bookmarked site. There was a section on portals in the middle of the page. "Listen to this. *Anecdotal evidence suggests that contact with places high in energy of similar genetic content may bring a subject into the time period of that energy."*

"What this means? Not understand." Regina leaned closer.

"Hmmm. Wait a minute. We had the DNA test, so we know we're related. 'Spots of similar genetic content' would be in Poland... or where our family lived in the U.S.! That would be upstate New York." I looked at her and smiled.

"Go there and find porthole to *Mała Łąka*?" She straightened her headscarf, ready to go.

"Well, it's an idea. Nobody from our family lives there now, but it would be something to do. While I try to figure out how to be ready, like Aniela said."

"Something to do?'" Regina's face flushed a deep shade of red. "Trouble with you people here." She looked up at the ceiling. "*Matka Boska*, so sorry I complain..." She shook her little fist at my face. "Daughter sick, needs Mama! Not want to *be* here!"

"I know, I know." I tried to touch her rounded shoulder but she jerked it away. "This page says contact with a place with your 'genetic content' might take you back in time. Maybe if we go to Amsterdam, New York, where our relatives lived we can find another wormhole or portal or whatever. And that portal will like us because our family's DNA is there. It's worth a try, don't you think?"

Tears spilled onto Regina's soft wrinkled cheeks and I ran to the bathroom for a box of tissues. She sniffled and wiped at her eyes and nose, and for once, I kept quiet and let her collect herself. It seemed like the best thing to do. I was tired of offering solutions that went nowhere. We each took a few deep breaths and straightened our shoulders. *At the same time. In the same exact way.* And burst out laughing.

Regina spoke first, catching her breath. "Okay. We go where your people came. And you try to be ready. Maybe..." her voice drifted off as she looked out the window. In the field across the road, pale stalks of wheat waved against the dark line of trees in the distance. Summer in the country. "Field like home," she said quietly, "wheat and trees. Where is place we go again?"

"Amsterdam, where my mother's grandparents settled in the 1890s. It's in upstate New York."

"We go now?" She looked as if she was trying to force hope down into her soul before it could run away.

"Not today. It's late. But let's pack a bag and leave tomorrow."

In the field outside, the wheat stopped waving and grew still.

That evening, after her favorite supper of ham and potatoes, I read to Regina from Jessica's high school history book about people coming to America to escape the pogroms and poverty in Europe in the late nineteenth century. Then I left her to study the black and white photos in the book while I packed for our trip. When I was done, I went downstairs to see how she was doing. She held a wad of tissues balled up in her fist and her eyes were red.

"So hard for them. Think my life bad! These people, how they suffer! Sickness, fall off boat..."

"I know." Her naked sorrow shamed me. This too was my fault. I had to make it go away. "Look. It was a long time ago. Most of them survived, and went on to start families and build homes, and have good lives." My frantic tone of voice, eager to reassure, embarrassed me, and I stopped talking. How did I know? I only knew what I learned at school. How many of the unhappy and unsuccessful made it into the history books?

Regina rested one hand on the page she had opened. "Make me sad. Maybe *Matka Boska* send me here to see how lucky. Punish me." A little gulp escaped from her throat. "Maybe Aniela right: not ready to go home. Not suffer enough for sins."

Oh, no. This would not do. Please God, no more suffering for this woman. I made my voice firm.

"Regina." I paused until she looked into my eyes. "I don't believe for one minute that you are being punished."

"You not know, Kat. Pray for help from Pawel, yes. But something else. Something hard to say." She looked down at her lap. "Pray also for getting away from children. Six get married but six still in home. No rest, but *not mean to leave them!*" Her voice was high and strained. "*Matka Boska* teach me lesson. Never again pray for getting away." She looked up at me, blinking hard.

"Oh, Regina, all mothers feel that way sometimes. You have had more than your share of hardship. I'm sure *Matka Boska* forgives you for wanting a break."

She turned away from me, her stocky frame folding in on itself. All she wanted was a little peace and quiet. Instead, she had been tossed into a complicated and alien future, far from everyone she had ever known and loved.

We left for Amsterdam in the morning. Three hours into the trip, Regina threw up at a rest stop on the New York State Thruway. We had barely made it inside the ladies' room.

"Sorry, sorry." She wiped her face with the wet paper towel I gave her. Her hands gripped the sides of the wall-mounted sink.

"No, *I'm* sorry. I should have given you something for car sickness. We can probably get some pills in the gift shop."

Her face was as pale as milk as we walked out into the busy food court. Travelers bustled past us, oblivious. I wondered how many times I had done the same, as others dealt with their own sickness and worry. We never know what people are going through unless they tell us. And then, we may not be much help.

"Come on. Let's get you some water and Dramamine." We bought two bottles of Dasani and a very pricey package of the motion sickness meds and took them outside to a picnic table. Tree branches flared with dusty green leaves, and thick underbrush lined both sides of the highway. The traffic's loud hum and the periodic crack and whine from the gears of semi-trailers gave the scene a sense of high urgency. Places to go, people to see. Everybody headed somewhere fast. I sent a silent prayer to the Universe that the Dramamine would take effect soon. Thankfully for both of us, it did. It was about time things worked in our favor.

After driving north for another two hours, we turned west at Albany and after another half hour, there it was: Exit 27, Amsterdam. My birthplace. Summer sunlight sparkled on the wide Mohawk River as we crossed the bridge into town. Regina was quiet, gazing out the windshield at the scene ahead. Dry stalks of Queen Anne's lace waved a dusty welcome on the roadside and blue chicory bloomed in the sidewalk cracks, but they did little to brighten the tarnished old city. Boards covered the windows and doors of abandoned factory buildings, the once bustling carpet mills where my grandparents had worked. The doors of two-story frame houses hung loose on their hinges, missing the large immigrant families once sheltered inside. Beside these sad-looking structures, tired-faced men and women sat on front steps or stood on dilapidated porches. My heart ached for my old hometown, so battered and worn. As we drove into the center of town, we passed a bank, a news dealer, and a cheap furniture store still open for business. A Holiday Inn dominated the small central square. I pulled into the lot and booked a double room for the night.

After depositing our bags in our musty smelling room, I took Regina on a slow driving tour. She wanted to walk but I had not climbed the hills of this town since high school. Now I was tired and feeling every one of the 32 years since then.

"The house where I lived is a mile from the river. All uphill." I looked over at her sturdy round face, her brown eyes like chestnuts. "Aren't you tired?"

"So? Always tired, what is new?" She smiled, but gave in easily. "Okay, back into car."

I was relieved to hear it. "So, the medicine is working?"

"Yes, medicine working." She nodded and patted her middle. "No more sick stomach. Let us go to your old home."

As my Jetta climbed the Church Street hill, I felt like a tourist in my own life. I had trekked many times to and from the downtown stores and from school to our house on Catherine Street. But on this summer evening, traffic was much heavier than I remembered.

"Look, here's the street where I lived." I turned the wheel hard right and traveled down the short block to the small white Cape Cod my parents had built in 1965. A wrought iron number 33 hung on the siding near the aluminum front door. I parked at the curb and turned off the engine. A few cars drove slowly past and the drivers peered at us with casual interest, but no one stopped. Regina looked at her hands, then out the window. A dog barked in a pen behind the house next door.

"Smaller than your house in Pennsylvania." Regina glanced at the adjacent yard. "Dog not like us. How we find porthole here?"

"Yeah, he does look a bit hostile. But this is where we lived, so there's got to be some of that 'similar genetic material.' Wait here, I'll see if anyone's home and if they'll let us inside."

I turned off the engine and walked around the front of the car to the sidewalk. The driveway was empty but a carport stood where my dad had promised to build a garage. He never got around to it. Bright red geraniums lined the short walk. I rang the bell and waited. I pulled open the aluminum storm door and knocked. No answer. I turned back to the car. Regina's eyes were on the still barking dog. I rang again, and listened, but if there were any sound from inside the house, the dog's frantic barking would cover it. A sudden urge came over me to throw my car keys on the ground and wail. Would nothing ever work out the way I planned it? I took a long slow breath and closed my eyes. Then I walked back to the car and got in.

"Doesn't look like they're home. Why don't you sit back and relax? I'll drive around a bit. Maybe we'll get an idea about what to do next, and maybe we can come back later when somebody's home."

"Find porthole," she reminded me, tapping a finger on the steering wheel. "We come to find porthole to *Mała Łąka*." She opened her door and before I could stop her, set off running down the driveway.

"Where are you going?" This day was getting out of control and fast.

"Backyard may have porthole like your house in Doylestown!" She tossed the words over her shoulder without a backward glance. I jumped out of the car and hurried after her. We had just reached the grass at the end of the drive when the dog broke through the rusted wire of his pen and charged at us.

"*Jezus, Marya!!*" Regina shrieked and cowered against me.

I backed away from the growling dog. "Stay!" I commanded in what I hoped was a firm and convincing tone. I held one hand up in the universal "stop" position and grabbed Regina's arm with the other. "Come on, let's get out of here." We fast walked back to the car, the dog snarling at our heels. Somehow, my heart beating like a hammer in my chest, I managed to get Regina inside, shut the door, then scoot into the driver's side and start the engine. I didn't exhale until we were halfway down the street, the dog running after us.

"So now what we do?" Regina turned her head and looked through the back window.

"We find another portal. One without an angry dog. There has to be 'similar genetic material' all over this town." My own words stirred a pang of loneliness. *Babcia*, and my aunts, uncles and cousins, had once lived here too, but now they were gone. All of them gone. Dead or moved away and out of touch with me. I had no idea how to find any of them, if they were still alive.

The place felt like a ghost town as I continued down Catherine to the stop sign at Lenox. I turned the steering wheel left and left again until we were back at Church. The road became Route 67 as it headed north through dairy farms and on toward the Adirondack Mountains. I wanted to follow it there, to lose the painful nostalgia churning inside me.

Instead, I turned south to another part of town, where old memories lingered.

For close to an hour, I drove through the deepening summer twilight. I drove through the Rockton Y, a crazy four-point intersection smack against an abandoned brick mill where a fast-moving branch of the Chuctanunda Creek flowed under the roadway. I drove uphill to the new high school, a sprawling one-story building of light brown stone behind the Kmart shopping center. I drove past the Tastee-Freez where on summer nights my teenaged friends and I made memories of love won and lost. With each remembered scene, a feeling: joy, tenderness, longing. My emotions came and went while Regina sat patient at my side, sometimes closing her eyes to rest or pray. I told her about these familiar places but the memories were all mine. To her they were only stories. It would soon be dark with nothing left to see, and so I turned down Division Street and back to the Holiday Inn.

Chapter Twenty

EARLY THE NEXT DAY, we ate the hotel's free continental breakfast in total silence. The previous day's failures had changed the energy between us. I refilled my cup with decaf from the buffet and went back to our table.

"Let's leave the car here today. Our people walked the hills of this town and we should too. We may see something on foot we wouldn't notice from the car, something that might lead to a portal."

"Works for me." She gave me a playful shove that broke my serious mood. I wanted to hug her but I smiled instead. We could do this.

"Glad to hear it. Let's get going."

We climbed the Church Street hill with the sun at our backs. As we passed Green Hill Cemetery, Regina spotted a deli across the street, and in its window larger than life sized photos of Polish food.

"*Pierogies, kielbasa, Gołabki.*" In an instant, she dashed across the street in front of an oncoming SUV. My shocked scream was lost in the horrifying screech of brakes. The man driving the SUV and half a dozen others in cars behind it waved their fists and pounded on their horns. From the opposite curb, Regina beckoned me to cross.

"Regina!" I screamed.

"*Tak, tak, tak,* Wait before crossing. Come on."

I hurried across, waving apology at the cars stopped in the road while I mouthed the word "sorry." By the time I entered the store, Regina was pointing at the food in a refrigerated case. I wanted to grab her and shake some sense into her.

"Are you crazy? You could have been killed out there!" My quivering voice betrayed my fear.

Regina pressed a palm to her heart. "Sorry, Kasia. Not mean..."

I was so scared I couldn't let my anger go. "Okay, we're in the store," I snapped. "What do you want?"

She touched the glass case. Gołabki, the stuffed cabbage rolls, lay on Styrofoam trays behind a little white sign reading "75 cents each, 3 for $2.00." A young female clerk opened the sliding door and pulled out a tray.

"No, we don't have a refrigerator in the room." I shook my head. "We don't even have a microwave." I tried to pull her away but she kept her feet firmly planted. Then her lips moved, and I leaned closer to hear. "Sorry, sorry. Mother taught me to make these."

Behind the counter, a door opened to a familiar sight. Aniela stood in the doorway, wearing a white silk blouse and black velvet skirt. She frowned at me and folded her arms across her chest. Then she strode to the display case and stood beside the young clerk.

"*Dzień dobry*!" Aniela said, her voice as stern as her face. Embarrassed by my anger at Regina, I turned it on Aniela.

"What the hell? Are you following us again?" My thoughts went back to St. Adalbert's in Philadelphia, and the way she had shown up there, unexpected, only to desert us again. Aniela lifted her chin.

"I am helping in the store." She turned to the young woman beside her. "Kat, Regina, I would like you to meet Stacia, my niece."

I stared at the girl. "I didn't know you had family up here. This is *my* hometown." Regina put her hand over her heart, and stood at rapt attention.

Aniela put both hands on her hips. "*Is* it now? What a coincidence!" Her smile was knowing, and the chill up my spine told me this was not news to her at all. Nor was it a mere coincidence. Aniela was here because we were here.

It occurred to me that I could have asked her to come with us. But I was so used to not depending on anyone but myself. My mother's leaving and my father's depression had taught me that. *Babcia* used to say I was too independent for my own good. And maybe she was right.

Aniela interrupted my skittering thoughts. "You are buying for Regina what she wants, right?"

I rolled my eyes but her look was unchanged, and with my cheeks burning, I paid Stacia for two *gołabki*. Aniela warmed them in the microwave behind the counter, giving the keypad firm self-satisfied pokes.

When the oven pinged, she handed us plastic knives and forks and we took our cabbage rolls to a small square table in the corner of the shop. Though breakfast had been less than half an hour ago, I was starved. I sliced off a piece of *gołabki* and put it in my mouth, the garlicky taste taking me back to Babcia's house. I closed my eyes, savoring the memory. Aniela stood behind the counter and watched us as Regina hummed to herself, comfortably wielding the plastic utensils. When we were finished, Aniela took our empty paper plates and tossed them into a trashcan.

"So, where are you ladies going today?"

"Aniela, I don't think it's any of your..." I began but Regina interrupted me.

"Find porthole to *Mała Łąka!* Want to come?"

"I do not mind. Give me a minute." She whipped off her white apron and fluffed her hair, the amber ring sparkling. Closing the glass-paned door behind her, she hustled us down the front steps. "Where is this porthole?"

"She means portal. You remember, we read you can go back in time through a portal." Though I was still a little embarrassed I hadn't invited her yesterday, I was glad she came with us. Sure, it was a little creepy the way she popped up when we least expected. But it was also kind of nice to have another woman on the case. Or adventure. Or disaster. I still wasn't sure what to do next or how to prevent another encounter with crazy Jurek if we got that far. Maybe Aniela could help.

160

The three of us walked up Church Street, me in my Reeboks, Regina in her trusty old boots and Aniela in leather Ferragamo pumps. As we rounded another long curve, I kept close to Regina. She would not jump into the road again, not if I could help it.

The sidewalk led us north to the five-point intersection my mother called Worse Corners. No traffic light helped cars or pedestrians make their way across. Never had, still didn't. And now there were lots more cars and we were the only pedestrians. I gripped Regina's hand tightly, looked all five ways and looked again. Aniela smiled indulgently and gave me an approving nod. I could tell I had moved up a notch in her regard, now that I was looking out for Regina instead of yelling at her.

When the coast was clear, we crossed to the sidewalk leading up the hill, past a trendy-looking candle and gift shop called The Old Country Peddler. At the next intersection, the sign for Butch's Tavern came into view. I recognized the old neighborhood bar on the first level of a two-story wood and shingle building. Its worn old stairs led directly up from the sidewalk.

"Is anyone thirsty?" Aniela asked. "Why don't we stop in here for a cold drink?" I held back. It was an old seedy-looking bar I had walked past on my way home from school. I had never been inside. But I was tired of walking, and it was the only place we would be able to sit down for a while. Regina, however, looked like she could go another ten miles. Still, she agreed to the stop.

"*Tak, tak,* cold drink," she nodded. Aniela smiled at me with her nose in the air and ushered us inside.

In the dark barroom, I could barely see. Regina forged ahead while Aniela gave my back a gentle push. I stumbled as my eyes began to pick out objects in the dark: a wooden chair, a long bar, a napkin dispenser. A trio of men in dark work pants and white T-shirts sat at the bar, their hands wrapped around tall glasses of beer. As if we were not there. Neither the men nor the bartender looked at us. A young girl with long dark hair stood up from a chair near the back and came forward.

"Can I help you ladies?"

"Um, yes, we'd like three Cokes, please," I said. We pulled out chairs and sat at the nearest table. The cold sodas felt good going down, familiar and sweet. Regina raised her glass to me and Aniela then took a big slug. She put the glass down hard on the darkened old wood. A swallow moved down her throat as her eyes widened. "Soda," I told her. "You haven't had that yet. It has sugar and air bubbles in it. Do you like it?"

"Soh-dah!" she repeated, nodding at the glass. "*Smaczne!*" Good. Something modern she liked. I leaned back and sipped from my own glass, enjoying the moment of respite from our crazy quest.

"Having hard day, Kat?" Aniela's voice was kind but her look still felt patronizing.

"No harder than anyone else who is trying to help a woman from another century find her way back home."

"You do not have to be sarcastic. I can be of some help if you will only ask." Her gaze went from me to Regina, sipping her soda through the paper straw. "It is her first straw." Aniela cocked her head at the older woman.

Regina giggled. "Straw but not hay!"

"The English is confusing, is it not?" Aniela glanced from her to me in turn. "Same words for two different things, words are spelled the same but pronounced differently, and so on."

"You're right. I'm sure it must get tiresome." I sighed and took another swig of Coke.

"It is not so bad. You take everything too seriously. You need to have all the answers all the time. Why do you not accept help? Regina prays to Blessed Mother for help every day."

"Yeah, and look where that got her!" I shot back.

"Kat, you do not know whole story." Aniela said each word slowly and precisely, maintaining steady eye contact all the while. She paused and looked over her shoulder at the men deep in conversation at the bar. The girl who served us was back in her seat, her head bent over a book. Aniela turned back to me and Regina, drawing herself close to the table. "I think perhaps it is time for you to know more."

"More of what," I squeaked and felt an involuntary shiver. Even then, I could tell it was one of those moments when you know something big is about to happen. You think about stopping it but you know you can't. Powerless, you wait while everything around you starts to change forever.

"Kat, you do not know who I am." Aniela's dark eyes flashed. She straightened her shoulders and gazed at the amber ring on her right hand, stroking it with one finger. Regina and I froze. Our eyes darted toward each other then back at Aniela.

"What do you mean?" My voice cracked. "You're not who you said you were? Who are you?" With each question, my anxiety grew. Regina did not move a muscle except to let her mouth open a little, no sound escaping, not even the sound of her breath.

"My name," said Aniela, "is Jadwiga Wegierski Jagiello, daughter of Ludwik Wegierski of Hungary, grand-daughter of Wladyslaw the Elbow-High, bride of Wladyslaw II Jagiello, and King of Poland. That is, until my untimely demise, but that is another story." She reached for her glass and took a long, deep sip through her straw.

My glass wobbled and soda spilled out as I set it down with a laugh. "Wladyslaw the *who?*"

Aniela frowned. "Very funny. He was short man. He was also great one."

I wiped the spill with a paper napkin and grinned. Aniela and Regina looked serious. "Wait a minute." I looked from one to the other. "Regina, you don't believe her cockamamie story..."

"*Święta Maryjo, Matka Boska!*" Regina blessed herself.

"Yes," said Aniela/Jadwiga as she centered her glass on a cardboard Schlitz coaster. "*Święta Maryjo* heard your prayers. She loves how you are so devoted to her. She saw your need but she is very busy. You should see how many requests are put before her every day. Unbelievable! She asked me to be her delegate. To see what I could do for you

163

both who are having such difficulties in your respective times."

She chuckled softly and clasped her hands together on the table.

"Oh-kay," I said, stretching the word out while my brain tried to take it all in. The Jadwiga of the statue in my childhood church wore an apron full of roses. And now that I thought about it, I remembered smelling roses when Aniela was around. I smelled them now, beneath the acrid stench of beer. Despite wanting to appear skeptical, I knew in my every fiber that the supernatural was visiting my life in a big way. Beside me, Regina laughed and clapped her hands.

"Help has come! I always know *Matka Boska* will help me! Take us to porthole!"

"Ah, Regina, it is not so easy," Aniela, or Jadwiga, replied. "There are things we must do. Or should I say, there are things you must do, and Kat as well."

"Me? What am *I* supposed to do, that I haven't done already?" I said in a petulant voice.

"Kat, you must watch that bitter streak of yours. Yes, you have done much for Regina, but *Matka Boska* says you have a few things you need help with too."

"Who *asked* her?" I said with my arms folded. "Not me."

"We can discuss later. For now, shall we see if we can help Regina?"

"That's what I've been trying to do."

"But maybe not so hard, am I right?" Jadwiga seemed to look right through me. "There are times you would like her to stay with you, to be your friend?" The kindness in her face made me feel understood. The woman got me. And I didn't know what to do with that.

"Maybe," I mumbled. "I don't know." The two women stared at me. Unable to meet their eyes, I shoved my chair back and stood up from the table. "Come on, whoever you are, let's get on with it."

Outside the tavern, I squinted in the blinding sunlight. Aniela's revelation had rocked me but I tried to pretend otherwise. I grabbed the metal handrail on the steps. Meanwhile, Regina chugged down the street, way ahead of us.

"What's the big hurry?" I yelled. I ran after her but, still disoriented, I tripped on a chunk of concrete in the broken sidewalk and stumbled against her. Regina wheeled around and grabbed my upper arms. Her face was so close to mine I felt her breath.

"Don't belong there," she gestured at the tavern. Gray strands of hair had escaped from her headscarf but she was oblivious, uncaring or both. The woman formerly known as Aniela came toward us at a slow dignified pace. Gray clouds moved across the sun.

I stood on the curb, hands on my hips. The air was still and I had that eerie sense of time slowing down when the world is waiting for a storm.

"So, what's our next step, Aniela, I mean, Jadwiga?" My challenge did not faze her in the least.

Jadwiga looked up at the darkening sky. "I am spiritual guide not time travel expert. But I do know this: window of opportunity is closing fast."

She rocked back on the heels of her pumps then folded her hands together in a formal pose. A pose like the statue of St. Hedwig in my childhood church, right here in Amsterdam. Of course. Hedwig is another name for Jadwiga.

I rubbed the back of my neck with one hand and blew out a hot breath that lifted the hair over my forehead. "Well, then, why won't you tell us what it is we 'must do'? How are we supposed to know if you don't tell us? And why didn't you say who you were in the first place, instead of pretending to be someone else?" Heavenly delegate or not, the woman was exasperating.

"Answers must come from within. I am only to provide bit of course correction. You know, it is not expected for me to show my true identity. But you two ladies have proven very difficult to lead. I consulted Blessed Mother and we felt it best to remove veil, so to speak."

"That's great." I kicked at a stone. "Just great. Can you remove a couple more of those veils, please?"

Regina grabbed my arm. "Come on. Get back to hotel, look in toplap. That is what *I* must do!"

And so, with nothing better in mind, I followed her downhill toward the Holiday Inn. Or rather, I trudged behind Regina and the woman formerly known as Aniela. Regina's boots could have been on fire. I had to hurry to keep up and all the while I argued with myself. *Don't be so gullible.* But what if it's true? What if the Blessed Virgin Mary really did send Jadwiga to help us? I was scared. But excited. Strong women helpers were a good thing, weren't they? I wanted to believe. It would be so great if it were true. Kind of like having a mother. Or being one.

Because my mom left when I was so small, I had few memories of her. The time she took me to the circus and rode beside me on the carousel. The time she helped me cut up her movie magazines to make collages. The time she taught me to throw a ball. I had nothing like that with Jessica. Why not? The circus was too noisy; I didn't want her to make a mess with cutting up papers; Alan took care of her sports lessons. Suddenly, I wanted a do-over. I wanted it now.

Even though Anna's need for her mother took first dibs, I could still reach out to Jessica. This was, after all, the 21st century! We got back to the hotel in twenty minutes. I pressed Jessica's number into my cell, then sent a simple text: I'm sorry. I love you. With the message, I sent a silent little wish in my heart. *Please call me back.*

Regina and Aniela were glad when I told them who I'd been texting. Now I had to do something else while I was waiting for my daughter's reply. Something to take my mind off it. I fished my laptop out of the trunk of my car and opened it with sweaty hands. Then I clicked through the web until I found the spot where we had left off.

"What next? What other travel ways?" Regina's questions met with silence as I paged down the screen. The air through the car's open window increased in pressure. Thunder rumbled in the distance, as if the Universe itself was warning us to hurry, but Aniela/Jadwiga took her time walking toward us with great dignity. Finally, she caught up and climbed into the back seat as if it were her royal horse carriage.

"Wait, other ways to time travel...let me see..." Reading fast, I became as excited as Regina. "It says in the 1980s the subjects focused on an electrical antenna and visualized the time they were in and the time they wanted to travel to. So... you would have to visualize the year we are in now, and then 1825."

"Aunt Anna?" Both women shouted in unison.

"Antenna. It's a big structure that conducts radio waves or electricity or something." The sky had darkened to gunmetal gray. "You know this is just plain ridiculous. The sky looks like a thunderstorm is coming. We are not going to look for an antenna during an electrical storm!"

But Regina was not about to wait any longer. "We find Aunt Anna, we take Regina to home."

"Regina, we could get struck by lightning. It's dangerous to be outside in a storm, you must know that."

"Stay in car, then. Drive to Aunt Anna and see what is there."

What the hell, I thought. *Why not?* My head hurt. I didn't want to sit here in this dismal motel parking lot. We had to do something.

Jadwiga sat silent in the back seat while the engine hummed to life at the turn of my key. A fat raindrop splattered against the windshield.

"So how will I stay in the 21st century while you are visualizing 1825? I don't want to run into crazy Jurek again. If this works, we'll have to separate. And what about Jadwiga here?"

I spoke her name with a touch of derision, not wanting to show I believed her so easily. Just in case. But truth be told, I did. I believed every word she said though I felt foolish showing it. I had seen enough by now to convince me something special was going on, and I wanted to be part of it. To be part of this motley little threesome, come what may.

"Do not worry about me," she reassured us with a royal wave. "I will report back to *Święta Maryjo* for next assignment. Just go on with your business." As she finished her sentence, the rain clouds opened and drenched the car, the street and the sidewalks. I turned on the wipers and drove through the downpour. Metal gutters on houses and stores poured water onto the sidewalk and street. A thunderclap, then a flash of lightning split the sky. Within seconds, my wipers were useless.

"I don't see how we'll find an antenna in this mess." I pulled over to the nearest curb as the rain pelted the windshield.

Regina touched my arm. "Now Kasia see how Regina feel: Stuck." She nodded in satisfaction. "Maybe drive car to future time!" She giggled. Her point was clear, but it wasn't quite so funny to me. When I scowled, she apologized. "Sorry. Keep try. We do it. Right, Jadwiga?"

The Queen in the backseat nodded and smiled, her chin held high. The rain showed no sign of stopping. But it had to stop eventually, and the time would come, I knew, when we would be on the next leg of our journey. For now, we were cozy and safe, cocooned inside my car. But if the antenna thing worked, Regina would be gone, and I'd be here. Alone again. There was no way Jadwiga was going to stick around after that.

As we waited for the storm to clear, I thought about the crazy situation I had gotten myself into. I was driving in a car with a queen and a peasant from two different centuries. I had accidentally traveled through time myself, spinning through a portal shot with light. The world had reeled around me and I had staggered, falling to the ground. I hated that spinning feeling. Regina, on the other hand, could hardly wait to do it again. I was going to lose her.

The rain slowed a bit and I could see through the windshield. Three or four people walked past under open umbrellas and a couple peered in at us through the windows then hurried on. I suppose I could have asked someone where we could find an antenna, but I just didn't think of it. My head was preoccupied with my impending loss.

I pulled away from the curb and drove around in the light summer rain, following parallel streets on either side of Church until at the end of Edson Street I spotted a tall electrical tower. The rain ended and weak sunlight poked through the clouds. The tower glinted where raindrops clung to its metal sides. I pulled as close to it as I could and turned off the engine. Regina jumped out of the car, leaving the door wide open. Jadwiga and I followed her through the wet grass.

She took a wide-legged position close to the tower's base. Standing firm as a fireplug, with eyes tightly shut, she chanted softly.

"2017...*nie, nie*...1825...1825..."

"Wait!" I cried, leaping to her side. "Don't go without me! Don't leave me here alone!"

"*Oj!*" she said, startled. A cloud shadowed her face. I grabbed her hand, and we repeated the dates together. "2017-1825." Regina held my hand tightly and stared at the tower. Afraid and nervous, I squeezed my eyes shut and braced for another dizzy spell. It never came. Instead, I heard the screech of a car's brakes and my eyes flew open. A black and white bearing the logo of the Amsterdam PD idled behind my Jetta, its radio squawking.

"You ladies okay?" the officer shouted. He walked across the grass to reach us.

"Hi, Officer, we're fine." Regina stood glum beside me, still holding onto my arm.

"*Psia krew!*" She muttered and stomped the ground with her boot.

The policeman peered at us through large black sunglasses. "You sure you're okay? What are you two doin' here anyway?"

I was afraid she'd spill the beans and I didn't trust the cop. He might think we were lunatics or worse, fugitives from an Alzheimer's ward. He might take us in and try to find help in the form of a strait jacket.

"It's okay, Officer, we were just talking." I tried to sound friendly. And normal.

"This here is private property." He popped his gum. "Belongs to the power company."

"Oh...We didn't know." Jadwiga stood in the background examining her nails. If only he'd leave. I looked at Regina and her eyes told me she totally agreed: *Get rid of the cop.* "We weren't hurting anything, Officer, just looking around. Nice day, isn't it?" I cringed as soon as I heard myself speak. This "nice day" had just had a thunderstorm. Just then the radio in the cruiser crackled.

"Eighty-two, come in, eighty-two. State your location."

"You ladies be careful, now." The officer trotted back to his car, spoke into a black receiver on a curly cord, then placed it back in the dashboard holder and put the car in gear. In the next second, he pulled away, lights flashing and sirens wailing.

Chapter Twenty-One

"YOU SAID '*PSIA KREW!*' My *Babcia* used to say that! What does it mean?"

"Means 'damn it!'" Regina's lips were prim and tight. "Problem for you?"

"No, no problem. Go ahead, curse all you want." Jadwiga had pressed her lips together as well but said nothing. The field around us was filled with the fragrance of wet grass while thick clouds blew across the late summer sky. A pair of sparrows wheeled around the electrical tower. It emitted a soft hum, as if waiting for us to act.

I blinked and shook my head to clear it. My stomach flipped. What had I almost done? Terrified Regina would leave me, I had tried to go back in time with her. Was I out of my mind? Should I go or stay? I couldn't move.

Regina ran up to the tower and squeezed her eyes shut. "1825..." she whispered. She might leave. We hadn't said goodbye. "1825." She said it louder. She yelled it, screamed. "1825!"

My legs shook and my back was drenched with sweat.

"Don't go," I whispered, closing my eyes. A deep quiet filled the air. No birds chirped. No summer wind moved across my face. I heard her voice again.

"*Psia krew.*" I opened my eyes as she scuffed the toes of her boots in the dirt.

Jadwiga was gone. I'm not proud to say I was relieved. I know I was being selfish.

"Come on." I put my arm around Regina's waist. "We can try again later. Maybe the timing is wrong or something. Maybe the cop wrecked the energy." I didn't say what I feared: that Jadwiga was right. We had missed our window of opportunity.

She looked doubtful but stepped away from the tower and followed me to the car. "Later," she mumbled looking back, "always later." She turned in a full circle. "Where is Jadwiga?"

"She can't have gone far. She's on foot, and we have the car. Although she seems to have found a way here from Doylestown all by herself." A queasy feeling came over me.

I started the car and drove off the grassy field and onto the quiet street. We traveled a few blocks north, then south, looking for Jadwiga. After a few minutes with no trace of her, I pulled over at the side of the road.

I needed to center myself and take some time to think. We flipped around that day like human Frisbees, and it wasn't much fun. *I am in the perfect time and place*, I recited, eyes closed. *All is well in my world*. When I opened my eyes, Regina was staring at me.

"What?"

"You are praying?" Her gray eyebrows lifted her forehead wrinkles up to the edge of her kerchief.

"I'm saying affirmations. They help me center myself."

"Okay, whatever. Let us try again Aunt Anna."

"Not right now. I need a break and I don't want to go back to that depressing hotel." Regina moved a hand over her mouth. "Want another pill?"

"No, I am fine." She smoothed her skirt and crossed her feet at the ankles. Her boots were coming apart, frayed bits of thread showing where the leather separated at the soles. How had I not noticed this before? I was supposed to be taking care of her.

"Let's get you a new pair of shoes. There are stores all along Route 30."

She rolled her eyes and folded her arms.

"Don't you want a new pair of shoes to go home in?"

"Fine. Still not going back home. Focus not working. Jadwiga disappear. Maybe we miss our chance. So...we buy shoes." She refolded her arms and turned away to look out the window. Sarcasm was not her best look, and it hurt me to be on the receiving end. But she wasn't refusing to go, so I forged ahead.

There was no shoe store left in the old downtown so I headed for the newer commercial district on the northern edge of the city. Traffic became heavier as if any life worth living happened there, outside of town. A huge Walmart sat far back from the highway among big box stores and restaurants from every fast food chain I had ever heard of. My mood lifted with the buzz of activity and the familiar names. I couldn't wait to see how pleased and comfortable Regina would be in her new shoes.

At the Walmart entrance, the automatic door opened though we were still a couple of feet away. Regina stepped up to it, her mouth half open, again and again as the door opened and closed. Shoppers smiled at her in her brightly colored outfit, then at me, as they walked around us. I smiled back sheepishly.

"She's not from around here, is she?" A dark-haired man in jeans stopped beside me. "Or, is she, you know," his voice lowered to a whisper, "dementia? My mom got like that."

"No, no, she isn't." I scrambled for words to explain without telling the whole truth.

"Hey, that's okay," he said, loud and cheerful. "It's good she has you to take care of her. Have a nice day!" With a quick wave, he left us and entered the store.

"Come on." I grabbed Regina's hand, pulling her forward. "We're here to buy shoes, remember?"

"Yes, shoes," she replied with a frown. Inside, I scanned the overhead signs and found the shoe department at the very back of the store. Row upon row of cheap footwear lay on racks higher than our heads, many more shoes, Regina said, than she had ever seen in her entire life. "What a country," she began, holding both hands up to frame what she saw.

"I know, I know. Can you just pick some sneakers to try on? Here's my size, which looks pretty close to yours. Come on," I called over my shoulder. "Sit down over here on this little bench."

Regina stopped walking, put her hands on her waist and gave me a look. "No, not sit down. First go to toilet."

"Okay, let's see." I scanned the signs hanging from the ceiling and located the rest rooms not far away. "The rest rooms are over there." I pointed and started walking but she stayed where she was.

"What next in this crazy place? Rooms to rest? Want toilet."

"Sorry, that's what they call the toilet. Come on, I'll show you where it is." Shaking her head, Regina scurried after me, upbeat canned music keeping time with her feet. The sharp odor of bleach stung the air in the hallway where the ladies and men's rooms were located.

While she was inside, I looked over the wide selection of shoes, all made in China. I could afford to buy her better ones, I thought, but that would mean driving miles away to the mall outside Schenectady. We were here now, and this would have to do.

My phone chimed the tune that meant Jessica and I scrambled to get it out of my purse. She'd sent a reply to my text: "Love you too, Mom." That was all, but it was something. My heart did a little dance as I hit reply but I never got to start typing.

A terrified scream broke through the piped in music. *Regina.* I dropped my phone into my purse and ran toward the ladies' room. A stocky fortyish man in work clothes streaked out with Regina close behind him waving a long metal piece of clothes rack.

"Idź stąd!!" She screamed, raising the metal rod above her head.

Just then a security guard stepped out from the housewares aisle and grabbed the man's denim shirt at the neck.

"Hey, I wasn't doin' nothin'! Lemme go!"

"What happened? What's going on?" I shouted.

"Girl in there, he goes after her!" Regina pointed back toward the ladies' room. I hurried to the door and pushed it open. Whimpering came from the second stall where a girl who looked about twelve cowered in the corner. Her dark hair hung disheveled over her wide, brown eyes.

"It's all right," I said softly. "They caught him. He won't hurt you." I stepped back and held out a hand, but she stayed there, trembling. "Can I call someone for you? Is your mother or somebody in the store?" My voice sounded hollow in the empty room. She sniffled and brought her hands down from her face. Then she stood shakily and smoothed a shiny black miniskirt down toward her knees. It had a long way to go.

Behind me, a short policewoman pushed into the room, followed by her male partner, both of them wearing the blue uniforms and badges of the Amsterdam PD. I seemed to be having daily encounters with the police. This time I was glad to see them.

"I'll take over from here," the female cop said. I went out to find Regina.

Back in the shoe department, she had propped the metal rod against the wall and stood with her arms still cocked and ready to fight. Shoppers milled around her, everyone talking at once. The male officer came out of the restroom and shoved the assailant forward, cuffing his hands behind his back as the security guard released his grip. After they disappeared around the racks of shoes, the girl and the female officer walked out of the rest room together.

"Where do you take her?" Regina asked. Her voice was loud over the weirdly bouncy music and the agitated voices of customers nearby.

"Amsterdam Memorial," the policewoman said. "She looks okay, but it's standard procedure. I'll need a statement from you, Ma'am."

"That's the hospital," I told Regina. "They'll take care of her."

Regina's eyes were focused on the girl. "I go too."

"It's not necessary, ma'am. We'll get a hold of a relative for her."

The girl looked only at Regina. "Please? Can she come with me?"

The officer frowned. "Don't you want to call your mom?" The girl looked at the floor and mumbled something none of us could hear.

The officer shrugged, pulled a pad and pen from her back pocket and stepped closer to Regina. "I need your statement. Spell your name for me, please. And I need an address for when this goes to court. You might have to testify."

Testify? My stomach clenched. Think, Kat, think. "Her name is Regina Wrozkowna. She's my aunt, visiting from Poland. She's staying with me." I didn't tell her we'd be long gone by the time this came to court, if it ever got that far, and I sincerely hoped it would.

"I still need an address and phone number." When I gave her mine, she raised her eyebrows. "Pennsylvania? What are you doing in Amsterdam?"

Oh, brother. Breathe, Kat. Remain calm. "We're visiting friends." I prayed she'd let it go at that. She turned to Regina.

"Ma'am, can you tell me what you saw in there?" She moved her head in the direction of the rest room.

"Girl screaming, I run inside, man push me and run out! I go after him!" Her face reddened as she demonstrated the shove he gave her with both hands. The officer jotted notes into her pad and slapped it closed.

"Thank you, ma'am." She turned to the girl. "Come with me. We have to get you checked out."

"Do I have to?" Her chin trembled as she wrapped both arms around herself.

"I'm afraid so. There are some bruises on your arms there, and I have to file a report. It's standard procedure but it won't take long. Meanwhile, we can call your mother."

As they walked away, the girl glanced back at us. Regina nudged my side.

"We go, too." I did not dare object, nor did I want to, remembering the horror story Regina had told us. Her rape had happened in a different time and place. But thanks to her, this story would have a very different outcome.

As I drove the short distance to the hospital, Regina kicked the inside of the car below the glove compartment with her little booted feet. Her lips pressed together in a hard line and her headscarf had slipped sideways. I waited at the red light on Route 30 and glanced at the hospital building already visible down the road.

Regina drummed her fingers on the dashboard until the light turned green. I took a deep breath and headed for the huge hospital parking lot. Lucky for us, we found a spot not far from the emergency entrance. We hurried inside where the officer was waiting for us. She waved at a curtain alcove behind her.

"There's a crisis center volunteer in there with her. She'll be all right. Nothing happened, thanks to you." She cocked her head at Regina. "She said you walked in just before things got ugly."

"I may go to her?" Regina's voice had a new and solid authority to it. The officer led us to the curtained area where the girl sat on a gurney. I flinched at the sight of the dark purple bruises on her arms. As it turned out, the girl's mother was at work and she pleaded with us not to call her.

"I don't want to bother my mom. She can't take off any more time." The crisis volunteer spoke softly but firmly as she explained the services her agency offered, up to and including counseling for as long as she needed it.

"You won't tell my mom? She told me not to wear this skirt." Her thin legs dangled toward the floor.

The counselor spoke up behind me. "Honey, your mom will be worried. You're under age, and we can't just let you go home. Someone has to be called."

Regina interrupted. "Excuse, I may say some things?" The girl looked directly at her, with tear-filled eyes. "Something like this happens to me, also, long time ago. Is not your fault. Remember this." She placed her hand over the girl's much smaller one and the girl's shoulders instantly relaxed.

"Promise you never believe is your fault." Regina's words were gentle. Nobody moved, nobody breathed until the girl spoke.

"Okay."

"Say to me." The girl raised her head, her hair falling back from her face.

"It was not my fault." Her voice broke but she turned to me, the crisis counselor, and the cop and repeated to each of us, louder each time. "It was *not* my *fault!*" Her chin trembled and tears came in a flood.

Regina took the girl into her arms and held her as her sobs echoed off the walls around us. When Regina looked at me, I saw that her own eyes were full and overflowing, the tears falling unchecked as she kept her arms around the girl. She was crying for herself, now, seeing herself in this young innocent girl, feeling her own pain and suffering. I went closer and leaned in with my arms around both of them, my own tears clouding my sight. Regina looked up at me.

"Not my fault," she mouthed without a sound and I knew she was thinking of another place and time. I coaxed her head onto my shoulder. After a while, the girl's sobs wound down to sniffles. The crisis counselor handed around a box of tissues from the counter beside the bed.

"All right now?" Regina asked the girl.

"Yes. Thank you." She nodded and wiped her nose with a tissue.

"Lady will call mother now. Will be okay."

The girl reached out both arms and gave Regina another hug.

The crisis counselor stepped close to the bed where the two sat side by side. She looked directly at Regina with a soft half smile. "You've been a big help. I feel as if you've been through something like this before."

Regina and I exchanged a glance, and she stood up beside me. "Happy I can help," she said, and turned away. "Come now, Kasia. Have to buy shoes."

As we walked toward the hospital exit, the scent of roses permeated the air. Jadwiga stepped out of an adjacent hallway and fell into step beside us.

"Where the hell did you come from?" I demanded. "Why weren't you there when we needed you?"

"Seems you did not need me at all," she replied with a regal nod. "You have done a good thing today. How do you feel?"

Regina squinted at her and gave a little snort. "Okay. Fine. Actually, feel good. Yes, feel very good. But why did you not come when there was trouble?"

"Ah, Jadwiga cannot be everywhere. I was called away." She smoothed her hair with both hands. "You have done well. I am pleased at your progress." She put one hand on her hip and leaned back a little, nose in the air. "And mine. Not bad for first mission."

"But we haven't made any progress at all," I cried. "Can't you just help her get back home? And what do you mean, your first mission?"

Jadwiga cupped her elbow in one hand and tapped her lips with the other. "Never mind that now. So, you are now ready to let her go?"

Part of me leaned back toward Jessica and Alan and another part clung to Regina. Being with her had awakened in me a longing to try again with the ones I loved and had hurt. To not give up so easily on my family. To not be like my dad. And maybe my mom. Maybe I would never know the real reason she left, but I didn't have to repeat the cycle. Still, if I could just keep Regina in my life, and reconnect with my family...I wanted them all. Because, in that moment, I knew the whole truth: I loved them all. And they had loved me. There had to be a way to work this out, but so far, it had eluded me.

I shoved my hands into the pockets of my jeans. "She's not fitting in here very well. And she does have a sick child, remember? I think this experiment or whatever it is has gone on long enough."

Jadwiga lifted both arms like a statue of Mary. Her amber ring shot beams of light in all directions. "It is no experiment. And I cannot do the work for you, even if I wanted. Remember, it is for both of you that I am here, Kat. You, too, have something to learn." She lowered her arms and smoothed her velvet jacket over her hips. "And my success as guide depends on it, so please hurry."

I forced a laugh. "So now I'm the reason for the holdup?" Our queen just stood there wearing a mysterious smile. Regina held up her hand to silence me and spoke to Jadwiga.

"Can you hurry this thing she must learn? Can you make it faster?"

Jadwiga let out a sigh. "All right, here is a clue: Kat, think about your choices. Why come here to Amsterdam? Your mother and grandmother, they are not here. No one who loved you is here. You came to look for a portal but was it not also for you that you made this journey?"

I opened my mouth to protest. To deny what she said. But I knew in my broken heart she was right. I was a grown woman with an abandoned little girl inside. And in a sense, my daughter and I had abandoned each other.

"I wanted to reconnect with my past." *Instead of my present. I shook my head to clear it.* "Okay, maybe I used that as an excuse to look for a genetic portal here. It could have worked you know." Then I saw the light as if it shone above her chestnut hair. "*Did y*ou know? Did you know it wouldn't work?"

"We novice guides do not know everything. But I see this: you run around doing, looking, searching for happiness with no success. In other realms, we know that all answers must come from deep within. They can only be accessed by taking time to look into the heart."

My heart, at the moment, was aching. And very tired.

"I do try. I have my affirmations, my Goddess cards, my altar of sacred objects..." My words trailed off, empty and futile.

"Kat, you are too easily discouraged by your multitude of choices. Learn to focus. You will get there. It is my job to see that you do." She reached over and gave my shoulder a little squeeze. Quite honestly, I was getting tired of her patronizing gestures but before I could come up with another smart remark, she went on. "Let me tell you something. My job depends on this mission. If we do not succeed, I cannot return to Earth. For this and for other reasons, time is running out."

"And that's a bad thing for you?" My sarcasm went into overdrive. "Not enough to do up there in the heavens?"

Regina gasped and blessed herself. Jadwiga tilted her head and smiled. "Do you know how old I was when I died?"

"Very young," Regina whispered. "After your baby is born?"

"Oh my god..." My hand flew to my mouth.

"Yes, I was twenty-five. How would you like to be forever twenty-five? Maybe you would say yes, but think about it. Never to experience life in all its wonder. Never to raise a child, or have women friends over many years...there is so much you take for granted, even sad times I would like to share, when you comfort each other. But I cannot. All I can do is apply to Blessed Virgin to be spiritual guide. This allows me to come back, to experience life with you, even if it is not my own." She brushed a tear from her cheek. "Don't you see? If I fail at this first mission, Blessed Mother will make me repeat spiritual guide course before I can return, and that could be long, long time."

Regina reached out to hold her hand. "*Pani* Jadwiga, you are good to us. We do our best now to help you as you help us. Come, do not cry."

Watching those two dear women, I ached to join the circle. I drew closer and put both arms around them. We shared a group hug just like I'd seen Jessica and her friends do so many times before. Before I knew how it felt, or what it meant. This was true friendship. And now it was mine.

"We'll do whatever it takes to make this work," I said. "Don't you worry, Jadwiga. You're going to be an excellent guide."

She smiled at me, not like the medieval queen, but like the much younger woman she was. *She's only three years older than Jessica,* I thought. *But she'll never have the life Jess will.* I wanted to be there, to see my daughter experience it all. We would do this thing, Regina, Jadwiga and I. We would learn our lessons, get our stripes, whatever it took to bring us where we all needed to be. I had never felt so alive. And less alone.

Jadwiga smoothed her hair. "Thank you, ladies. I am sure that things will move forward now. At least, I hope so. I will check on you both later." With that, she swept out the door. By the time we reached the parking lot, only the lightest scent of roses remained.

Regina stood up taller and pushed up her sleeves. "She is little bit embarrassed, I think. But it is okay. We do not give up."

I loved her even more then, for what she had done for the girl and for the way she had talked to the young Jadwiga. I straightened my spine and tried to mirror her stance.

"No, we do not give up." And speaking the words aloud, I believed them.

With no immediate plan, we decided to go ahead with the shoe-buying mission. Neither Regina nor I wanted to go back to Walmart, so we bought a pair of sneakers at the outlet store on the corner of Golf Course Road. Afterwards, we drove again through the old neighborhoods, looking for another likely portal. And all the while, I thought about what Jadwiga had said about my choices.

On Catherine Street, the dog still barked behind the neighbor's house, but someone had put him back in his pen. The antenna still loomed in the field off Edson Street and the tavern still had stairs to the sidewalk. But nothing felt the same. This town was all off somehow, not quite right. Neither Regina nor I wanted to get out of the car and look for a portal again. All the streets and buildings looked sinister, as if they could at any moment turn on us, breaking into fragments of another less welcoming world. There was nothing for me here. Not anymore.

We checked out of the Holiday Inn that afternoon and headed south to Pennsylvania.

Chapter Twenty-Two

AS THE MILES UNFOLDED behind us, words spilled from Regina like water from an open faucet.

"That girl, mother should be with her." And yes, I thought, I should be with Jessica. But she was a grown woman now. Maybe I should have been there for her more when she was a teen. Instead of telling her what to do, correcting her at every turn. Regina's voice broke into my thoughts. "And where is father? We do not ask." She pounded the dash with her fist.

"Hey, give yourself a break! We did the best we could. She'll be all right. And you were amazing. I'm so proud of you." But not of myself. Not as a mother.

Regina gave me a long lecture on how the priest, the parents, the family and the village should have taken care of the girl, not strangers like us. She acknowledged the female cop, the nurse and the crisis worker were kind and that the girl seemed okay for now. But the whole episode was wrong and appalling and I couldn't disagree.

When she was done venting, the hum of tires on the road was the only sound we heard. The signs indicated we were getting close to New York City and I had to concentrate as cars merged onto the highway from both sides. But soon Regina tapped me on the shoulder. She wasn't done yet.

"Where is father? Mother work, but where is father?"

"Maybe her father is not in the picture. Don't you have a problem with *your* children's father, Regina? Isn't that how you ended up here?"

"Pawel good father. Work hard. Feed family. Okay, drink too much, sometime hit me or boys." She fingered her skirt and looked out the window at the trees whizzing by. "Never hit girls."

I glanced in the rearview mirror before changing to the slow lane. "That's no excuse, you know. He hits *you*." Boy, did I have it easy with Alan. A little boring, maybe, but sometimes boring was good. What had I been thinking?

Regina leaned back against the headrest. "Pawel is beat by overseer many times. I see it myself, for not paying dues. He has paid dues but they lie to get more money."

"That's got to be hard. But just because he got beat, it doesn't give him the right to hit you, too."

"Ah, Kasia..." she sighed. "It is how life is. Men work day and night, get angry, frustrated. Women must be strong."

"What? It doesn't have to be that way. You do not have to put up with him beating you." I stole a quick look sideways as she stared down at her lap. "How can you stick up for those two girls – the one at the mall and the one at Walmart – and yet not stand up for yourself?"

Out of the corner of my eye, I could see her lift her chin. "In Mała Łąka, women are strong. Polish women are strong. How do you say it? We handle things."

"But surely you must see..." I glanced over for a second and stopped talking. Her face was tight with her lower lip sticking out like Jessica's when she closed down at my lectures. I bit my tongue. *God grant me the serenity to accept the things I cannot change.*

The road wound its way south and as I guided the Jetta along, my back began to ache. *...the courage to change the things I can.* After a few moments of quiet, I tried again.

"There's a lot you don't know. Things get better for people over the years. We have human rights. It's not fair for people to live in poverty while others grow rich from their labor. It's not right for men to beat their wives..."

"*Tak, tak, tak,* Kasia, not fair but how it is. Suffer on earth. Reward in heaven."

...and the wisdom to know the difference.

Regina gazed out the window at the Catskill Mountains as if heaven lay just beyond their softly rounded peaks.

Back at my house that evening, we were too tired to do anything but unload our suitcases from the trunk of the car. We ate peanut butter and jelly sandwiches for supper on my enclosed back porch. It was still summer and still light well after eight. Tiny sparrows, wrens and chickadees flitted through my herb garden. We laughed when a wren climbed over the top of the plastic birdfeeder and dove in for a beak-full instead of eating from the perches like the others. I handed Regina my binoculars, but she waved them away.

"*Nie. Dziękuję.* Not need to make bird bigger." She brushed crumbs off her skirt with her gnarled hands and began to knead the fabric. "Make bread in morning, while everyone they sleep except birds," she said. "Many loaves when children are small."

An image of the bakery shelves at Wegman's flashed before my eyes. She had seen the huge variety yet I could see on her face it was her own simple loaves she longed for. Or maybe just that simpler time. Tonight, I wanted to know more about it, and the people who were my ancestors.

"How did you meet Pawel," I asked her. She leaned back in her seat on my old wicker couch and her gaze seemed to travel far beyond my garden.

"Always know Pawel," she said. "Grow up together in *Mała Łąka.* Krystyna and Józef have wedding, we dance. He is handsome, tall, and wavy hair." She smiled fondly. "*Matka* say time to marry. Need my bed and food for little brother. Pawel very nice to me, polite. Go for walks at evening, time goes by, then go to parents. Soon wedding for us too."

She warmed to the story, and I sat back and listened. Like all peasants, Pawel owned no land of his own. The couple was given a cottage to live in by Pan Zalewski, but he still held ownership. They were only renters, paying with their labor. Working from sunup to sunset soon destroyed what romance had existed between them.

"Some days like two horses together, work and work, at home, in field." She gestured the shape of a yoke around her head and that of the imaginary Pawel close beside her. It didn't sound like my idea of a good marriage, but who was I to say? Apparently, that was beyond my grasp, as well. I had dreamed of romantic adventures like the ones in my books, but now I saw they were worth nothing compared to what I had and may have lost: a solid partnership where both husband and wife were free to follow their own paths while supporting and loving each other.

Outside the screened porch, a blue jay perched on a rhododendron branch. Fat green buds stood stiff and tight among the big shiny leaves, but they would not open again until next spring. The jay squawked and took off for the woods and the branch shuddered and grew still.

For the rest of that week, Regina and I stayed close to home. The humid summer air felt like a heavy blanket but inside my air-conditioned house, I felt closed in. Alan called and said that Jessica wanted to talk to me, so I called her cell, but she was at work.

"I'll call you tonight, Mom," she said. "I promise." Tonight, for her would be very late for me, but I didn't care. I was desperate to hold on to the ball she'd tossed me. Especially after what Alan said.

He told me he had decided to take me at my word that there was nothing more going on between me and Chuck. But he was dating someone he'd met who worked at a convenience store on his route. I gathered my courage and asked him point blank on the phone if he'd consider moving back home, but he said no. Not now. Not just yet.

"Let's give it some time, Kat," he said. "Take some time to think about what you really want. I don't want to go through anything like this again."

I fingered my wedding ring. I had never taken it off. The back of my throat hurt.

"Okay, thanks," I said and clicked off. I sat in a kitchen chair and stroked *Babcia*'s shawl, thinking about Alan, repeating his words in my mind. He was dating, and had every right, but there was no one else for me. Chuck had been a stupid diversion, and maybe one of my poor choices that Jadwiga had alluded to. I stayed up until midnight waiting for Jessica's call. She apologized for calling so late.

"I just got off work," she said. "It's almost nine here."

"It's okay," I said. "I'm so glad to hear your voice."

She was quiet so long I thought I'd lost the connection.

"Are you?" she said in a small voice. My cheeks burned and I was glad she couldn't see my face.

"Yes, I am, and I wanted to say how sorry I am about the bike. I don't know what I was thinking...well, I do know, but..." I had been so afraid for her, of losing her in a motorcycle accident, that I had pushed her farther away from me.

Jessica let the empty silence stand for a minute before she spoke.

"Look, Mom, I get it. You were afraid I would crash and get killed or something. I had a helmet you know. And it's my life...."

"I know, you're right," I said, my voice shaking. "I'm sorry."

I was so tired of trying to control her and everything else in my life, with little to no success. I didn't know what else to say. Which was a good thing. Because sometimes "you're right" and "I'm sorry" are exactly enough. Especially when speaking to your daughter. I wished for a one-way mirror so I could see her reaction. Finally, her voice came through the darkness.

"It's okay, Mom," she said. I let myself fall backward onto my bed, still holding the phone to my ear. "But I need to stay here and figure out what I want to do. I'm not coming home."

A little flip of fear and worry teased at my brain but I let it be.

"Can we talk more often? I'd love to hear how you're doing."

"Sure thing. I'll call again soon. Bye!" And she was gone. But not so far away this time. The distance in miles was the same yet we had closed the distance between us just a tiny bit. And it was good.

Regina continued to pray on her knees to the Blessed Mother every morning. The following Sunday I took her to Mass at the Shrine. At the gift shop, I bought her an icon of the Black Madonna and hung it on the wall in her room. During the days that followed, she climbed the stairs to visit it, but after the first time I saw her from the hall, standing forlorn before her idol, I gave them some privacy.

On hot sunny days in my backyard, she examined every plant and flower and taught me the purpose of every one. The cones on an evergreen could forecast the weather. The fir tree's branches could avert plague. Mugwort was good for every ailment known to man. Burning sprigs of thyme would disperse storm clouds and lightning. It worked whenever she tried it. My plants never looked so good or had such loving care. Regina talked to them in Polish as if they had ears, encouraging them to grow. And every day, she prayed before the icon for a way back home.

One hot morning in August, I pulled up a weed and tossed it behind me onto the grass. Regina was watering my petunias with a hose, a process she delighted in because it was so much better than filling and carrying a wooden bucket numerous times like she did back home. I wiped the sweat from my forehead with the back of my hand.

"Want to take a ride to the plant nursery? We could use some annuals to fill up those bare spots. And maybe some zinnias! My *Babcia* loved zinnias. Every year on August fifteenth, we took bouquets to church so the priest could bless them."

"*Święto Matki Boskiej Zielnej*! Beautiful feast day honoring Blessed Mother!"

Of course! I had forgotten about this day many long years ago. I went inside and looked at the calendar on the wall beside the fridge.

"The fifteenth is tomorrow. Let's get some bouquets together."

She clapped her hands to her chest. "Cut hay from field across road?" She began to rummage in a kitchen drawer for a pair of shears.

"What? No, not hay, flowers." She lowered her head and chewed at her lip. I had seen that look before. "Okay, bring the shears. We can do both, flowers and grains, why not? I'll call the Shrine to make sure they still do the blessing."

The next morning, I confirmed the Shrine would indeed have a blessing of flowers. Regina and I went across the road and cut a small bundle of wheat. Back in the kitchen, we tied it with twine. On the way to the Shrine, we stopped at the supermarket and bought a bouquet of zinnias, daisies, snapdragons and black-eyed Susans. The store display of cut flowers was huge and I let Regina take her time choosing what she wanted. Oddly, none of the blossoms had a fragrance, though I checked them all myself. Regina kept holding them up to her nose and sniffing while I paid the cashier, as if she thought we just hadn't found the right blossom, the one that smelled good.

At the Shrine on this hot and humid morning, we joined dozens of women and children and a few older men at the altar rail. A different elderly priest from those we had seen on our other visits sprinkled holy water from a silver holder onto our bouquets. Regina's face glowed as she held her wheat and flowers, the petals trembling in her tight grasp. She bowed her head as the priest glided past and I felt a pang of envy. If only I could be as nourished as she by this lovely ritual.

The next morning, I drove back to the market for groceries. Regina had started the first day of a personal novena to the Blessed Virgin, a nine-day petition for a permanent trip back home.

While I waited in the checkout line, my cart full of groceries, I glanced at the magazines on display. Glossy photos of desserts on the covers beside titles like "Six Weeks to Weight Loss" and "Walk Yourself Thin." I made a face at the mixed messages, placed my items on the conveyor belt and paid with my credit card, then pushed my cart out the door and headed for home.

Regina was standing just inside the laundry room when I entered from the garage.

"Come in, Kasia." Her grave expression and tone frightened me.

"What's wrong?" I looked behind her for a clue but no one was there.

"Please." She took the grocery bags from my hands. "Go sit down. Have news."

"What is it?" My legs felt like they belonged to someone else. "Is it Jessica? Has something happened to Jessica?"

"*Nie, nie*, not Jessica. *Proszę*, come with me." I followed her through the kitchen where she took my bags and set them on the counter, then led me by the hand to the living room couch. She sat beside me while the moment settled around us like gelatin, cold and shimmering. I did not want to know this news. She took both my hands in hers.

"Alan call on phone. *Matka* have accident. Die in car crash." A weight descended and pinned me to the couch. "Very sorry, Kasia. Very, very sorry."

I hadn't heard from my mother in how long? It must have been years. The birthday cards she sent never had a return address, and the postmarks came from all over the country. The last card came when I turned eighteen. There was nothing after that. Rusty old hurt circled my heart and stayed there, wrapped in bitterness "Why should I care?" I muttered through the knot in my throat. "She left me and my dad, never bothered to tell us where she was. I haven't seen her since I was ten." I pulled my hands away to swipe at my eyes, filling now in spite of myself. "I thought she was dead, and now..."

"You should care because she is mother." Regina stroked my hair. "No matter what she does, we always love mother. We are sad when she is gone."

"She's been 'gone' for a long time." Anger rose in my throat to mingle with the tears. My voice sounded like an ill-tempered child's and I struggled to bring it under control. "How did Alan find out she was...killed?"

"Read news online," she said, as if she heard such things every day and I marveled at her composure. She must have answered the phone by herself. I would need to call Alan and get the details. Slowly, I stood on orphan's legs. I was a different woman now, one with no parents. Even though my mother left long ago, and I told myself she was dead, I had always harbored the hope she would come back someday. Now that would never happen. All this time I'd been helping Regina I could have been searching for my own mother. I might have found her.

At the wall phone in the kitchen, I punched in the number of Alan's cell. He would be in his truck at this time of day, but he answered after two short rings.

"Kat! Hold on, let me pull over." I waited as the sounds of distant traffic passed through the receiver. In a minute, his voice was back. "Listen, I wanted you to know right away. I was surfing the web at lunchtime on my iPad. There was a car crash in Lancaster last spring. There was no ID on the woman driver, she was killed instantly, drove right into a tree. They just ID'd her yesterday and it was your mom, it has to be. How many Anastasia Kowalski's could there be? Her age sounds about right. She was living right there in Lancaster, in some trailer park."

"Wow, I can't believe that. She was so close. Why didn't she call me?" More tears spilled down my face. "What kind of mother does that?"

"I don't know, Kat, maybe she didn't know you moved here from New York after we got married." Static and road noise in the background, then "I'm sorry. Kat, I really am. Want me to come over?"

"No, that's okay." I took a deep breath and wiped at my face with my free hand. "So, what am I supposed to do with this information?"

"Well, you could call the police in Lancaster. You should probably have a service or something. You said years ago there weren't any other relatives left." His voice dwindled away.

"Okay, thanks for letting me know." My voice broke and I started to sniffle again.

"I'm sorry, Kat. If there is anything I can do, help you with…"

"I know. Thanks. Really, I appreciate it." We each ended the call as if on signal, with no word of goodbye. My mind was already in Lancaster, where I would have something to do other than feel this pain. I would do my duty, unlike my mother. I would take care of things.

I called Jessica and gave her the news. She was sympathetic, but she'd never met my mom. "I know she was my grandmother, but she left you, didn't she? I'm sorry, Mom. But I don't have the money for a flight back East."

Of course, I understood. At her age, I would have said the same. When I contacted the police chief in Lancaster, he used a gentle tone to fill me in. The following days felt like a movie about someone else's life. I had a small death notice published in the *Lancaster Journal* as well as the newspaper's website. Somehow, though I had no prior experience, I managed to hire an undertaker to perform a graveside service in the cemetery where my mother's body had been buried by the coroner's office, marked only by a number in a central Pennsylvania potter's field. My mother's life was a mystery. Where was the man she had left us for? No one came forward, and I didn't have the heart or energy to search for him.

The day of my mother's funeral was warm and sunny. Blue jays screeched a raucous accompaniment to the undertaker's words. Regina and Alan were the only other people in attendance. My mother's numbered, nameless grave seemed to hold all my questions at ten, fourteen, twenty-one, and even now. How could she leave me and Dad? Why didn't she take me with her? What kind of mother refuses to take care of her child? My questions lay buried now, with her.

Alan and Regina moved closer to my side. "The Lord is my Shepherd," the undertaker read from a worn black book. "He maketh me to lie down in green pastures..." Beyond the fence of the graveyard, a real pasture held a herd of dairy cows, black and white. A calf strode up to its mother and nosed under her for milk. Tears flooded my eyes and Alan handed me his handkerchief. Embarrassed, I cried bitter tears, not of loss but of anger. Not grief, I thought, not ever again. As soon as the service was over, I spun around and marched to my car.

"Kat, are you okay to drive?" Alan asked.

"Yeah, yeah, I'm fine. Don't worry."

Regina gave him a sympathetic smile and climbed into my passenger seat, buckling herself in. I drove away from the cemetery without once looking back.

At home, I headed for the photo albums in the attic, the ones I never looked at. The ones with pictures of Mom, Dad and me. I ripped the pictures from the album and tore them to shreds with my bare hands. Then I dumped them all into a wastebasket, took the whole basket into the garage and emptied it into the large metal garbage can. I slammed the lid so hard it hurt my hands and I cried out my pain all over again.

Regina had followed me out to the garage but made no move to stop me. She gave me a sad little smile. What a fool I had been! But that was all over now. I was moving on. All through the last few days, I had considered my options, and now I had made up my mind.

"I am coming with you," I said. "There's nothing here for me."

"No, Kasia, you must not! What about wonderful life here? Alan, Jessica, job in library?" Regina held her arms out to me but I ignored them, hugging myself instead.

"Jessica has her own life now. She doesn't need me. And Alan is going on without me. He has a girlfriend!" I started to cry again, my throat thick with care.

"Do not cry so, child." Her gentle voice was what I had longed for, and never heard, after *Babcia* died. A mother's voice. I broke down at last, right there in the garage, weeping buckets of tears as she held me in her arms.

Regina stayed with me until my sobbing ended. Then she led me back into the house and turned on the teakettle. While she got teabags and mugs from the cupboard, in the routine we had perfected together, I got out the tissues and wiped my face. Then for what felt like the hundredth time, I pulled out my laptop and clicked on the website we had used before. For the next two hours, we sat at my dining room table sipping chamomile tea and comparing various time travel techniques. It was truly amazing how many there were.

The summary at the bottom of the last page drew my attention. The most successful "intentional" time travel, it said, took place on a full moon, with a visualized date and destination. It made sense to me, but so had all the other suggestions, and look where that had led us: nowhere fast. Still, we had to stop flitting around and focus. Focus, Kat, I whispered. Focus. My breath deepened. This must be what Aniela meant, what I needed to learn: I needed to focus!

Of course, I had second thoughts. I would be taking a big risk. I might never be able to return here. But my life was already a mess. I had no friends, an estranged daughter and a floundering marriage. My job was unfulfilling. What could it hurt to try living a simpler life in the 1820s?

Regina strongly disagreed. "Stay home and live your life, Kasia," she pleaded. "Talk to husband. Call daughter, talk again. You must try."

"I *have* tried. Alan wants me to 'give it some time' and Jessica wants to stay in California. I'll just stay with you for a few weeks," I lied. "I think we have found how to do this right. After a short visit, I can come back here."

Regina closed her eyes for a moment and moved her lips. I assumed she was arranging her English for another argument. The house creaked around us and once, I heard another incessant dump truck rattle down the highway. Regina blessed herself and eyes open, looked straight at me.

"Okay, ask *Matka Boska*. You must promise not to change anything in *Mała Łąka*."

"So, you'll let me come with you?" My heart beat a happy tattoo.

"Not wanting this, Kasia," she replied. "But maybe it helps you to see my place." I pushed up my sleeves and grinned at her. She returned the smile, shaking her head all the while.

That night, I slept better than I had in months. I had lost my mother, for good this time. My husband and daughter were fine without me, thanks to my own bad behavior. But I could start anew, in a place where things were simple. And I would have a friend who loved me there.

The house was quiet when I woke the next morning. Selene jumped onto my bed and pawed at my pillow. I stretched my arms and petted her, then swung my legs over the side and padded to my closet for my robe.

Regina's door was closed and I decided to let her sleep while I went down to the kitchen and put the kettle on for tea. When the water was ready, I made a cup for myself and carried it to the table. A ray of sunlight touched a small bunch of zinnias in my shrine above the sink. I closed my eyes and said a healing affirmation. *All shall be well and all shall be well and all manner of things shall be well.*

The clock on the wall showed nine. She was sleeping late. I carried my tea upstairs and knocked on Regina's door. No answer. I called her name. Nothing. I turned the doorknob and went in. Her bed was made and in the center of the quilt a pure white envelope lay waiting.

Shaking, I walked closer and read my name. *Kasia.* Not Kathy. No. My heart raced. This was not happening to me again. I managed to open the envelope and read the words inside.

"Sorry must go alone. Praying for you. Regina."

The block letters seemed to rise from the paper and slap me in the face. That's what it felt like as I reeled and landed on my back on the quilt. Then the tears came. Again. The familiar lump of pain and betrayal lodged in my throat and I couldn't get it out. I staggered to my phone and unplugged its charger from the wall. I wiped away just enough tears so I could see Alan's photo and pressed the speed dial feature beside it. When he answered I could only sob, a deep hiccup from way back when I was ten.

"Kat? Talk to me. I can see your number. Kat?"

I struggled for breath. "She left me!" Then I sobbed again.

"Okay, let's calm down. Take a breath. Who left?"

"Regina, she's not here!" It came out as a high-pitched wail.

"Oh, no, did she run away again? Shall I come over?" The concern in his voice was enough to make me lose it totally. My throat felt so thick I couldn't swallow. I sat down on the floor with my phone clamped to my ear. I couldn't stop crying. Alan said my name over and over. "Kat. Kat. Kat. Okay, stay put. I'll be there in fifteen minutes."

By the time he arrived, I had managed to dry my face and comb my hair. A bit embarrassed at my earlier display of emotion, I waited at the front door and opened it as soon as he parked his truck. I tried to look semi-confident and in control.

"Okay, tell me what you know." Alan was all business now. The concern I'd heard on the phone was overshadowed or hidden or gone, and I didn't know how or if I wanted to bring it back. But I didn't want him to see me all helpless, that I was sure of. I took a breath and stood up as straight as I could.

"She left a note this time. She must have found the portal she came through in the backyard. Oh, Alan, I think she's left for good this time. She's not coming back." I could have been speaking of my mother as well. In a very short time, I had lost them both. Alan stood in the hall just inside the house and ran a hand through his hair.

"Well, isn't that for the best? It's what she wanted, right?" When he caught my eye he tilted his head as if to coax an answer that would settle things once and for all. But I didn't want them settled. Not like this.

"She betrayed me, Alan, just like my mother!" A screech that was my voice surprised me, and I tried to tone it down. "After all I've done to help her..."

"Hey, hey, hey. Regina is nothing at all like your mother. You know that. She cares about you; otherwise why would she have listened to you for so long? You have to stop trying to control people, Kat. You have to let us live our own lives...I mean..."

I took a step back. "I know what you mean. I wasn't trying..." but I couldn't say it. I didn't have the heart to defend myself for one more second. Whatever I did or said, nothing worked out the way I wanted it to. My many jobs, my quiet marriage, my impetuous daughter. And now, my last chance at a family who loved me had slipped through my fingers. Maybe Alan was right. It was partly my fault. "I guess I was still hoping she would stay here with me." I stepped aside and motioned toward the kitchen. "Want a cup of coffee?"

"No, that's all right." He moved backwards to the door and put his hand on the knob. "I gotta get back on the road. Why don't you make one for yourself, though? And try to relax. Maybe get something to eat, okay?"

So that was that. From the doorway, I watched his white truck turn around and head back down the drive before it turned right onto the highway and disappeared through the trees.

Selene rubbed against my legs. I picked her up, carried her to the kitchen and filled her bowls with fresh water and kibble. Coffee, tea, what did I want? I was too upset to eat anything.

I went back upstairs to the meditation corner of my bedroom, got out my deck of cards and searched through my box of candles on the floor beneath the low wooden table. Tea Rose. My fingers touched the pink votive among the dozen in the box and I knew it was just what I needed.

The scent of roses. Always a comfort, and now, imbued with another meaning, the memory of a woman who had helped us, or tried to, when I wasn't being so difficult. The candle fit neatly into a curved glass bowl. A tear fell onto my hand as I struck the match and held the flame to the wick. A deep inhale of the floral aroma, then another, and I closed my eyes. Maybe, someday, I would be all right.

At home alone, with nothing to do, my mind spun in circles. I needed to be out, among people, doing meaningful work. The next morning, I drove to the library. It was busy, as usual for a Friday, and someone else was at the reference desk, someone I didn't know. I found Cary in her office.

"Kat, how nice to see you!" she said, standing. "What brings you here?"

"I'm ready to come back," I said. "I can work today. This afternoon."

Her look of pity gave me pause. "We have hired someone to fill your shifts," she said. "We didn't know how long you'd need." She came around her desk and put a hand on my shoulder. "You don't look well, Kat," she said.

"I'm fine." Her kindness almost broke down my defenses. I couldn't say another word for fear I'd end up in tears.

"I don't think so. Take a few more weeks, then come back. We'll talk then." She walked to her office door and gestured me out. I'd never been fired before. Well, maybe that weird job at the courthouse, and that time...I shook my head, confused and embarrassed.

"Okay, that's a good idea," I said. "I'll be in touch." With all the dignity I could muster, I walked from her office through the library, feeling eyes upon me as I moved, until the blessed sight of the glass exit door beckoned me through and into the parking lot where I sat in my car and cried.

Back at home, I called my friend Karen to find out when the book club was meeting next but she said it was the night before.

"Actually, we thought you quit." She sounded annoyed. "You haven't shown up for like the last six months."

"I've had a lot going on. I would like to come back, though." She told me the book and the date of the next meeting, a month away. Then I suggested we meet for coffee.

"Sure, let me check my schedule. I'll let you know."

The quiet after she hung up pressed against my ears. I went out for a long walk and picked up a ready-made dinner for one at the gourmet supermarket.

Yoga class on Saturday morning was nice, and the instructor welcomed me back after my long absence. But what would I do with the rest of the day? The County Theater always had a good indie film or two, but who could I get to go with me? It felt like too much work to find someone, so I went alone. That was a mistake. I chose a French subtitled story that turned out to be a study in one woman's lonely descent into madness. After I sat through the whole thing hoping for a happy ending that didn't materialize, I had to get an ice cream at Nonna's next door to the theater just to feel better.

The little coffee and dessert shop was packed with couples and teenagers, nobody alone like me. I took my cappuccino cone outside and walked down State Street, licking the drips from my hand. When I reached my parking spot, I sat in the driver's seat of my Jetta eating the ice cream and listening to NPR.

The late summer sun, close to setting, glinted off the row of parking meters and the chestnut hair of a woman in high heeled boots on the other side of the street. I sat up, stunned at the sight of the woman I knew as Aniela. As quickly as I could open the door and toss my cone into a trash can, I called out.

"Aniela!" The woman and everyone else within the sound of my voice turned and looked at me. Her face wore a questioning look but my heart fell. She wore huge black-framed glasses perched on a long thin nose. It wasn't the Queen of Poland, not by a long shot. "Sorry! I thought you were someone else." I went back to my car and drove home, thinking I'd call Aniela. But what would I say? With Regina gone, I didn't need a translator, and I worried she'd think I was as inept as I felt.

All the rest of that weekend, I tried to read but couldn't concentrate. I took a long walk in Hansell Park and practiced yoga in my bedroom but my thoughts were full of images of

Regina and Jadwiga. What were they doing now? Did they miss me? And, late Sunday night, it popped into my head: the question that demanded an answer. Could I really find out?

Regina had already left on her own, without me. But I could follow her, to a better, simpler world. I could leave the present, where I had screwed up so badly, and start anew. And just as I had helped her here, she would be there to help me adjust. I called the woman I'd formerly known as Aniela and told her what had happened. She was sympathetic and, to my surprise, agreed it was probably okay for me to follow Regina back in time.

"Not going so well for you here. You may learn better what you need if Regina is near. I shall consult with higher up and get back to you."

The next morning, she called back and said she'd gotten approval from her boss, the Blessed Virgin, to help me follow Regina back in time.

"Just get better clothes for this," she said. "Portal in bakery is good one for you, not backyard. That one is only for Regina."

Elated, I prepared for my trip. I researched Polish folk costumes on the web, but the cost of "vintage" clothing was high and I couldn't wait for the mail. I decided instead to wear an outfit I found in Jessica's closet: a long blue cotton skirt and a white long-sleeved blouse. I hoped they would disguise me as just another nineteenth century Polish peasant.

I addressed and stamped an envelope to Alan and enclosed a short note explaining where I was going. I wished him well and asked him to feed Selene but did not say when I'd be back. I put it in the mailbox with another, longer letter to Jessica in which I told her the whole story from start to finish. She had put a lot of distance between us, but I loved her and unlike my own mother, I wanted her to know what I was doing and why. With a kiss to her name for good luck, I flipped up the flag on the mailbox. It would be picked up in the morning, when I'd be gone. My heart skipped at the thought, and I almost lost my nerve.

My previous trip to *Mała Łąka* had been pretty scary, so I renewed my prescription for Valium, telling my doctor it was for an upcoming flight to Europe. I just didn't tell her how I'd be flying. The next morning, I drove south on 95 to Port Richmond and parked down the block from Szypula's Bakery.

When I entered the busy shop, a small group of tourists occupied the attention of the two women clerks and I slipped by unnoticed. Once I reached the old brick building behind the back garden, I wasted no time. I stood in front of the huge wall oven, closed my eyes tightly and focused on 1825, and my vision of the outdoor shrine in *Mała Łąka*.

At first, nothing happened. I started to open my eyes for a peek when a white flash of light blinded me. A whooshing sound filled my ears and a warm wind blew around me. A second later, the wind subsided and the light diffused. I was standing in the pale light of winter, in front of the little wooden shrine on the snow dusted hillside behind Regina's home. And standing right beside it, wearing a white fur cape over a light green gown and a satisfied smile was our friend Jadwiga.

PART III

Chapter Twenty-Three

STUNNED AND A LITTLE SHAKY, my stomach lurched, and I threw up a little in the grass at her feet.

"Sorry." I wiped at my mouth with my sleeve. "I didn't expect that to happen."

Jadwiga nodded once and took a step forward. "Good job! *Wiedziałam, że możesz to zrobić.*"

"What? *What? English*, please!"

She drew herself up to her full height and spoke with perfect elocution. "Sorry. Myself, I am polyglot. I speak Hungarian, Russian, Latin, German, Serbian and Bosnian. English, too, and of course I am quite pleased to be speaking Polish for little while before my next assignment." She lifted the hem of her silky gown and gave it a little swish.

"Oh, how nice for you." I didn't bother to keep the sharpness out of my voice. "But what about me? How am I supposed to get along here with the little Polish I know?" Even to my own ears, I sounded needy. Why hadn't I thought of that before I left?

"Do not worry. Regina and I, we will help you." She stepped aside to reveal the old woman I loved and came here to see. Regina stepped forward, arms outstretched. I cried a little as we hugged.

"I know you didn't think I should come, but I missed you. I'll just stay a little while, for a visit. Is that okay?" I held my breath, waiting. The two other women exchanged a look.

Then both spoke at once, waving their arms. Jadwiga finally said I could learn what I needed here better than at home, and that I was a brave woman to come here on my own like this. Regina said she'd make room for me in her home for however long I wanted to stay. But they still looked worried.

"What?" I sat down on the grass, as tired as if I'd run a marathon. "Is there a problem?"

Jadwiga sat down beside me. "There is just one small thing."

"Okay, what is it?" Something told me it wouldn't be small at all.

"Now that you are here, there is no going back right away." Panic flooded my brain.

"What? What? What?" I couldn't stop saying that one word. What had I done?

"Calm yourself," Jadwiga said. "All is not lost. But now that you are here, you cannot return to your home until you have learned your important lesson."

Okay. I could do this. My heart rate returned to almost normal. Not quite, but almost. "So, Regina was sent to my world to realize it was not her fault she was assaulted, and that's why she was allowed to come back here..."

Jadwiga nodded. "Yes, it is just like that. And we will help you. But you must arrive at knowledge on your own. Through your own action."

Regina glanced at Jadwiga then spoke to me. "I will help any way I can. First, I will explain to others who you are."

"What?" It seemed my vocabulary had shrunk to one word. She couldn't mean she'd tell them the truth. These people would never understand. They'd kill me for sure.

Regina patted my hand. "Do not worry. I will think of something, along same lines as when you met priest. You know, widow lost in forest story."

A chill wind moved across the stiff brown grass. Little flurries of snow swirled around us and I shivered in my thin peasant blouse. "You didn't tell me it would be so cold. I could have brought a shawl or something." An inner voice spoke only to me. Was I never happy anywhere? I had wanted to come here, after all. I had better make the best of it.

"Sorry, sorry." She put an arm around me. "So long in Doylestown, I forget it is winter when I left here. And we have to go back to same time, for some reason." She was dressed in the old clothes she had on when I found her in my kitchen. The new sneakers were gone, the old worn boots back on her feet. And wrapped over her body was a long cloak of a dark brown coarse material.

"Why weren't you wearing that cloak the day you left here by accident? Wasn't it winter then too?"

Regina shrugged. "Upset, run outside crying, thinking I will get away for just one minute to pray." She rubbed my shivering arms with her hands and gave me another hug.

The snow flurries had stopped and all around us lay a quiet, deeper than any I had ever known before. Jadwiga broke the silence with a sigh.

"Let us not stand here being cold." She adjusted her fur cape around her neck. "We shall get a shawl for you, Kat. Sometimes I worry about the two of you. I am not sure you can pull this off. But my own future depends on it. I want to stay here on Earth, so I will do everything I can. Quite honestly, Kat, I am amazed anyone in your time manages to get anything done." She tapped her finger against her lips. "But that is neither here nor there." A slow grin lifted her cheeks. "A joke. Neither here nor there?"

"Very clever. Can I get a little hint about my lesson?" Since I was here, for better or worse, it might be good to get this over with. Then I'd decide whether or not to go home.

Jadwiga looked away for a moment. I waited, scarcely breathing, ready to grasp at any clue. Finally, she turned and faced me again.

"Do not think so hard. Be where you are." The woman was exasperating.

"What's that supposed to mean? It sounds like something from one of my self-help books!"

"Sorry, Kat, I cannot do this work for you. But I will remain close in case of emergency as always."

I closed my eyes and lifted my face to the sky. *May I be safe. May I be strong. May I be where I am.* Part of me thought of my country house, my cat, my quiet meditation corner. My husband, my daughter. My life. How could I be present when my mind flitted from one world to another?

Beyond the hillside, the faint tinkle of a bell mingled with the cries of children. Jadwiga reached out her hands to grasp mine and Regina's and on either side of her we walked over the crisp brown grass. A few yards along, Regina whispered, dropped Jadwiga's hand and blessed herself then broke away. Jadwiga and I watched her climb ahead of us up the hill. Would she forget about me now that she was back where she belonged? As if to confirm my fears, she lifted her head and broke into a trot. Jadwiga's hand slipped away from mine and I turned to look but she, too, was gone. Now what?

I had to catch up to Regina. As I trudged up the hillside I saw the dirt path leading into the tiny village, the path we had walked on our short accidental visit. Now I saw a church and a few buildings and farmyards. On either side of the path, tall linden trees with sparse snow-dusted leaves fluttered a silvery welcome. Where the trees ended, two rows of cottages lined the road.

Far head, Regina stood before one of the houses, its thatched roof covered with dark green moss. Brown stiff weeds stood haphazard between bare spots in the thatch. The little house reminded me of a fairy tale cottage in a children's book. A fallow patch of garden took up the space behind a twig fence. Goats bleated from a pen at the back of the garden.

Outside the front door, an elderly man sat on a bench cleaning mud from his boots with a trowel. When he saw Regina, his deeply lined face clouded with anger. Her whole body drooped, her head bowed, and her hands clenched in front of her. I shivered and looked around for Jadwiga. She was gone, as surely as if she had never been there.

"Where have you been all afternoon?" the man demanded in Polish, waving his trowel in Regina's face. He spoke pretty fast but his body language conveyed his meaning all too well. "Who is she?" he waved the trowel in my direction. I forced myself not to cringe and met his eyes with what I hoped was a friendly and confident smile.

"She came from far away," Regina said, and I was surprised to realize I understood her words. I imagined wheels turning in her head as she formulated her half-truthful response. Yes, I thought, I'm from far away. *Very* far, and I wish I was back there right now.

"Hah!" He stood and faced me. "Where is your husband?" Spittle flew from his lips. I blinked rapidly, and scuffed my shoes in the dirt, buying time.

"*Miło pana poznać,*" I stammered in my feeble Polish. I am happy to meet you. *Not.* Desperately, I wracked my brain for the right words to placate him.

"*Jestem wdową,*" I stammered, my tongue catching on the unfamiliar phrase. Recalling his wife's earlier story to the priest, I told him I was a widow who Regina kindly offered to help. My hands and feet were freezing, and I wondered if I would ever be warm again.

Pawel peered at me through narrowed eyes and spat on the ground. My legs trembled under my long skirt and I longed to sit down. Or run away. Or be safe. Why, oh why, had I come here? I turned all the way around looking for Jadwiga, willing her to appear. A white duck squawked at my feet, making me jump. Pawel turned away from us and stomped into the cottage.

"Franciszek, Zofia, Monika, Mikolaj!" He shouted their names inside, a bitter anger pervading his voice. "Mama has a 'friend' with her!" He spat out the word *koleżanka* as if it tasted bad in his mouth.

Four children came through the open doorway. The oldest, Mikolaj, had a faintly visible beard on his chin and upper lip, and when Regina introduced us, he blushed and ducked his head. Then she walked past him into the house, calling for Anna. The others moved aside for me to follow her, bowing their heads as I passed.

Inside, a low fire burned in a hearth in the middle of the room. My eyes slowly adjusted to the dimness as I tiptoed toward the sound of Regina's voice. She sat on a low narrow bed, holding a little girl of five or six, her hand on the girl's forehead. The child's face was red and sweaty but she smiled weakly. A sweet, familiar smile. The smile on my face in my kindergarten school picture. Trembling, I walked closer to the bed and stared at myself.

The child's eyes were glassy, reminding me of Jessica's brush with the flu when she was small. I could see Jessica in her eyes, but it was me Anna resembled. No, more than resembled. Anna was the exact spitting image of me as a little girl.

I opened my mouth to speak but nothing came out. I could not think. Heart palpitations hammered against the inside of my chest and I could barely breathe. It was me, there in the bed, gazing with love at Regina. The little girl me. But no, it couldn't be. This child, little Anna, lived over a hundred years ago, long before I was born. So, who was she? Regina and I were related, so this child must be my ancestor too. I touched my throat. My DNA was in this child, or rather hers in me.

I closed my eyes, wrapped my arms around myself and inhaled deeply. My heart still pounded. I looked again. The girl stared back at me and gripped her mother's shoulders. If she dies...fear swept across the space from her bed to me and settled in my stomach. She had my face, my hair, my body as a child. She had to be my ancestor. If she did not live through this illness, I would never be born. We had to save her.

From somewhere deep inside, I found a way to smile at Anna, tilt my head in a friendly gesture and reach out a hand but it was shaking. I grasped it with the other and held them both at my breast. All the Polish words I knew had fled from my brain and as much as I wanted to reassure the child, it was for the moment beyond me. All I could do was struggle to keep the smile on my face and my eyes back in my head.

I whispered in Regina's ear that I needed to pee and she told me in Polish to go outside, where to my great relief, I found what I was looking for. The wooden outbuilding was cold but I was fast. Afterward, I went back into the house.

Regina called over her shoulder in a flurry of Polish. A brown-haired girl who looked about nine ran to a high recess in the mud wall, and picked up a small wooden chest. She opened it on a table, took out a small bundle of dried roots and broke off a piece and crushed it with her fist into a white mug. Next, she poured water from a clay pitcher into a black iron pot and carried it to the middle of the room, where a fire pit held a few charred pieces of wood. She lit the fire and when the water was steaming, poured it into the mug and carried it to Anna's bed. Regina took it from her, held it to Anna's lips and coaxed the girl to drink.

"What's wrong with her?" I whispered, moving closer. Regina shook her head once and turned her eyes toward Pawel standing in the doorway. *Crap.* Had he heard me speaking English? I held my breath and ran a hand through my hair. My dyed blond-layered hair. He stayed where he was, glaring at me with arms folded.

Anna was quiet now, the mug drained, her head lying back against a small pile of folded cloth. Regina took the cup from her hands and we watched as her eyelids fluttered, and her little mouth lay slightly open. In a few minutes, the child's breath blew wisps of her pale blond hair away from her face in a gentle rhythm. She was asleep.

Regina stood and rubbed at her lower back. She walked to where Zofia and Monika watched from a corner near the window. She spoke to them quietly and when she had finished, they went into the adjoining room and came back with arms full of straw. They then spread the straw over the packed dirt floor between two beds. Next, they went to a stack of blankets and quilts in the corner and carried them over to cover the straw.

That night I learned the girls normally slept in one bed and the boys another, but as a guest, I would get the boys' bed and Mikolaj and little Franek would sleep on the straw-covered floor.

"Guest in home is God in home." Regina's tone was solemn. We wrapped the plain woolen blankets she had taken from a high shelf around our shoulders and stepped outside. "Polish proverb. Guests bring blessings so we treat them well."

I glanced back at the house behind us. "Does Pawel know that?"

Regina patted my arm. "Of course, it is tradition. Why do you think he let you come in? Man is head of house, but sad to say he has little means to show this. Harvest not good last fall and we never know how much we keep after paying landlord." She looked down at the dead grass beneath our feet. "Pawel is good man. Anger shows he is head of family."

Oh, brother. I breathed a heavy sigh. "Good thing you didn't wear your new sneakers. That would have rocked his world."

A quiet chuckle started in her throat but she stifled it at once. From inside the house, Anna coughed in her sleep.

"Do you know what's wrong with Anna?" I whispered. Dusk had fallen. Windows glowed from within most of the cottages along the deserted street.

"She has sweating sickness." Regina looked back at her doorway. "Give her *pokrzywy* for strength. You have this too in Pennsylvania, not in garden but growing like weeds by the side road." As she went on to describe the plants with prickly leaves, I thought of stinging nettles, an ugly weed. Was that what she was feeding her child?

"Shouldn't we also call a doctor?" How long before it was too late? For little Anna and for me?

"*Nie,* doctor in Kraków and only for *szlachta.* We know things to do. And we pray. If God's will, she will be made well."

This was not the explanation anyone heard from me when Jessica was Anna's age. She survived the flu, though I worried the whole week she was sick. Did I pray? I don't remember, but I know I called her pediatrician. Often.

And so, on my first night back in 1825, because I didn't know what else to do, I tried to understand Regina's strong faith. That and a bunch of dried herbs were all she had to save her daughter's life. And probably my future existence.

Inside the house again, I pulled off my short leather boots and climbed into the boys' square bed, still wearing my clothes. Tomorrow I would talk to Regina about Anna being the unsettling mini-me. A thin muslin curtain separated the area I shared with the kids from a larger, double bed about two feet off the floor. This had to be the bed Regina shared with Pawel. Would I be able to hear them? Would they hear me? I shuddered at the lack of privacy.

"*Czy pani jest zimna?*" Monika, the nine-year-old, asked if I was cold. She sat on the other narrow bed with Zofia, her eight-year-old sister, and looked at me with concern in her lovely brown eyes. We were so close we could whisper and still be heard.

"*Nie,*" I said, relieved I understood her. She untied a red and yellow scarf from around her neck. "*Bardzo ladny,*" I said, pointing. I hoped the words for "very pretty" hadn't changed very much over the years. She smiled shyly and looked at the floor.

"*Dobranoc,*" I whispered.

"*Dobranoc, pani.*" She giggled and ducked under the covers.

It wasn't easy to sleep that first night. I'm sure I was the last person in the house to close my eyes. Pawel and Regina snored. Anna woke up crying several times, and Regina and Monika got up to comfort her. I wanted to help, but was too unsettled and unsure to move from my bed. Finally, exhaustion set in. The next thing I heard was Regina's voice a few feet away.

When I sat up, I saw Monika's silhouette in the dim morning light as she went outside carrying a big pitcher. A snuffling noise came from behind the house and I tiptoed to look out the window. A small goat and two sheep grazed behind a fence. A shaggy brown dog wandered across the yard and stopped before eight-year-old Zofia. I went out the door to join her.

I asked her the dog's name. In Polish. So far, so good.

She tenderly stroked its brown fur. "Piotr," she whispered without looking up.

Behind me, I heard a masculine chuckle and turned to see her brother Francizek, a blond boy of about seven.

"She gives the dog a boy's name!" He laughed again and pointed at his sister. I didn't understand his exact words but I got the meaning from his gesture.

Zofia pushed her equally blond hair behind one ear and stuck out her tongue at him.

"It's a good name," I said in Polish. "I like it."

Zofia put her hands to her hips and stuck out her chin. "See, Franciszek! Pani says Piotr is a good name for a dog."

"Let's get some breakfast," I said, suddenly nervous about continuing in my halting Polish. I didn't want to start an argument my first morning here. "Where's the kitchen?" The kids stared at me round eyed then followed me back into the house.

Regina sat on Anna's bed brushing the child's hair. Her gentle rhythmic motions lulled Anna into a peaceful little smile, my smile. Even her hair was mine as a kid, blond and fine. What was in that herbal drink her mother had given her? It had worked faster than my flu medicine back in the twenty-first century. She looked a lot better than the night before, her cheeks a light pink, her eyes clear. Thank you, I whispered to the Universe.

"Matka Boska answers prayers," Regina said in Polish. How was it I could understand her so well? A flash of heat came over me just before I smelled roses. I looked around for Jadwiga. Was that a flash of green silk at the window?

With a knowing look, Regina told me she believed healing Anna was a miracle from the Black Madonna. Would the tea have done the trick if someone else had made it, if Regina were still in Pennsylvania? I had no idea. I wished I had brought my Goddess cards, so I could consult them. Regina looked over at me.

"You are hungry after your long journey?" she said with a grin. Relaxed and at home, her sense of humor had returned. And though I understood, mine was still somewhere back in the future. I pieced together some Polish words to say I wasn't hungry and that Anna looked exactly like my kindergarten picture. And that I was extremely relieved she was better.

"*Naprawdę?*" She smiled. It was nice, she said. We all had the same DNA, so why not? I pulled her aside so I could speak English.

"She doesn't just *look* like me. It's like looking into my own face when I was small. And it's kind of scary."

Regina patted my hand like the reassuring mother she was, now that she was back here in her own time and place.

"No worries," she whispered. "I am scared in Doylestown but you help me. Now I help you."

"Okay. I know you will do your best." I wanted to do something, too, now, something to pull my weight. "I was wondering where you store and cook your food? I thought I could help feed the kids."

Regina motioned to Monika, who had just stepped into the house with the heavy pitcher of water in both hands. She walked with great care and placed it in the center of the table, then hurried back outside. I followed her as she made a beeline for what I recognized as a spring house nestled into the hillside. I had seen others like this in the Bucks County countryside built of large flat stones. In past centuries, they were used to keep dairy products cold before the invention of electricity. This one was a type of half-underground cellar made of dirt and wood.

Monika ducked her head through the low wooden doorframe, and a moment later, emerged with a package wrapped in cloth. She motioned for me to open it. I lifted a corner, releasing the pungent aroma of pale yellow cheese. My mouth watered and I peeked past her slim body into a dim space that smelled of damp and old wood. A couple of rough wooden shelves held more cloth bags. Monika opened them to show me small amounts of coarsely ground flour. We brought the packet of cheese back to the house and put it on the table next to the pitcher and a basket of bread. While all this was going on, the rest of the family worked around us. Everyone seemed to have a job to do.

From the doorway, I watched Monika go back outside to pump water into a wooden bucket Zofia had positioned on a large flat stone directly under the spigot. She held the bucket with both hands as water dripped, then poured from the pump. When the bucket was full, she grabbed another from a pile beside her. I went out to ask if I could help, but they shook their heads shyly.

"*Nie, pani, dziękuję,*" Monika said. She stepped away from me, and my heart sank. She didn't trust me, and why should she? My Polish words were as halting as a child's and I worried they told her there was more to my story than her mother had shared.

I pressed on, insisting. I wanted to do my part, and to show them I meant no harm. Of course, they had to tell me what to do every step of the way, which added to my strangeness in their eyes. Who didn't know how to lay and light a wood fire?

By the end of an hour, I was exhausted. But there was more to do. Tending and feeding the animals, cooking, eating and cleaning up afterwards, all day long. There was literally no time for anything other than working, eating and sleeping.

All through the day, I attracted wary looks from everyone but Regina. I might be her new best friend but only one person held the power in this family. Pawel frowned whenever he looked at me, and the children were edgy, uncomfortable. By evening, muscles I hadn't heard from in years were crying out for help. Bed was all I wanted after our supper of thin chicken broth, bread and cheese.

Before Regina blew out the lamp, I let my sleepy gaze travel across the room. A cross woven of wheat and a small wooden shrine to the Virgin hung on the back wall. Muslin curtains embroidered with red and blue hearts met across the only window. No glass or screen covered the opening, and only a wooden shutter kept out the cold. The lowing of cows in the distance and the shuffling of the goats in the shed were my odd lullaby. I pulled the covers up to my shoulders and fell fast asleep.

Chapter Twenty-Four

I COULD HAVE SWORN only a few minutes had passed before I was aware of light beyond my eyelids and movement in the room around me. I felt more rested than I had in years. If only I could have a nice hot shower and shampoo. Even without my blow dryer.

I rose and looked around for Regina, and found her outside tossing corn on the ground for the chickens. Her hair was covered by a clean white kerchief. I looked around to see if there was anyone close enough to hear me speak English.

"Do you think I could wash up?" I whispered.

"*Tak, tak*, not a problem." She told me Pawel and the boys had left at dawn. "*Dobrze spałaś?*"

"Like a top." Her eyebrows squished together as she tried to figure that one out. "I slept very well, thank you. *I ty?*"

"*Dobrze, bardzo dobrze.* Good to be home."

She led me back inside the house, where we heated a pot of water for my bath. It was quite a production involving feeding pieces of wood from the pile near the door into what she called the *stara baba*, the open fire pit in the center of the house, and lugging buckets of water from the pump in the yard. Regina handed me a rough hard lump of brownish soap and shooed the girls out of the house. Rather than stand there naked, I lifted my long blouse and skirt and washed the skin I could reach. After I dried myself with clean rags, I refastened my bra. Regina blocked the door with her body. How would I explain a bra if someone saw it? More proof I didn't belong

216

here. What had I been thinking? No more baths for me, at least not anytime soon. I would have to get used to body odors, including my own.

As it turned out, the lack of showers and deodorant was a small concern compared to the dark looming cloud that hovered over Regina and her husband. Alan and I had our problems, but this was something else entirely. Pawel was always on the verge of anger, and Regina and her children tiptoed around with eyes averted like downtrodden medieval serfs.

That night, as I was about to fall into bed again exhausted, Pawel stumbled through the doorway, banging the door against the wall. All six children scattered into darkened corners like actors who had played this drama many times before. Only Regina remained in the open, standing to face him with a fat wooden hairbrush in her hand. I saw her fingers tighten around its handle.

Pawel lurched forward, his heavy boots pounding the hard dirt floor. Alcohol fumes polluted the warm air. The savage look in his watery gray eyes turned my legs to jelly. I looked around for a way to escape, but his body stood between me and the only door. Trembling, I backed away and fell onto the bed, flailing my arms in the air. I struggled to sit up again as Pawel advanced on Regina.

"Out of my way, stupid woman!" He flailed at her with an unsteady arm. Regina tried to move aside but she tripped and fell. Her hairbrush flew across the floor and under the bed where I sat. I jumped to help but before I could get to her, Pawel kicked her in the side.

"Stop," I screamed in English. "Stop kicking her!"

Pawel yelled drunkenly at his wife. From what I could make out, he shouted that the whole village was talking about her stupid story of a widow wandering in the forest who thinks she can eat his food and take a bed in his house. Suddenly, Pawel's boot struck Regina's head with a sickening thud. In a dark corner, the little girls whimpered.

"Stop it!" I yelled and pulled at his arm. He turned and grabbed me by the wrist, wrenching it until I knelt at his feet. He held on, his legs wide apart as he fought to keep his balance. Pain shot up my arm like a hot wire and I cried out.

From the shadows, Mikolaj sprang at his father, pulled him away from me and pinned both his arms behind him. Pawel struggled for a few seconds in Mikolaj's grip but the teenager held on. Time stopped for a beat. Inside the cottage, there was no sound but Pawel's heavy breathing. Then a loud wrenching sob broke from his throat. His shoulders curled and he stumbled, snot running from his nose as Mikolaj pushed him outside. I peered out into the darkness to see him stagger down the street, the only sound the lonely call of a single crow.

Behind me, Regina cried softly. I checked her head for cuts as she moaned and wiped tears on her sleeve. Monika, with lips pressed together and a frown furrowing her pretty brow, went to a pile of rags in a wooden bin, pulled out a few and wet them with water from the big white pitcher. She carried them to Regina, who held one against her head. Mikolaj put his arm around little Franek, who stared at his mother with widened eyes.

"Regina, I'm sorry I caused this," I said in English. Now that the adrenalin was leaving my body, my hands shook uncontrollably. I sat down on the bed, gripping the straw bedding tightly on either side.

"Not your fault, Kasia," she answered me, also in English. "Pawel worries."

"Don't make excuses for him," I answered, too upset to find the Polish words. In the corner, Mikolaj rubbed at his jaw and lowered his head.

"I am all right," Regina whispered. She winced and held the cold compress to her head. The bright red mark on her face would, I knew, turn into an ugly purple bruise. Tears filled her round eyes.

I took her hand and held it between my own as she sniffled and wiped her nose on her sleeve. When she lifted her head, the tears on her cheeks glimmered in the candle light.

Her children stared with open mouths as their mother and I spoke a language they had never heard before.

Soon Regina collected herself and urged her children into bed. She and I lay awake long after midnight as she tried without success to find a comfortable position. I tried my lovingkindness mantra: *May we be safe, may we be strong, may we be happy, may we live with ease.* It wasn't working. I couldn't get my mind to release its terror. But somehow, by some miracle, my body gave up the night watch and I fell asleep.

The next morning, loud snoring woke me on the edge of dawn. I lifted up on my elbows and stared at a pile of clothing near the door. The pile moved and exposed Pawel's head and boots on the dirt floor. Quiet shuffles told me everyone else was already up. The children at the table were tearing off hunks of bread and pouring steaming cups of tea.

Nobody spoke a word. My knees protested when I stood next to the bed, massaging my lower back with one hand. Last night's incident had wrenched a few muscles and my left arm still hurt from being twisted.

On the floor, Pawel rolled from side to side but did not wake, even as Regina came in, silent as her children. They glanced at him every few seconds while they ate and I took my cue from them, quietly taking a place on one of the long benches.

"This is silly," I finally whispered to no one in particular. I waved a hand in the direction of the sleeping man on the floor. "We didn't do anything wrong."

"Hush," Regina whispered back. "No trouble!" She led me outside. The girls and Franek tiptoed around their father's body as they went out to feed the animals. Mikolaj took a steaming mug of chicory outside, looking back over his shoulder. With her left hand, Regina beckoned me to the rustic garden fence.

"Pray to *Matka Boska* last night. Everything all right, except for headache this morning. Hurt so bad I do not sleep." She folded her arms and looked cautiously around her.

"Oh, really? Has it occurred to you that praying to her is what got you into trouble in the first place?" I still didn't get it, me with my mantras and goddess cards: we each did what we believed in, regardless of the outcome.

She ignored my question and went on. "Many men are angry. Not enough food for family, because Zalewski take what we grow. By the way," she said, using a phrase she'd picked up somewhere in my world, "Pawel never hit girls, only boys."

"Well, he hit *you*. Surely the Blessed Mother doesn't approve of that."

She stared at me, unblinking and held on to her sides with both hands.

"Does it hurt where he kicked you?"

"Only little. Barbara helps." She waved toward her friend's cottage up the street. "She is good like saint whose name she carries. Put *bobkowe listki* on this morning then clean bandage. Better." She leaned forward a little and pulled up her blouse on one side to show me a poultice of what looked like mashed leaves. "Healing fast."

"Hmmm. Remember that time you burned your hand at the homeless shelter, and when we took the bandage off the next day, there was no sign of a burn..." My words drifted away as I realized I had never understood that little miracle.

"Tak, tak, tak. Hope it now happen always for me." She crossed herself and straightened her blouse. Then she leaned closer to my ear. "We must be careful."

A deeper voice interrupted in Polish. "What are you saying?" Mikolaj was so close behind us we both jumped and Regina let out a tiny cry.

"Mikolaj! Do not scare me!" she admonished her son in his language. He retorted in words so clipped and fast I could only watch as mother and son argued back and forth, their arms waving in the air. Finally, I poked Regina on the shoulder.

"What?" I whispered.

"*Bądź cicho!*" She told me to be quiet but it was hard to stand there, watching their body language, not knowing what tale she was spinning.

"Regina, what is going *on*?" I said in English. Mikolaj nodded his head and reached out and before I knew what was happening, he had planted a gentle kiss on the back of my hand and walked away down the road.

"Okay, what did you tell him?" I demanded when he was out of earshot.

"I tell him your parents take you to America as baby, and you forgot most of your Polish language. I say you are teacher there, and you are teaching me to speak English."

"Hmmm..." I rubbed my hands together. "This could work. Maybe."

Regina put a rough hand on the shawl covering my shoulder. "Come, no time to waste." She beckoned me to follow her down the street to Barbara's house, where her friend opened the wooden gate and ushered us in. I tried on a few expressions a visiting teacher/widow might wear: lofty, distant, sad. Barbara narrowed her eyes and cocked her head to one side.

"*Czy boli panią głowa?*" She asked if I had a headache, and I understood her, a miracle in itself.

"*Nie, nie,*" I answered with a smile and basic Polish. "But Regina has a bad one."

Just then, another woman came up to the fence. Red-faced, with long tendrils of dull gray hair escaping her brown headscarf, she shook a fist and pointed a finger at me, calling me a Polish word that I knew meant "witch." As soon as she stomped off in the direction of the little wooden church, Regina spoke.

"Genka is a troublemaker. She runs to the priest all the time." She said it in perfect English.

My stomach flipped as Barbara squinted at me, and Regina, realizing she'd spoken English in front of Barbara, covered her mouth with her hand. A puff of wind blew dirt up from the road, and behind us, a door creaked on its hinges.

We turned toward the sound, and although no one was there, I felt a pull toward the other side of the house.

The hem of Jadwiga's pale green gown was barely visible among the dull brown weeds. Making a quick gesture toward the outhouse behind a stand of evergreens, I hurried there. Jadwiga stepped from the bushes and shook her head at me.

"You are not doing so well. You must let me help you."

"Oh, *please.*" My voice quavered. "Yes, yes, help me! People aren't buying me as a poor widow who speaks English. I'm afraid of what might happen next. That woman called me a witch!" I didn't even want to think about it.

"Remember, Kat, you decided to come here. You must make best of the bad situation. I shall be nearby, ready to pull you through. Pay very close attention to what is going on. You will be all right." She nodded and folded her hands into her long silken sleeves.

"I *am* paying attention, Jadwiga. I'm scared!"

"Do not be. I will fix things to keep you safe." She stroked her amber ring with the index finger of her opposite hand.

"Is that your magic ring? What about Regina? Can you keep her safe too?"

"Yes, you might say amber holds magic for those who know how to use it. It is not for amateurs, so do not try." She put her hands behind her back. "Regina, she behaved very well in the Walmart. She comforted the girl and told her it was not her fault she was attacked. Now we will see if she knows how to apply what she learned."

"Her husband is insane! He beats her up and she just takes it. Can't you do something?" Panic fluttered through my chest.

"She must find her own strength. And you must focus on your own predicament. That is why you were permitted to come here. Can you do that?"

"Uh...I guess. I mean, sure. I can focus." I inhaled, held it three seconds then let the air go. Surely, she didn't expect me to handle this entirely using my own devices. Jadwiga stepped close to me and put her hand on my shoulder. The stone in her ring gleamed as if lit from within.

"Good job, Kasia. Focus. Pay attention. You will find what you need within yourself." Before I could react, she stepped behind the outhouse. I wanted to tell her about Anna and me, how we looked alike, but when I ran after her I found nothing but trampled grass.

Chapter Twenty-Five

WHILE I WALKED BACK to Barbara's garden, loud voices carried from up the road, where Father Marek strode toward us, brown cassock swinging around his legs, closely followed by a smug-looking Genka. She clasped her hands together and flicked an expectant look at the priest, who scanned our faces through his small round spectacles before settling his gaze on me.

"*Dzień dobry, pani.*" His cordial greeting did not fit the harsh tone of his voice. He asked me who I was and where I had come from. Afraid to give myself away, I kept silent as Regina told him I was Katarzyna Kowalska, a poor widow she found wandering in the forest, stricken mad with grief. I held my breath.

Father Marek straightened his spine while Genka took a little step away from him. He cleared his throat and raised a hand to point at me. The words I understood – "speaks English" – chilled me to the bone. The three of us glared at Genka who looked back with defiance. Across the road, a large bush trembled and beneath it, I spied an inch of light green silk. Jadwiga's silent support gave me courage, and mustering all my dignity, I reached out to shake his hand.

"*Miło pana poznać. Jestem z Ameryki.*" So far so good. I had told him I was from America. Now I would find out how well he understood English. "*Czy pan mówi po angielsku?*"

A tall white goose ran squawking from the bush across the road. The priest licked his lips.

"No speak English good. Hello. Our Father who art in heaven." His face flushed beet red. He explained in Polish that he had studied at the seminary in Kraków with a British priest but English was not part of the curriculum. He remembered just a few phrases he learned from the priest in that time long ago.

Regina translated for me, and he nodded and smiled as if he approved of what she said, but we all knew he was trying to save face. He didn't understand what she was saying at all. Finally, Regina took a breath and reverted to Polish.

The words I could make out from my limited store were *Święta Maryjo, Matka Boska Częstochowska*, forest and grief and mushrooms. She waved a hand at me and all eyes turned in my direction. There was more about *Święta Maryjo*, then a wave at her ear in the universal sign for crazy in the head, followed by the words for widow, sadness and home.

What was she talking about? She knew my home was in another time. She sounded almost like *me,* explaining *her* to Alan just a few months ago. Or a century and a half ahead. Genka and the priest eyed me warily but Regina gave him her sweetest smile and wished him a good day.

"*Tak, tak,*" the priest mumbled. He bowed his head, blessed us quickly and departed. Genka and Barbara stepped closer to me and Regina.

"Holey moley!" I whispered then switched to my very basic Polish. I told Regina she sounded just like me when I took her in.

"You took Regina in? Where?" It was Barbara and now I could understand her completely. Regina cringed and raised her eyebrows at me. I was tongue-tied, and my face felt hot. "I thought you were a poor widow. You are from America?"

She said all this in Polish but my comprehension was suddenly a thousand times better. Jadwiga's language lessons came back, clear as glass. My grandmother's voice filled my head as all she had taught me of her native tongue returned in force. I covered my ears but still the words rushed in. My heart raced, and in the air, I recognized the sweetly welcome scent of roses.

Regina looked around to see if anyone was watching. A few people worked outside their homes in gardens and animal pens but no one was close enough to hear us. Still giddy, I looked down at my feet. Regina coughed. When Barbara spoke again, I understood every word.

Regina was her friend, and if she had invited me to stay with her, it was good enough for Barbara. But she wanted to know who I was, really, and why I was in *Mała Łąka*. She and Genka could keep a secret. She tilted her head and raised her eyebrows, waiting. Genka gave a solemn nod of her head and put one hand over her heart.

I looked at Regina. Regina looked at me. The goose waddled up to our feet and poked its beak into Barbara's skirt. Barbara beckoned us to follow while she fed the hungry bird and so the three of us and the goose trailed Barbara into the enclosure beside her house. When we were all inside, she closed the gate.

She and Genka took handfuls of corn from a wooden bin and scattered it on the ground. Our feathered friend pecked away while we watched. Finally, Barbara spoke again.

"Please, Genka and I can help. But you must tell us who you are." They looked very serious but I wanted to laugh out loud. I understood Old Polish! It must be another of Jadwiga's miracles, the magic of her amber ring. Regina still didn't know. She cleared her throat.

"Remember when I was gone for few hours the other day?" She paused and waved at the road. Barbara and Genka silently nodded. "I prayed to *Matka Boska* and a big wind came, a flash of light, and I was in her yard." She waved a hand at me. "In America. In the future. More than a hundred years from now." Her voice went very quiet at the end, and we had to strain to hear her. Barbara laughed.

"I thought you said you went to the future!" She and Genka exchanged nervous smiles. The goose waddled through a flock of white chickens at the far end of the yard. It was time to speak for myself.

Regina's mouth fell open when she heard my perfectly accented Polish. "*O Jezus*," she said and blessed herself.

I told them what Regina said was true. I really lived in the 21st century, in America. And I came here to be with her because there was nothing for me there. As soon as I heard myself, I knew how ridiculous my story sounded. The sun went behind a cloud and a gust of wind kicked up the dirt in the road, twirling it in the air. In for a penny, in for a pound. "We found out something else. Regina and I are related. We are from the same family."

Genka asked how we knew, folding her arms in front of her. Man, this was complicated.

Regina stepped in to put an arm around my waist. "In the future, they have special science to show this. It is hard to explain. But *Matka Boska* sent me to her because we are family and I had to learn something. Then I came here but Jurek knocked us down and we were back in America..." She stopped to take a breath.

Barbara's eyebrows went up about a foot. She wanted to know why, since she prayed to *Matka Boska* too, she was not also taken into the future. I didn't know at that point if Barbara and Genka believed our story, but at least they weren't freaking out. In fact, they were quite calm. I wondered if, unlike modern folks, they still had a sense of the mysteries of life.

Genka's harsh cough broke the silence. "Marek is not the best pastor we ever had," she said in Polish. "He does nothing to help us with Zalewski, only goes to have dinner with him in the manor house. Sorry I said anything about you to him." Her eyes moved from my face to the small stones at her feet.

Barbara spoke up next and of course, I understood her too. "Father Marek is allowed to keep rabbits, but never shares them with us. I don't care what he says. If you have trouble, come here. To my house. You too, Regina."

My instinct was to trust these women I hardly knew. I liked Barbara's common sense, down to earth attitude. And Genka was not as threatening as she had first appeared. She quickly brought up a subject we still needed to consider.

"Witches do tricks like speaking other tongues. We have to beware if Father Marek brings up witches." She frowned at me. "You are not a witch, are you?" I shuddered and shook my head. Not me.

Nervously, I glanced toward the bushes for Jadwiga's telltale green skirt. Nothing. If she was still there, she had hidden herself well. Genka's frown deepened, but Barbara put a hand up to her chin.

"Regina has never hurt us, and we have counted on her in the past for help." She touched Genka's arm. "Remember your sick baby? How she made the medicine for her?"

Her head down, Genka murmured a barely audible *"Tak."*

"Let us see how things go. It will be all right." Barbara gave her a little sideways hug and jostled her playfully, and Genka's face creased in a tiny smile.

"Dziękuję bardzo." I put out my hands. First Barbara, then Genka, clasped my fingers in theirs. Their eyes met mine but they were harder to fathom than their words had been. Behind Barbara's head, a branch moved and through its leaves, I saw a glint of amber.

Regina and I worked all the next day in her house and garden, sweeping the floor and preparing dry herbs. As we worked, she told me how she would use them.

The tips of *skrzyp* or horsetail were boiled for soaking swollen feet. Comfrey, or *żywokost,*, was for rheumatism and tuberculosis. We cut the roots into pieces. When needed, they would be cooked in fat and a spoonful of honey, and applied to the sore parts of the body to promote healing. Some of the roots were placed in a bowl of fermented alcohol. After a few weeks, she would strain the mixture and pour it into a bottle to use as an arthritis liniment. Because by then I would be gone, she said. My visit would be over. I wasn't so sure about that, but for once I kept my mouth shut.

A few days later, on a cloudy afternoon, I was straining a batch of comfrey roots into a bowl and thinking about my life. Compared to what Regina went through, there was nothing wrong with my marriage, not really. Alan helped me when Regina ran away. He saved her from the river. And when he talked to Jessica, he urged her to return my calls. I pushed my fist down on the cloth holding the wet roots to get the last healing drop. My husband might lack ambition, but I knew he would never hit me. I had nothing to complain about except the lack of passion. Was this the way my mother had felt before she left for another man? Was I doomed to repeat history, and reenact her story? I'd never taken the time to look at myself in this way, as if I were someone else. This trip into the past was at least giving me a new perspective, and for that, I was grateful. And a little bit ashamed of my past behavior. But no one here, except Regina, knew about that. I could be who I was in the moment, free of my other life story.

The next day was Sunday, and I joined Regina's family for the morning Mass at St. Bartholomew's, a little church surrounded by a small grove of very tall evergreens at the edge of *Mała Łąka*. The entire village seemed to fit into the wooden sanctuary, with everyone dressed in clean but simple clothing. Here and there, a young woman wore a gaily embroidered vest over her tunic. A few of the older men stood at the rear and ducked out to smoke their pipes as soon as the service had ended. We followed them into the sunlight.

"Regina, wait up!" I turned to see Barbara in the doorway behind us. Smiling, she drew closer. "Is it your name day soon?"

"Next Sunday." Regina ducked her head and rubbed at her nose.

"Is that like your saint's day?" I remembered something about this from parochial school. The feast day of the saint whose name you were given at baptism was more important here than your actual birthday.

"*Tak*," she said with a nod. Barbara put an arm around her shoulder and leaned in with a question.

"Will Marianna and her family come here or will you go to her house?" We walked along the path away from the church, other parishioners going around and ahead of us as we talked, and I was relieved to see they appeared to accept the story we'd put out in the village, that I was Regina's houseguest.

She said her grown daughter Marianna, who lived a few miles away in Lipinki with her husband Andrzej, would come the next Sunday for a family meal. *Great, more people to deceive.* By now, my trip back in time was looking way more complicated than I had foreseen. It began to dawn on me that I had never thought very far ahead about anything I did.

The following Sunday, Marianna's family rode into Mała Łąka on a wagon pulled by the biggest brown horse I had ever seen. Its muscles bulged with every step and when Marianna's husband Andrzej pulled back the reins, its head lifted with a loud snort. The horse stomped its feet kicking up dirt everywhere, but nobody but I seemed to mind. I stepped back, coughing, and brushed specks of earth from my face and clothing.

The next few minutes were chaotic and joyful, with hugs and kisses on both cheeks all around, and a formal introduction of me, which caused the inevitable raised eyebrows between Andrzej and Pawel.

We stuck to the grief-crazed-widow-wandering-in-the-forest story, and added a bit about my parents taking me as a child to America just in case they heard me lapse into English. Actually, Regina told the story, while I confined myself to nodding and sheepish smiles. Even though my Polish comprehension had miraculously improved, I decided it was too risky for me to speak, after my slip-up with Barbara and Genka. Only they and Regina knew the truth.

Marianna's younger brother and sister were not at all interested in their mother's long story about me. They ran into the pen to play with the animals, and their laughter amid the bleating of goats and sheep warmed me in places that had long gone cold. Anna, especially, captured my interest. I felt as though I was watching myself run around as a child, decades ago – or rather, sometime in the next century. You'd never know she'd been so sick.

As I watched her, a bud on my family tree, I wondered what her place might be in history. Maybe she would do great things, far beyond what I might accomplish in my confused and lonely life. I hoped she would find a path that suited her, and unlike me, stay the course. I wanted to stay there, watching her, but busy noises from inside the house reminded me there was work to do. I reluctantly turned away and entered the cottage.

Regina and Marianna were placing wood onto the *stara baba* in the middle of the room. I pulled the iron pot from its shelf in the wall and placed it beside the wood. We made a hearty stew right in the pot and hung it over the fire from a hook in the ceiling. At first, the slowly cooking pork mixed with cabbage and mushrooms smelled tantalizing, but very gradually, smoke began to fill the cottage, so we went outside, intending to go back and check on the pot every few minutes.

Across the road, Pawel and Andrzej leaned on the fence and sipped beer from stone mugs. The air held the promise of spring but at this time of year the afternoon sun still hung low in the sky. Andrzej had some of the same mannerisms as his father-in-law: the cocky bearing, a little swagger, and a sneer for their wives. When Regina, Marianna and I scurried out of the house, coughing from the smoke, they laughed at us. Marianna and Regina ducked their heads and went into the side garden. I followed them, not sure what to do. I didn't like the way the men looked at us and laughed. I was angry and hurt for Regina and her daughter, but afraid to interfere and make a bad situation worse. I knew Pawel was a bully, and I didn't know Andrzej well enough to know what to expect from him.

I suggested we take a walk, and Regina smiled and took my arm. We strolled with Marianna toward the lane of linden trees at the edge of the village. I loved this peaceful setting, and the ease among the three of us, the surly men growing smaller as we left them far behind. Twittering wrens flew among branches that stretched across the road and met above our heads, providing a latticed canopy. Dried remnants of wheat and barley lay in the nearby fields. I asked Regina if she went here to gather the herbs she used and she showed me some of her favorite spots. When we stepped away from the road, I was surprised to see old clumps of mugwort and dandelion, and bushes of rosemary growing freely for anyone who cared to look. Though it was still late winter, I recognized their shapes from my own herb garden.

"Time to check on the stew," Regina said. We walked back along the road, Marianna humming a little song that came to an abrupt halt when we were close to the cottage. I recognized the sharp smell of burnt meat. Marianna ran inside, grabbed a long wooden spoon and poked at the mess at the bottom of the pot. Regina pulled it off the fire, waving at the smoke. Her special name day stew was scorched and ruined. My throat burned with disappointment and a deeper dread of what would happen next.

In a flash, Andrzej rushed through the door to his wife, grabbed the spoon and threw it into a corner. He yanked at her hair, slapped her across the face and yelled something about talking instead of staying in the kitchen, where she belonged. Tears filled her wide brown eyes and fell onto her cheeks. Pawel's face was the picture of confusion. He moved toward her, then stopped, threw his hands in the air and stalked away.

"It is all my fault," Regina insisted, pulling at Andrzej's sleeve. I was sickened to see the red mark on Marianna's face, and jumped in to say in Polish, *blame me, I was the one who took them for a walk. I was the one who kept them talking instead of watching the cooking pot.* Andrzej flicked a hand in front of his nose and my stomach twisted. Anna's little round face peeked into the open doorway. I put a finger to my lips and she withdrew.

In awkward silence, Marianna and her family left in their wagon. There was no dinner for any of us that night. Stomachs growled all over the cottage. I tossed left and right but could not sleep. After a long while, I heard a sob outside the window and got up to see.

Regina sat in the yard on an upturned water pail, staring up at the crescent moon. The sky was filled with stars. It might have been close to midnight. I sat on the edge of the animals' water trough and waited. Darkness cloaked our sadness, and I could barely see her face as my eyes adjusted to the pale moonlight. Her voice came to me through the still night air.

"Hurts to see daughter like that," she said, keeping her voice very low. "Cannot sleep. Want to do something, but what?"

"*Wiem*," I said. I know. The more I practiced my Polish, the more I remembered. It was funny that way. They say when you dream in a language, you have mastered it, but I wasn't there yet. In *Mała Łąka*, I had no dreams.

Regina and I heaved a deep sigh at the exact same time, and even in the dark, I felt her smile. "Glad you are here, Kasia," she said. I put my hand on top of hers in her lap and we sat there for a while, the stars twinkling like Jadwiga's amber ring. Regina looked up at the sky one more time, then rose stiffly and massaged her lower back.

Life was suffering and heaven, the reward: that was her belief. But when it came to her children, that belief must have been very hard to accept. As a mother, as would any mother, I understood and felt her pain. But there was nothing more to say. Gathering my woolen shawl around me, I followed her back into the cottage.

Chapter Twenty-Six

LATE IN THE AFTERNOON following her unhappy name day, Regina prayed at the wayside shrine of the Black Madonna. She stood with hands folded and eyes closed, a living portrait of intense peace I could only envy.

My constant thoughts of the danger here had given me a bad case of heartburn. Regina and Marianna were physically injured by their own husbands, the men who had pledged to love and care for them. And my presence here required a new explanation every day. Was I helping Regina as I intended, or was I adding to her troubles? And what did the Madonna want me to learn from this?

Pondering these questions, my hands tightened into fists as frustrated tears came to my eyes. Back home, I might consult my goddess cards for guidance. Here, I had nothing. And what did these dear people have? A strong abiding faith in God and the saints.

They were the *chłopi,* the peasant class, below the family who lived in the manor. There was a certain pride in that. The people of *Mała Łąka* lived close to the land and took care of it. Yes, it belonged to the *pan,* lord of the manor. But the *chłopi,* knew it best.

"*My wasi a ziemia nasza.*" This was the ancient saying they lived by. "We are yours, but the land is ours."

The truth was a lot more complicated. The *pan* of the manor owned the pasture where the *chłopi,* grazed their cattle. If you wanted to build a house, you cut timber in the manor's forest, and paid for it in goods or labor. The *pan* had final say on everything you did, yet every household in the village managed to keep a little patch of carefully tended vegetables, herbs and flowers.

While Regina continued to pray, I sat down on a smooth flat rock and thought about this lovely place. I loved our time in the garden, getting it ready for spring when we'd sow the plants she relied on for curing ailments, and the flowers I knew she loved. I knew it could be a beautiful and simple life, if only it were safer for these people, my ancestral family.

I closed my eyes and opened my palms to the Universe. *May all beings be safe. May all beings be strong. May all beings be happy. May all beings live with ease.* I repeated the loving-kindness mantra over and over, substituting the names of Regina and her daughter, but instead of relaxing me, it soon turned into frantic pleading. *May Marianna be safe!* I shuddered to remember how her husband had yanked her by the arm, and a warm rush of air passed across my face, startling me.

My eyes popped open. In the empty meadow below the shrine, a gigantic white stork flew back and forth, quite low but never touching down. Her long neck seemed too thin for her body, and her sharp wings created a breeze each time she passed. She glided left and right, her movements unbelievably graceful for such a large and awkward-looking bird. After another pass, she settled onto a boulder and turned her long, pointed beak toward me. Her black eyes focused on mine. I did not move a muscle for fear she would fly away. I wanted her to stay. Her eyes sent compassion straight to my center, and I sensed all was well, as it was meant to be. She peered at me for a moment, as if to be sure I knew. Then she opened her enormous black-tipped wings and lifted off the rock and into the sky. I sat and watched the clouds long after she was out of sight.

From the corner of my eye, a shadow moved across the dry grass. Regina walked toward me, the bottom of her skirt brushing the ground.

"Kasia is praying, too?"

"No, I was meditating." I stretched my arm to the pale blue sky. "Did you see that stork?"

"*Tak.* Not usual to come so close, they stay on roof or treetop. Like to be near water. Legend says when stork visit, good things happen."

"I hope so. Marianna needs some good things to happen. And, so do you."

Regina's eyes took on a faraway look. She glanced back at the wooden shrine and sat down beside me on the rock. She had prayed for her daughter, she said, asking the Virgin to protect her. She leaned over and touched my knee. "Gives me idea to help her."

"Great! Let's hear it." I folded my arms.

"Idea comes during prayer. Jadwiga say *Matka Boska* send me to you to learn something, right? I see how women are still hurt in your time. What I learn is this: It is not our fault. And I must do something to stop it."

I wondered if this was my lesson too. Could I stop the hurt I'd caused at home? Could I get my husband and daughter to forgive me? My hopes raised, I sent the *Matka Boska* a silent prayer of thanks. Regina stood and reached out a hand, and together we walked back down the road to her home.

That evening, after the dishes were put away and the animals were in their shed on the side of the cottage, we were exhausted, but we knew neither of us would sleep until we figured out how to help Marianna. We went outside to talk.

"Barbara's husband is kind man, never hits." Rustling sounds came from the animal pen as Regina kept talking. She alternated between Polish and English for me, but now I understood perfectly, either way. Ever since the scent of roses moment in Barbara's garden which held not a single rosebush, I had gradually become bilingual. It was so subtle, I didn't notice. Tonight, discerning the meaning of her Polish words was effortless to me.

When I told Regina, she was not surprised. It was another miracle, a sign the Madonna was helping us. The Black

Madonna, archetypal Mother. I wanted to believe like Regina did. And why not? Maybe the Virgin cared about me too. I closed my eyes on my sudden, unexpected tears and inhaled the sharp tang of the coming spring.

Regina tugged at my arm. "Cyprjan never believe in hitting. Their house is safe place for women. Like shelter where I stay before you come and get me."

A little light went on inside my head. "Was there somebody in that homeless shelter that was beaten up by her husband?"

"*Tak, tak, tak.* I see it on their faces: black eyes, *siniak* all blue and purple, I know what it is from." She kicked at the ground with her boot.

"Sad, isn't it?" I looked down at my own dusty boots and traced a circle in the dirt with one toe. "Even after all these years, women are still abused. Kind of makes you want to throw up your hands and give up, doesn't it?"

"*Nie, Kasia,* it does not." Her tone was defiant. "Do you not see? I have a mission from *Matka Boska.*" She lifted her chin and gave me a curt nod. "Let's see if Barbara is still awake."

We hurried down the street under the sliver of moon in the darkening sky. There was still enough light for us to see Barbara's figure moving around her garden.

When Regina told her what she had in mind, her friend was eager to help. "I have never liked the way Pawel treats you." she said in Polish. I was thrilled to comprehend her every word. "Neither does Cyprjan. You come over here when Pawel starts to yell. Just walk away."

"Or run," I mumbled. The plan sounded too simple. What if he ran after her? Regina and Barbara looked at me for a second then turned questioning faces to each other.

"Maybe run," Barbara said and bit her bottom lip.

"What about Marianna?" She lived miles away and I wondered how we would we know when *she* needed help. It would be *when,* I realized with a shudder. Not *if.*

"That is something we shall have to work on," Regina said. "But we will find a way. We *must* find a way." A cloud blew across the moon, bathing us in shadows.

A few weeks passed before I knew it, as we cooked and cleaned, went to church, and visited with friends. Pawel behaved himself, though he continued eyeing me with suspicion. Winter slowly released its hold on the land until one morning, everyone in the village, kids included, headed for the fields. It was time to prepare the land for spring planting. A man stood at the head of a rough path, his beefy arms folded. Regina quietly explained to me that he was the *pan*'s overseer. Tall and swarthy, with a long black mustache, he struck a pose, feet wide apart, until we formed a line before him.

He handed out scythes and rakes to the men and women, while the kids grabbed large straw baskets from a pile at his side and headed for the orchard. What looked to me like a dozen men built small brush fires from the chaff on the ground. Soon the air filled with acrid smoke. Most of the women stopped to cover their noses with white rags they tied behind their heads.

Regina whispered that last fall, the wheat had been gathered and stored, and today the entire village would work to glean the very last of the chaff left behind, preparing the ground for the crops. A hive of people moved back and forth, shouting across the rows of earth. One man broke into song and a few others joined in, so much like a crowd scene in a Broadway musical, I giggled. But it wasn't long before I didn't feel like singing, and neither did they. Grunts and the occasional shout floated across the field. This was hard work, and my back ached like never before. I stopped often to straighten up and stretch and was rewarded by sympathetic looks of pity. I was obviously not used to hard work, poor crazy American widow that I was.

Regina signaled me to wait until the overseer went to a far edge of the field where it met the forest. He waved his arms in anger at a couple of older boys, shoved them away from him and followed them along the tree line until we could no longer see them through the haze of smoke from the brushfires. Regina beckoned Barbara to join us over a little hillock.

In case anyone saw us, we made a big show of being hot and thirsty, wiping at our brows and drinking from metal cups we dipped in a tub of warmish water. In the space of a few minutes, talking as fast as we could, we worked out a plan. Throughout that day, as we passed the message to every grown woman at work in the fields, none of us suspected we would be put to the test that very night.

The waning light at sunset brought with it a sense of foreboding, as though the world was closing in on us, and I had never felt so far from Doylestown, Pennsylvania, where on evenings like this I enjoyed the cozy comfort of a warm sweater, a fireplace, and hot cocoa. As we walked back to the village, I daydreamed of spring, my favorite season back home.

At bedtime, my clothes and hair still smelled of smoke, but so did everyone else's. Just as I climbed under the covers with the house settling down around me, a scream from somewhere outside cut through the night.

More screams, a man's loud curse, and a sickening thud. I knew that sound. By the time I sat up, Regina was already scrambling down from her bed in the darkness. We heard the noise come again from a few doors away, but Regina and I ran past it, straight to Barbara's, according to our plan. As we reached her house, we saw her figure in the yard, ringing a cowbell with both hands. She raised it up then brought it down with the full force of her arms, her face flushed with anger. A little frisson of energy went through my body. We were in for it now, for better or worse. As we ran toward Barbara, doors flew open and women ran out filling the street with outrage. If harnessed, their pent-up fury would have lit the sky.

"*Chodźcie!*" Regina yelled. Come on! She headed back down the row of cottages, her skirt flying around her legs, with the rest of us close behind her. We bore no weapons. We would not need them. Each woman carried the frustration, pain, and humiliation she had borne inside her for years. But this time, instead of bearing our burdens sadly, we boiled over with righteous anger. I, too, was caught up in the crowd, my body taut with rage at anyone who would dare to harm these dear women, my friends.

We were a storm roiling down the street toward the pitiful sounds, pushing open the door of the cottage where the commotion had started. The scene inside nearly broke my heart. She was young, I guessed still in her teens. Her nose dripped blood as her young husband stood with his fist raised above her head. Regina leapt through the doorway and jumped at his back, twisting his hand so hard he cried out in pain. Right behind her, Barbara pulled his other arm and pinned it behind his waist. More women, me included, threw him to the floor and turned him over. Genka sat on his chest.

His eyes widened as he turned his head from side to side, shook it once as if to clear it, then clenched his eyes tight and opened them again. I think every grown woman in *Mała Łąka* had crowded into his little house that night. And every one of them directed her fury straight at him. I saw firsthand the powerful strength in our number. My life at home was, by comparison, so lonely, so isolated. So unnecessary. I wanted this for myself, a community of women. Barbara got to her feet when she saw he could not escape. She took a clean rag from a shelf, wet it in a bowl of water and gently wiped the blood from the young woman's nose.

"It will be all right now, Amalia." She stroked the young woman's hair. Amalia's eyes filled.

"I didn't believe it," she said. "When I heard you had a plan." On the floor, her husband squirmed, but we held on tight.

"Be still, Roman," Genka tossed over her shoulder, rubbing her lower back with both hands. She faced his feet from her seat on his chest. "You are giving me a backache." Somebody laughed and soon we were all giggling so much we had to work hard to hold him down.

Regina let go of his arm and turned his cheek towards her. She held his jaw in her free hand while she told him that if he ever tried to hit Amalia again we would swoop down on him like a flock of geese and peck out his eyes and some other body parts. Then she released his jaw and gave a fierce nod, but she couldn't keep from laughing. Neither could I, or anyone else but Roman. We laughed so hard we cried, hands pressed against hearts, slapping knees, rocking back and forth. Tears of relief clouded my eyes but not before I saw a figure in green silk pass by the window.

Barbara took Amalia home with her that night to give Roman time to cool off. She and Regina also wanted to talk to the young woman, to let her know she could call on us if it happened again.

As we left the cottage, a small crowd of men stood in the street, watching. A tall sandy haired man with a long mustache slouched against the fence, smirking at Roman who stood in the doorway rubbing at his wrists.

"What happened?" the man called out. "Finally meet some resistance?" Roman's ears turned red. The rest of the watchers laughed, a little too loud, like you do when you are nervous.

"Come on, Józef, that's enough," they called, and the handsome man with the long mustache pushed away from the fence and joined them. But not before he smiled at me.

Chapter Twenty-Seven

THE NEXT MARKET DAY in Lipinki, the story spread. A mob of crazy women in *Mała Łąka* had knocked a man down in his own home. The story was carried back to every surrounding village. And so, it was no big surprise to anyone in Lipinki when one windy Sunday morning right after mass, Barbara, Genka, Regina and I arrived in town. We had borrowed Cyprian's horse and cart to travel the few miles to the town where Marianna lived with her husband Andrzej. It felt so good to be part of this mission, riding with strong women who had purpose and meaning. Without Regina and her village, I never would have known just how good, and how powerful it was to have support and direction. To work together with others.

When we got there, we stopped at Regina's instruction, not at her daughter's cottage but farther down the road at the home of her mother-in-law. A crowd of men gathered around the cart, shouting up at us. Women blessed themselves and knelt in the road. Some of the men shook their fists at me, and I looked at them over my shoulder and squirmed in my seat. By the tone of their fear-tinged voices, I knew they had all heard a very embellished version of our story. The four of us had superhuman powers, and had cast a spell over every man in *Mała Łąka*.

One dark-haired man shouted that we were all witches. A stone of fear settled in my breastbone. I wanted to turn around and go back before this got out of hand. What did they do with witches in Eastern Europe in 1825? I didn't know and didn't want to find out.

Genka, God bless her, was not so easily frightened. She held up both hands. *"Uspokój się!"* Her voice was deep and strong. "Calm down. We stopped one man beating his wife. Is that such a miracle? Some kind of magic trick?"

The man yelled out that we had cast a spell to paralyze Roman. Otherwise we would not have had the strength to knock him down. His friends nodded beside him, arms cocked at their sides. Old movie images of peasants with pitchforks running at the stranger, the monster, filled my head.

From her seat in the cart, Genka shook her finger in the air. *"Matka Boska* and Queen Jadwiga perform miracles we cannot explain. Are they witches too?"

The dark-haired man growled from deep in his throat. "You are not the Madonna or Jadwiga."

One of the Lipinki women stepped forward to give Regina a hand climbing down from the cart, and her friends closed around us, edging the men aside.

"Witamy." Welcome. From the back of the group, an older woman came forward.

"Dzień dobry." She kissed Regina on both cheeks. "Welcome to my home. I have some things for you to eat and drink."

The men let us pass, muttering to each other as they walked away. The woman led us to a little wooden cottage with darkly stained wood and ornate carvings on the shutters that reminded me of a Bavarian cuckoo clock.

"Come in." The four of us walked inside as she held open the door. Like Regina's, this place had only one room. A teenaged girl with long blond braids on either side of her face stood beside the hearth. She looked just like Andrzej. Round face, wide eyes, high forehead. A Polish face. My people.

"Miło poznać," I said. Pleased to meet you. The older woman introduced the girl as her daughter Danuta and Regina introduced me as a friend who had spent most of her life in America. I grasped each of their hands in turn and tried to gauge their attitudes from their facial expressions.

They were serious and for the moment, more focused on the purpose of the visit than on me.

"*Dzień dobry, Elzbieta*. You have heard? You know why we have come?" Regina asked. "Your son is good husband and provider, but he pushed my Marianna. He slapped and punched her. And he yelled at her for burning dinner, which was not her fault."

"*Tak, tak*," Elzbieta said. Without a pause, she launched into a long apology and explanation about his rough childhood and his deceased father. Regina held up a hand.

"We understand. Many husbands hit because their father hit and so on. But now it must end. It is up to us, the mothers." She stood firmly planted in front of Elzbieta, a much taller woman. Of the two, Regina had taken on the steady confidence of a leader. Danuta watched her mother. In the silence, a clock ticked on the mantel.

"You have a clock!" Barbara gaped at the small wooden timepiece. Danuta blushed and nodded happily while her mother heaved an exasperated sigh.

"We have the only clock in Lipinki. Her fiancé gave it to us. Now people want to come and see it, day and night." She drew herself up taller while I stared at the black metal hands pointing to twelve and two. Ten after twelve. It was the first I knew the exact time since I'd left home, and I smiled inside, thinking how little it mattered.

"Her fiancé will not hit, correct?" Regina pinned a pointed look on Elzbieta and tipped her head toward the girl. Elzbieta's face flushed. The clock ticked on. Danuta looked down at the floor, then up at her mother. Finally, the older woman spoke.

"*Nie,*" she said, her face a deepening red. "He will not. As we shall teach him, for his mother has died. As I should have taught my Andrzej."

Regina laid a gentle hand on the taller woman's arm. "None of us taught our sons. Certainly not I. But now we make it right. Will you help us?"

In all my feminist workshops, I had never been as moved as I was that day by the solidarity in Elzbieta's storybook cottage. As one body, we four from *Mała Łąka*, plus Danuta and her mother marched down the road to the house where Andrzej and Marianna lived.

When he saw his mother coming, Andrzej took his pipe out of his mouth and stared. He stood outside his front door with another young man whom Elzbieta politely asked to leave. The man ducked his head and walked away as Andrzej stared after him. He was a lone man with five stern-faced women, and his sister Danuta gave him her own wary version of the same look.

Marianna came around the side of the house from the backyard. When she saw all of us, she stopped and wiped her hands on her white apron.

"Come here, child," Regina said. "You need to hear this."

"Let me do it," Elzbieta said. Regina stepped aside to let her approach her son. Genka, Barbara and I were spellbound. "You know what they are saying about you?" she asked him. Her head to one side, she put both hands at her waist. "I did not teach you to hit your wife."

Andrzej kicked at the fencepost. "And yet when my father hit you, you said nothing." Genka gasped. I took a step toward Elzbieta but she didn't need my comfort, not then.

She took a deep breath and stepped closer until her face was inches from her son's.

"That was then," she said. "Today is a new day."

Andrzej peered at his mother through the brown hair hanging over his face. She pursed her lips and waited. A light breeze ruffled his hair, lifting it. In the linden tree behind him, a cuckoo called. Andrzej lowered his head. *"Przepraszam."* I'm sorry.

His mother waved a finger at him then tilted her head toward Marianna. "Tell *her*."

Marianna twisted her hands in her apron and looked up at her husband. He took a step toward her and she walked forward to close the distance between them. The look in his eyes told me she was safe with him, for now. The moment was a private one between the two.

We left them together and headed back to Elzbieta's for tea. Sweet bread and *herbata*, the herbal tea I loved, made for a nice little victory celebration. At Elzbieta's dark wooden table, we pulled up chairs and Danuta listened, rapt, while Regina retold the Black Madonna's message, received in a prayer. All women must be protected.

Late the following morning, the warm April sun rose high in the sky. We were back in Mała Łąka again. After a tiring and tedious laundry routine, using a contraption that resembled a large bucket with a handle to push clothes around in soapy water, I was worn out. We had just finished hanging the clothes out to dry on a rope tied at both ends to tree trunks, and I was looking forward to a rest when I heard footsteps on the packed earth outside the fence.

Józef, the tall man watching us the night we rescued Amalia. I remembered his laughing taunt at her husband. His moustache curved up at the ends like my grandfather's in old photographs. This morning he wore a white muslin shirt over dark trousers and shiny black boots. I was thinking about how much more care he took with his appearance than the other men in the village when he introduced himself and invited me to take a walk. Regina shot him a disapproving frown but I pretended not to see.

Józef spoke slowly for me but thanks to Jadwiga's magic, his Polish was easy to understand. His eyes were kind as he easily shared information about himself. He was widowed like me, he said, and childless. His wife had died in the previous year, and when he told me the story of her long illness, sadness clouding his eyes, I felt a little guilty for passing myself off as a bereaved spouse.

He had always liked Regina, he said, and his wife had looked up to her. Now she had risen even higher in his esteem, because of what she had done for Amalia. His own father had shoved him around once in a while but never delivered a real beating. And Józef and his brothers, who lived in other villages in the Małopolskie region, never hit

LINDA C. WISNIEWSKI

a woman. I wondered if it went without saying that striking one's equal, a male peasant, was still an option.

Because he seemed a sympathetic man, I asked him about crazy Jurek, the nobleman's son. My Polish felt effortless and I was grateful that the magic still held. We hadn't seen Jurek since that first day we'd gone back in time, and I wondered if he would again come riding down the road, whip in hand. Remembering Regina's shame, I wanted her to be safe.

Józef told me not to worry. Jurek had been sent away. His lips pressed together as if to close the subject.

"What do you mean, 'sent away?'"

"I mean, Katarzyna, that *Pan* sometimes sends Jurek to the Baltic coast where he is not well known. *Pan* has a brother with a manor house there." He pulled up a long blade of grass and chewed on the end as we walked.

"And Jurek goes along with it?" I remembered the wild look in his eyes as he rode toward us. He didn't look like the kind of man who would take orders easily, or quietly go away.

Józef stared toward the line of poplars bordering the fields. Barn swallows swooped down across the sky, their long brown wings like shadows in the sunlight. A few of them landed in the field and picked at the furrows as Józef spoke.

"Jurek knows he must obey his father. He's not a good manager. When his father is annoyed by complaints about him, off he must go, to one uncle or another. His father has many friends who owe him favors. They see that Jurek goes where he is told."

The flock of swallows lifted into a slow circle dance high in the air. We stood and watched until they settled on the very top of Barbara's barn. A crowd of children ran past us, laughing, and I saw Anna's blond head in the middle of them, her face, my face, the picture of innocent joy.

"I hope he never comes back." I shivered and rubbed at my arms. The white blouse I'd borrowed from Regina was a bit large and slipped off my shoulder.

"Don't worry. If he does, you'll be safe." He reached out and straightened the blouse, and a shiver of delight went through me. It was a nice feeling, having him near, protecting

247

me. But it wasn't just me who might be in danger should crazy Jurek return. Regina, Barbara, any woman who worked the *Pan*'s land. And the girls, too, one day: Anna. I couldn't bear the thought of it, and said so.

"That's why they have men, to protect them." Józef looked off into the distance, his sandy hair blown across his face. The sun had gone behind a cloud and the air was growing chilly.

Chapter Twenty-Eight

ALL THAT SPRING AND SUMMER, Józef and I walked together most evenings. I felt safe with him, and I liked being away from Regina and Pawel and their busy household, where I wasn't much use and didn't really belong. Alan intruded into my thoughts from time to time, as I tried to imagine his life moving on without me, a thought that left an empty hollowness around my heart. Would I ever have the chance to see if we could work out our differences?

Regina insisted I could stay as long as I needed, but the village was not what I had once imagined it to be. Even here, I felt the same lack of purpose and the sadness I had carried with me all my life. Always leaning from one foot to the other, back and forth, wanting to do the right thing, the best thing, but trapped in my indecision.

Józef was easy to talk to, and very interested in the time I had spent in America. It was all very sweet, but I knew it could not last. I was often tempted to tell him the truth but at the last minute, something always stopped me. I wondered if my mother had felt this way, torn between two men, unable to choose the path that would make her truly happy.

One day in late August, Józef showed up at Regina's house to present me with a little bouquet of wildflowers. When I took them from his outstretched hands, Regina gasped and turned away. The three of us were alone in the house, and I looked from one to the other of them, and down at the flowers in my hands. Sky blue cornflowers, orange red poppies, a cluster of pale pink yarrow. I lifted them to my nose and inhaled the smell of summer, sunlight, and a world of beauty. What was Regina's problem with that?

When I looked up at Józef to thank him, his crooked smile gave me a clue. For me, we had been having a friendly little flirtation, but for Józef, a man without a woman in an earlier century, it was much more serious. The air grew thick and close around me.

Regina's story of how she met Pawel came to mind. Like me, she had found an attractive man of the same age, one who was nice to her, and took her on long walks, and all at once, I saw my mistake. Walking together must be a courtship ritual here. And I had stepped right into it. My face felt hot. I stole a glance at Józef from the corner of my eye. He rubbed his forehead, pushing back that gorgeous sandy hair. His broad shoulders shifted in his muslin shirt, and I imagined his arms around me.

Life with him could be so pleasant, my place in the village clearly defined, secure. No hard decisions about umpteen choices. All my issues back in the future could stay there. Alan and Jessica could go on with their lives without me. *And it would serve them right!* Something sharp and sour touched the back of my throat. I coughed and felt my chest tighten.

When had I become so bitter? Did it start the day my mother left, with her note on the kitchen table? It still hurt me, all these years later, and now that she was dead, I would never be able to ask her why she never came back for me. Would my husband and daughter have to live the rest of their lives with the same unanswered question?

I turned this over in my mind until Józef cleared his throat and Regina started banging pots and pans around on the table. I wanted to get out of the cottage, to think for myself without her noise and the distraction of Józef's deep brown eyes. I didn't want to give up the flowers, though, or the pleasant feeling of having him so near. I transferred the bouquet to one hand and took the arm he offered with the other. He turned to one side and led me out the door in an Old World gesture that almost stole my heart. I had never been treated this way, like a treasure, a princess, a delicate flower. I wanted to hold onto the feeling as long as I could.

We walked down the road and took our usual path through a dry field. The late summer evening was warm and peaceful, the sky as blue as the cornflowers in my bouquet. Bales of hay lay in the field, ready for storage in the manor's huge barns. Some would go to the workers' animals, including Regina and Pawel's goat. The fragrant aroma of the grain relaxed me, and I took a long deep breath. Beside me, Józef stopped walking, put his hands on my shoulders and gently turned me to face him. In the hazy light, his face turned somber. He lifted his chin, and took both my hands in his. Then he murmured a question I couldn't quite make out.

I shook my head to clear it, to help me understand what he had said. It had sounded like "Would you be my wife?" My heart pounded. By the questioning look on his face, I knew that my translation was correct. I smiled, I stammered, I stuttered. I took a step backward. He was such a sweet man, gentle, courtly, and handsome. But I needed more time to think. This did not feel right. I was already married. Okay, my estranged husband lived in another century, but still.

The day had started out so well. Why couldn't it stay that way, sunny and pleasant with no obligations? *Because it can't, Kat. Life is change.* I looked up at the sky. Same white clouds on that cornflower blue, but now it looked as flat as poster board.

I struggled to find words, but I took too long. Józef threw up his hands and paced around in a circle. He said I didn't know what I was doing. His voice cracked when he said that a woman of my age would not have many offers. How would I live then, alone, without a man to protect me?

When I heard his last few words, my mouth went dry. What kind of statement was that? I thought he was different from the other men in *Mała Łąka*, but here he was, trotting out the old traditional women-are-helpless-without-a-man garbage. Józef didn't know me at all. Or maybe he did, and I didn't like what he saw.

I pushed at his broad muslin-covered chest. I cried that I had been without a man for some time and was doing just fine. Suddenly, I needed to get away from him, either that or pound his chest even harder. Or dissolve in a puddle of angry, frustrated tears. I turned on my heel and ran off toward the woods.

Józef called my name, but he didn't come after me, and that hurt. I ran and ran, my cheeks hot and my eyes burning. I felt naked and exposed and I didn't know why, I only knew I had to get away, to hide from him and the rest of this world, judging me. I ran until I tripped on a root and fell to my hands and knees. For a minute I sat, brushing at my skirt and checking my palms and knees for cuts. I was all right on the outside but my stomach was a bundle of knots and my head pounded so hard I could barely think. Damn Józef for spoiling our little romance with his rush to propose. Why couldn't things stay as they were? Why couldn't things ever stay as they were, the way I wanted them? *If only I knew what I wanted.*

The feeling wasn't new. When Chuck and I flirted, it went as far as I wanted it to go. But Alan found out and ran away. I covered my eyes with my hands. Why had I hurt him? What had happened to my life? I hugged myself, longing for comfort. Which I would not get if I stayed there sitting on the ground. Like that day in my father's house, long ago, I needed to get up and find someone like my Babcia. I would go back and talk to Regina, and hope she'd understand.

As I pushed myself up to stand, the wind blew dry leaves around my skirt. I looked for the path back to the spot where I had run from Józef. It was gone. How could that be? How long had I been running? The dark and lonely forest closed in around me. I clasped my hands together, closed my eyes and took a deep cleansing breath. It didn't help. When I opened my eyes, my hands were shaking. I took slow steps in the direction from which I had come, though the path had disappeared. One foot at a time, I walked on, my head as heavy as my heart.

I'll never know how long I walked until the brush and trees grew thicker and my legs began to ache. I thought of turning back, but I wasn't sure which way to go. I wondered if I should keep on, just a little farther. Nothing looked familiar, though our walks had taken us into these woods many times before. Frustrated tears sprang to my eyes as I turned in a slow circle, looking for a way through the trees. My foot caught on a tangle of roots and I fell to the ground, crying out. But there was no one to hear me. I felt as if the earth itself had pulled me down. My long skirt and peasant blouse were torn and dirty. My palms were scraped and bleeding. A sob escaped from my throat. I thought of Jessica, on the other side of the world, in another century. My child who I loved more than myself! Would I ever see her again? And Alan, the kind man I had married who wanted a quiet home life. Was this what I had come to, all the weeks and months of trying to help Regina, all the years of trying to make sense of my life? I sat on the ground and bawled.

"What am I supposed to do?" I screamed at the sky. I wanted, needed someone to hear me, find me, lead me out. I screamed again, a frustrated angry wail from deep inside my body, a cry that felt as if it had lived in me forever, trapped and fighting to be free.

Chapter Twenty-Nine

ALL AROUND ME was a soft green darkness. Quiet. Pine needles carpeted the forest floor and I inhaled their scent deep, deep into my lungs. Again and again, I breathed in the aroma. *May I be safe. May I be strong.* Close to my spot on the ground, each tiny pine needle, each grain of dirt, showed itself to me, all parts of the planet supporting my body, holding me, anchoring me to this place. Quiet. Peace. My panic began to recede.

A few feet away, a grey squirrel scampered onto a fallen log and watched me. Little birds settled on the surrounding branches. I thought of Snow White in the Disney movie. No handsome prince would rescue me here. Was that what I had wanted all along? Had I always expected Alan to take care of me? How like my father he was! I once believed they were passive and lacking in ambition. But they were good men. Pawel's face came to mind, then Roman's and Andrzej's. My husband and my father were better than most. Had I flirted with Chuck and then Józef to escape my dull life? I thought of my mother's note on the day she left. *I have met someone who makes me happy.*

From the trees to my left came a sudden rustling. I turned and caught my breath as a dun-colored deer placed her forefeet on a flat stone and slowly turned her head to face me. Her liquid brown eyes held mine and looked straight into my confused and aching heart.

Long ago, I had needed my mother to look at me in just that way, but it was not to be. Now, I was a grown woman and I was tired of the longing. Maybe it was time to stop wishing for a better yesterday.

When the doe walked away, my tears went with her. The tears I cried today, the lonely ones when I was ten, and the bitter ones when I was fifty. My mother had made a poor choice, but she longed for happiness, just like me. I might never know her reasons for what she did, just as I never really knew her. But I could let that go and forgive her. She was human and just like me, imperfect. Maybe it was time to forgive myself as well. To stop searching for the perfect life and embrace the one I had. To create my own happiness.

My growling stomach called me to action. Get up off the ground, find the village. The sun was much lower in the patch of sky barely visible through the trees. The path out of the forest was here somewhere. All I had to do was find it.

I walked at a deliberate pace, searching for signs like cleared brush or footprints in the loamy dirt. The soughing of the wind grew louder, like the sound of a faraway train. I tried not to be afraid, but a hint of panic crept in. The trees were so thick, their trunks so dark. I had no way of knowing how large this forest was. My breath grew ragged. I stopped to collect myself.

It's okay, Kat. You'll be okay. Just think. Look for moss on the tree trunks. It will tell you which direction is west. Or is that east?

A rattling on hollow wood made me jump. High above my head, a woodpecker rapped on an old gray trunk with her sharp beak. Squirrels scampered away but did not hide. One sat up and watched me, then resumed her grubbing through the leaves. I forced myself to stop and think again.

Barbara once said she and Regina learned signs as kids to keep from getting lost. *What were they? The angle of the sun...it was setting, so that must be west. I knew the woods were west of Mała Łąka, so I needed to go east, keeping the sun behind me.*

I reversed direction, mindful of the setting sun, and trudged along for what seemed like hours. As evening deepened, the moon revealed itself from behind a cloud, casting shadows on the tree trunks. Low murmurs reached my ears, below the wind, under the crunch of my footsteps on the matted leaves. A clearing appeared, and with it, the feeling I was not alone. I stopped and looked around me: no animals or birds, just the wind and my own pulse in my ears.

To keep from panicking again, I imagined the wooden houses of *Mała Łąka*, the people, the fields and the flower and vegetable gardens. I pictured Regina and Barbara smiling and opening their arms to me as I walked down the road into the village. And when I looked down at my feet, I saw it: a scrubby kind of path, barely visible in the underbrush. I peered ahead but couldn't see where it led. Squinting in the pale moonlight, I bent down to see where the brush was trampled and made my way step by step. My feet and ankles ached.

Suddenly, the path divided. One section went straight ahead, another banked off to the right, and yet another to the left. All three were distinct and well-traveled. Which was the correct path? My skin tingled and my head whirled. For a second, naked fear touched my shoulders. In the next instant, words from deep within me brushed it away. *Just pick one.*

Could it really be so easy? Wasn't I supposed to analyze their different tangents by the light of the moon or try walking down each one to see if it was right? My head felt so heavy. I was tired of arguing with myself. Tired of living my life afraid. Afraid of making the wrong choice. Afraid of making a mistake. Enough.

Tonight, I would move forward. Tomorrow would take care of itself. Stroking my upper arms, I closed my eyes and raised my face to the moon. When I looked again, her cool light bathed the middle path, the one where I had placed my feet.

After I had walked for a while, the distant sound of women's voices drifted closer. At the base of the trees ahead of me, the horizon turned pink. Overhead, a white stork appeared, flying closer and lower as I reached a meadow filled with the smell of wood smoke. When I left the woods behind, she spiraled high into the sky and I knew she must be the one who had visited me in the meadow where Regina prayed. Far ahead in the yellow grass, dawn lit the shadowy figures of three women gathering twigs into large bundles. I hurried forward, knowing they would see me and show me the way to the village.

Back in *Mała Łąka*, Regina warmed a bowl of soup and pulled a chunk off a round loaf of dark bread. Her children sat on benches around the table and stared at me. Anna's face was solemn, and I smiled to reassure her.

"We had no idea where to look for you." Regina waved her arms in the air. "Józef told everyone you ran away from him and would not come back."

Pawel gave a loud snort from where he stood leaning in the doorway.

"What's the problem now?" Regina put the soup on the table in front of me and turned to him, her rough hands on her stocky hips.

"Józef is no good." I was thrilled I still understood his every word. "You should never leave a woman alone in the forest. Wolves, bears, who knows what animals are in there at night? Good riddance to him. He's not good husband for you."

"No, I guess not," I mumbled over my soup. Pawel's standards for male behavior surprised me. Apparently, hitting was okay but abandoning to the wolves was not. When I tore off a piece of bread, he picked up a clay dish of butter and a small wooden spreader and brought it over to me.

"*Dziękuję*," I said.

"*Nie ma za co*," he replied in a gruff voice. It's nothing.

Regina's eyes met mine with a twinkle. She followed up with a smile for her husband, who lowered his head and busied himself cleaning his fingernails with a pocketknife. The energy between them had changed, I was pleased to see. It was up to Regina now. And from what I had seen her accomplish with her son-in-law, I had a feeling she would be just fine.

Without being asked, the girls turned down the bed covers for me, and I climbed in. Despite the sounds of the busy village outside, I slept for hours.

It was mid-afternoon when I finally woke up and walked out through the propped open door. Regina was on the other side of the road, leaning on a fence with Barbara and looking out over the gently rolling hills. On the hillside to the north, a family of sheep grazed alongside two huge workhorses. Baby lambs scampered around each other on spindly legs. One of them scurried to the ewe and tried to nurse while she walked to the watering trough. All the lambs were creamy white except for a little black one chewing on a clump of grass, green shoots hanging from the sides of its mouth. Regina called me over, and Barbara, after checking to see that I was all right after my adventure, left us to tend her garden. After we watched her walk away, Regina pointed to the animals in the field.

"If you look carefully, you see each animal has its own personality, just like people in family. That lamb over there, see how jumpy? And other beside him, how easygoing?"

I looked where her arm pointed. A small white lamb startled and bleated every time another animal moved, while another quietly munched on the grass at his feet.

Kind of like the members of a human family, each with his own purpose. Or hers. I thought of Jessica, so headstrong and smart. So willing to take a risk to follow her dream. And of Alan, content with his quiet creativity. I longed to love them the way Regina loved her family, selflessly and without judgment. And to be loved by them in the same way. My place, my purpose, lay with them.

"I wish I had time to do this more often." I smoothed the wrinkles in my skirt. It was still a little dirty, and I had worn it all summer, but now I didn't care.

Regina smiled. "I know what you mean. Sometimes feels good to do nothing."

The sun warmed our backs and the backs of the sheep and the two horses, the wood of the fence, the soil under the grass. The same sun that had warmed our ancestors and would warm our descendants on two continents thousands of miles apart.

"Still wondering what to do, Kasia?" Regina placed her rough hand over mine. "Still looking for your purpose in life?"

I thought for a long time before I answered her. A tiny sparrow landed in a nearby aspen tree, and the branch bowed so lightly with her weight I looked hard to see if it had really happened. She chirped at me and flew away, and the branch sprang back an inch or two.

"You know, I don't think I am. When we first met, I believed your life had no choices. But you do have them, and you do your best to live with them." I looked across the field at the family of sheep. "It's time for me to get on with my life, too. Back in 2017, where I belong." We faced each other and burst out laughing. "I mean *up ahead* in 2017. In the future... or something."

Regina grinned. "Whatever!"

I rolled my eyes and leaned back against the fence. "I sure am glad I chose the right path out of the woods this morning. If I'd gone left or right, I might still be walking." Regina started laughing again. "What is so funny?"

"All paths lead to village, Kasia. One path ends up by church, one through meadow to schoolyard, and third becomes street where more houses are." She gave me a grin so wide the sunlight glinted off her teeth.

I was stunned. "You mean it didn't matter which one I chose?" She shook her head and pointed a finger at me, and before long, I had to laugh too, a healing belly laugh that left me gasping for breath.

When we had finally settled down, I told her about the popular slogan in my world: Bloom Where You Are Planted. And the ad for the running shoe: Just Do It. I didn't need to worry about the perfect way to live. I just needed to choose a path and stick with it.

We turned away from the fence and walked over to her garden. "I really like the way you use herbs for healing. I'd like to do that at home, and maybe teach others. I don't know if anyone would be interested, though."

"Only way to find out is..." she paused with a mischievous grin.

"Ask!" we shouted and collapsed against the fence, laughing hysterically again.

Chapter Thirty

NOW I WAS READY to time travel home, according to a very relieved Jadwiga, who stopped by the very next day, when Regina and I were home alone.

"I must tell you," she said, "that you caused me much worry. I was not always confident in my ability to steer you the correct way."

"What will you do now?" I asked. "Can you stay here, or go back to the time when you were queen?"

Jadwiga looked down at her shiny boots. "Perhaps. It is not for me to say. Matka Boska will decide where to send me next."

Regina patted Jadwiga's shoulder. "We will pray to her for you. She must know you were good to us and we are grateful."

"Yes, thank you so much, Jadwiga," I said. "We couldn't have done it without you!"

She drew herself up to her full height and folded her arms. "That is for sure!"

Of course, she was right. We all knew that. Regina and I had grown to love her over the past months, and wished her well. We would miss her. Now, we had one last task: to get me back home where I belonged.

We made sure all the elements we had studied were in alignment: a full moon, visualization of the destination and year, and a good steady portal. Since it had worked for Regina, we decided I would use the outdoor shrine.

On the night of the next full moon, the women of *Mała Łąka* held a farewell party for me. Regina told them I would be heading back up north, to the port where ships left for America. I had relatives there, she said, and how true that was, only she, Jadwiga and I knew. We sipped the *wodka* Barbara's husband got from his cousin in Kraków and ate Genka's freshly made *chrusciki,* a delicate pastry tied in a bow, and munched on slices of Cyprian's smoked *kiełbasa.* Father Marek stopped by to give me his blessing, then waved goodbye while stealing a quick glance at the moon overhead. Józef didn't come, and I was okay with that. I hoped he would find a good wife soon.

The women told a few last stories and gave me some more tips on using herbs. We talked until the moon was directly overhead us in the night sky. Then it was time to say goodbye. Each woman embraced me in turn, all of us smiling through our tears. They believed I was leaving for Krakow at dawn, in a wagon Regina's son in law Andrzej would drive. From there, I would travel by carriage to the Baltic Sea and the ship that would carry me across the Atlantic. It was a lie, of course, added to the story we made up about the *Pan* giving me the money for the trip to atone for his son's behavior. Jadwiga said sometimes a little fib was better than exposing the truth to people who were better off not knowing. Like the little wayside shrine, an escape hatch to another world, but only for those whom the Madonna chose.

When the last woman returned to her home, the bushes rustled and Jadwiga stepped out wearing her lovely green silk gown and carrying a huge bouquet of roses. She held them out to me with a regal nod.

"*Matka Boska* and I, her surrogate, are very proud of you, Katarzyna. Go forward now and live your happy life."

"Thank you." I held out a hand and she clasped it in both of hers. "For all the little miracles. Don't think I didn't notice." Regina would still be struggling to learn English if not for Jadwiga and her amber ring.

"*Nie ma za co,*" she said, beaming. "It has been my pleasure to work your case as my first mission for Blessed

Mother. You were successful in learning what you needed to know. And now I can report back for next case. I hope it is with another good woman like you." She gave my hand a firm squeeze then let go, a glint of tears in her beautiful eyes.

I turned to Regina and put my arm around her. "Thanks to both of you, and to the Madonna. *Bardzo, bardzo dziękuję.*" All of a sudden, looking at these two dear faces, I wanted to stay, for just one more minute. "I sort of wish I could pop back and see you sometime. You know, check on how Anna is doing."

Jadwiga's eyes widened. "Oh, no, no, no!" She waved her arm at me, her amber ring glinting in the moonlight. "No, you do not! It is not meant to be."

Regina tilted her head to one side. Her scarf still covered her soft gray hair, and I remembered my first sight of her, in my kitchen only six months ago. How much we had learned together, and how I loved her now. She held me in a long embrace, then stepped back, keeping her strong rough hands on my shoulders.

"Thank you, dear child, for all you have done for me. May happiness be yours always."

The three of us walked up the rise of the hill to the weathered old wooden shrine with its gold trimmed icon of the Virgin. I felt the urge to hurry now. Clouds scudded across the face of the moon and moved on through the vast black sky. I did not belong here, but I would leave part of me behind, among these strong and hardy people. Regina loved me and always would, through all the pages of time. I knew that as surely as I knew I loved my daughter. And yes, my mother. Looking at the Virgin's painted face, I made a silent vow that Jessica would know I loved her without condition, just as she was.

"*Szybko!*" Jadwiga whispered. Quickly. I closed my eyes and visualized my Plumstead Township backyard, and in the next second, warm air whooshed over me. My eyelids filtered a light as bright as the midday sun, and as the wind stopped, I opened my eyes on my green and wooded backyard. I was back home where I belonged, still clutching Jadwiga's roses. It seemed as if no time had passed at all. It was still late summer here, and I wasn't even dizzy.

Alan gave me a ride down to Szypula's to pick up my car, which was right where I left it, including all the tires and hubcaps. That was a miracle from Jadwiga, for sure.

"Meet me back at the house?" I asked. "I have some things I'd like to talk about."

"Sure," he said then cracked a smile. Beside him, my heart grew a few millimeters. I loved everything here, everything I saw. The smokestacks, the brick churches, the narrow streets filled with row houses. Even the traffic on 95, people traveling with me toward home, work or any of life's myriad destinations.

That evening, Alan and I talked for hours. He knew I'd always loved books. Ever since I was a little girl they've been a comfort to me. My favorite part about my job at the Township Library was helping people find the information they needed.

"I think I'd like to go to grad school, get a library science degree," I said. "Would there be enough in our savings for that?"

He shrugged, unconcerned. "Should be. If not, I'll help you get a loan."

"Thanks, Alan," I said. "You don't have to...I mean, after all the trouble..."

"No problem. I've had some time to think, driving around these past few months. I could have done a better job paying attention to you at times." He rubbed his hands together.

"We could both have done better," I said with a smile. "Let's have lunch on Saturday after I figure out how to apply for classes."

"Okay, I better get home. Early start tomorrow."

I watched his truck's tail lights leave my driveway and turned back to the house, this time not in sorrow. Definitely not in desperate panic. Whatever came next, the searing loneliness I had carried all my life was gone.

My phone lay on the kitchen table. I walked to my little altar and touched each sacred object with my fingertips – a stone, a feather, a string of beads. Today was the day I might begin redeeming two women: myself and my mother. I called Jessica.

"Hey, Mom." She answered at once.

"Hi, honey," I said. "I've missed talking to you."

"Since the other day?"

Of course. No time had passed for her in the 21st century while I was back in *Mała Łąka*. "Yeah, since the other day."

Time was a riddle to me now. What was the past, really? And what did it mean to be in the present? I only knew that my daughter and I were in the here and now, and I had another chance with her. A chance to be the kind of mother I had always wanted. Forgiveness worked both ways. My mother wasn't who I needed her to be, but I loved her. And at last, I could break the chain around my heart. I could be a loving mother to my daughter.

"I was wondering. Do you think you might come back for a couple of weeks' vacation?"

"I don't know, Mom, Maybe. Let me check with the manager." She didn't argue, as I half expected she might. Progress, in slow halting steps.

"Did you get my letter?"

"Uh, no, no letter. When did you send it?"

What did it matter? Time was such an impossibly vague concept, wasn't it? "Never mind, I'll explain when you get here."

"Okay. Talk to you later."

Now a month has passed, and it's late September as I sit in my study watching a doe with dust-brown fur meander through the woods out back. Soon there are two of them, flicking their white tails, noses to the ground foraging for acorns and seeds, munching on the tops of weeds. Reminding me of the quiet countryside I left so far behind.

The day before I left *Mała Łąka*, I wrote up a condensed history, so Regina would know what happened next. If she couldn't read it herself, she could get someone she trusted to do it for her. I wrote about the First World War, the short-lived independence of Poland, the 1939 German invasion from the Baltic Sea. I wrote about the Holocaust and the concentration camps. I covered the Communist years, and the changes that began after Lech Walesa and *Solidarnosc* brought democracy to Eastern Europe. I folded the papers in half, put them in my skirt pocket and wandered around the village for an hour looking for a good place to leave them. As I watched Regina in her little cottage and in the village with her friends, content with their families and their place in the world, I saw what I had to do. On a day when almost everyone worked in the outer fields, I opened the gate into Regina's garden, tore the history I had written into tiny pieces and buried them under the beets.

Last night I found myself missing her. I thought about Anna and searched out my kindergarten picture in an old scrapbook. I gazed at my little face and wondered what became of her after I left *Mała Łąka*, and how her life had turned out.

This morning, right after breakfast, I went online to a genealogy site and entered her name. This is what I found. In 1840, at the age of 20, she married a young man named Maciej Czelusniak. They had four children and ten grandchildren. The website listed all their names and dates. The youngest, born in 1882, was named Angelika, my grandmother's name. Because, of course, Anna's youngest granddaughter *was* my grandmother. She married the man who became my grandfather, and they had one child: my mother.

The moment I understood all this, I felt as though a shining beam of light and love had traveled across the years from Anna to me. Because Regina went back home and nursed her little girl back to health so she could live a full life, I was born one hundred and thirty years later. Our mitochondrial DNA continued on. Anna was my great-great grandmother. In a very real way, Regina had saved my life.

Now I pull grandmother Angelika's soft shawl around me. Yes, even today, I feel her comforting warmth. My Goddess cards are spread before me, three cards bearing images that bring a smile to my lips. A haloed woman with large brown eyes and a straight aristocratic nose gazes off into the distance. An old woman and a young stand side by side. And on the third card, three hands are clasped together like spokes of a wheel.

Regina and I are back where we belong. But sometimes even now, when sleep will not come, I listen for her footsteps.

THE END

About the Author

LINDA C. WISNIEWSKI is a former librarian and journalist. Her work has been published widely in literary magazines and anthologies, and on her blog, www.lindawis.com. She is the author of a memoir, *Off Kilter: A Woman's Journey to Peace with Scoliosis, Her Mother and Her Polish Heritage.* Linda lives with her husband in Bucks County, PA.

CPSIA information can be obtained
at www.ICGtesting.com
Printed in the USA
BVHW032018090421
604372BV00009B/5